My Mother's Child

My Mother's Child

Dwan Abrams

www.urbanchristianonline.net

Urban Books, LLC
97 N18th Street
Wyandanch, NY 11798

My Mother's Child Copyright © 2010 Dwan Abrams

ISBN 13: 978-1-60162-771-1
ISBN 10: 1-60162-771-8

First Mass Market Printing October 2013
First Trade Paperback Printing September 2009
Printed in the United States of America

10 9 8 7 6 5 4 3 2 1

This is a work of fiction. Any references or similarities to actual events, real people, living or dead, or to real locales are intended to give the novel a sense of reality. Any similarity in other names, characters, places, and incidents is entirely coincidental.

Distributed by Kensington Publishing Corp.
Submit Wholesale Orders to:
Kensington Publishing Corp.
C/O Penguin Group (USA) Inc.
Attention: Order Processing
405 Murray Hill Parkway
East Rutherford, NJ 07073-2316
Phone: 1-800-526-0275
Fax: 1-800-227-9604

This book is dedicated to Alex

Acknowledgments

Thank God for blessing me to complete another novel. Thanks to my husband, Alex, and daughter, Nia, for giving me the time and space to write. I owe them a debt of gratitude for all of their love, support, and encouragement.

Much love to my mom, Gwendolyn Fields. Thank you for always believing in me. To my dad, Gary Abrams, I love you. To my sister, Ireana, I love you for just being you. Thank you for blessing me with my adorable little niece, Carrington. To my sister-in-law, Cordella, and her husband, Gerald, I love you! A special thanks to my cousin, Omar Scott, for always reading my work and giving me honest to goodness feedback. Love you!

Thanks to the dynamic ladies of Faith Based Fiction Writers of Atlanta. Your critiques and feedback were so helpful and greatly appreciated.

Thanks to ReShonda Tate Billingsley, Lurma Rackley, Rhonda McKnight, and Marisa Jones for all of their valuable input while I was putting this story together. A special thanks to Dr. Sherri Lewis, Tamara Angela Grant, Attorney Stan Gregory, and Aleta Barnes for consulting with me on various scenarios. Thanks to Joylynn Jossel and Kendra Norman-Bellamy at Urban Christian for all of their hard work.

To my glam squad, my friend and make-up artist, Shawnteé Robinson, Mrs. Sylvia and the ladies at Shear Madness Salon, and Shaunita Blake. Thanks for hooking me up!

To Vickie L. Brown at Victoria Belle, thank you for making my Valentine's Day celebration the most amazing and enjoyable day ever! Very special thanks to Michele Kraft DeBlois and the entire staff at Forrest Hills Mountain Resort in Dahlonega, Georgia, for providing my husband and me with the most memorable and romantic honeymoon destination imaginable.

Thanks to the talented authors on the roster at my publishing house, Nevaeh Publishing. You inspire me. Keep doing what you do.

Thanks to my attorney, Sheila Levine, for always having my back. Thanks to Dee Stewart, Rhonda Bogan, and Terrance Wooten for helping me along my literary journey. I appreciate you so much!

To my pastor, Kerwin B. Lee, thank you for sharing your anointing with the Berean Christian Church cousins. We love you! To my spiritual mother, Minister Adrienne Swearingen, I thank God for you. Love you.

I enjoy receiving emails, especially from readers. I would be remiss if I didn't thank the readers who took the time to email me about my books. Thank you so much for your testimonies and feedback. Nice to hear from you.

Last, and certainly not least, a very special thanks to every book club that has selected one or more of my novels as their book of the month. Thank you; thank you; thank you!

Prologue

Present Day

"Dear God, no!" Consuela struggled to digest what she saw. Her chest pounded so hard; her ears throbbed so loud from the fright of the scene before her. She thought she would explode. But God moved the scream that sat at the pit of her stomach and helped her get the fear out. She roared in agony. Her voice boomed back and forth on Lyric's walls. Yet her employer didn't move despite it all. What had happened here?

Mrs. Johnson, Lyric's neighbor, tapped Consuela on the shoulder, startling her. Consuela felt like punching someone.

"You live next door; how could you not have heard anything?" Consuela wanted to know.

"I haven't been at home most of the day," she said. "Surely you don't think I could've had anything to do with this. Lyric is my friend."

There was Lyric. Semi-naked. Unconscious. Lying on the floor. A colorful nylon scarf squeezed her neck like a vice grip. Consuela wanted to scream again, but only pitiful whimpering noises emitted from her mouth. She leaned down closer to Lyric, extending a hand to her, but jerked her arm back when she noticed purple and blue bruises on her arms, right breast, and thighs. Remnants of dried up crimson and black colored blood stained the area above her upper lip.

"Sweet Jesus," Consuela said.

Consuela wanted to cover up Lyric's battered body, but Mrs. Johnson told her not to touch anything. Consuela looked around the room, although it was hard to see. Her tears blurred her vision. What she could see was that the room was in complete disarray. Lyric's palatial estate usually looked like a model home. Today, broken glass and overturned furniture replaced the tidy abode. Consuela felt as though she was having an asthma attack, only she didn't have asthma. Then she glanced up and saw a man hanging by the neck near the balcony overlooking the sitting room where she'd found Lyric.

She ran screaming out of that house like a wild woman. Mrs. Johnson stared in shock. Consuela got in her car and locked the doors. Her hands were shaking like a rattle; she was unable to put the key in the ignition. Through her hysteria, she couldn't remember the number to 9-1-1. After fumbling with her cell phone, she stared at the phone before remembering the number. She pressed the keys and pushed the send button.

One

Fifteen Months Ago

Lyric couldn't understand why God wouldn't bless her with a son. If only she could get pregnant. She really wanted to give Michael, her husband of fifteen years, a son, a namesake. No matter how much Michael assured her that he was happy with her and their twelve-year-old daughter, Autumn, a part of her felt as if she were less than a woman because she couldn't give her husband a son.

On the surface, she didn't lack for anything—big house, fancy cars, and money. She didn't know whether she was the luckiest or unluckiest, woman in the world. With her eyes still closed, she ran her hand across the vacant side of the bed; her husband was already up.

Feeling the loneliness that she had come to know all too well, she sat up in the king size bed and looked around her master-bedroom suite.

The room was elegantly decorated in deep mocha with gold and beige hues. Her magnificent eight-bedroom home in Grand Cayman Estates located in Lithonia, a suburb of Atlanta, was everything she had ever hoped for and dreamt.

Autumn skipped into the room still dressed in her pajamas. Lyric glanced at her digital clock and the time read 9:30 A.M. No matter what time of day, Autumn seemed to have an unlimited supply of energy. "Mom," Autumn said as she made her way over to the bed, "are we still going Christmas shopping at the mall?"

"That's all you care about," Lyric teased, moving her feet so that Autumn wouldn't sit on them when she plopped down on the bed. She knew that Autumn enjoyed shopping just as much as she did. They didn't need a specific season, and there didn't have to be a reason.

Smiling, Autumn said, "Can Heavyn come with us?"

Autumn and Heavyn had been best friends since kindergarten. They were both only children and liked to pretend that they were sisters. Both of their fathers worked as cardiologists and heart transplant surgeons at Emory University Hospital. Their mothers volunteered as room parents and ran in the same social circles. Lyric and Chloe oftentimes chaired fundraisers together.

The two women had so much in common that they became good friends too.

"I don't know why you're asking me; you know that you and Heavyn have already plotted this whole thing out. Don't try to play me." Lyric laughed.

Autumn giggled and fell back on the comforter. She rolled over on her side and propped herself up on her elbow. "So she can come?"

Lyric had a hard time telling her daughter no. By no means was Lyric a pushover. As long as Autumn's requests weren't detrimental to her physical, emotional, or spiritual well-being, Lyric liked to indulge her. When she looked at Autumn's sweet face, Lyric saw her baby. The adorable, doe-eyed, chubby-cheeked bundle of love that she used to cuddle and play with for hours on end. Not the fiercely independent pre-teen that she had become.

Lyric smirked. "What do you think?"

"Thanks, Mom; you're the best." Autumn scooted herself off the bed and stood barefoot on the carpeted floor. Placing her index finger on her chin, she said, "Can we catch a movie too?"

Lyric picked up a decorative pillow and tossed it at her. Autumn stepped out of the way, and the pillow bounced off the back of the leather couch located in the sitting area of the room.

Laughing, Lyric said, "Fine. Now get out of here."

Before she left, Autumn gave her mother a hug and kissed her on the cheek. After Autumn left, Lyric yawned and stretched her arms high above her head. She then removed the satin scarf from her hair and placed it on the nightstand. She picked up the cordless phone next to her bed and dialed her friend Chloe's number. Chloe answered on the second ring.

"I was wondering when I was going to hear from you." Chloe sounded upbeat.

"Girl, I don't know why we even bother to try and spend alone time with our daughters because it doesn't work," Lyric chuckled. "When those two are apart, they act like they're being punished. Since Michael went to play cards with the fellas last night, I thought it would be good if Autumn and I watched some movies and ate popcorn. It seemed like fun when I thought of it." She paused and took a deep breath. Exhaling, she said, "That child refused to understand why Heavyn couldn't come over and hang out with us." She shook her head in disbelief. "So of course, first thing this morning, she came in asking if Heavyn could go with us to the mall and movies."

They both laughed.

"You know I know," Chloe chimed in. "Heavyn did the same thing to me. So what do you say? I've already gotten my Christmas presents. Shoe shopping and lunch for us while the girls are at the movies?"

"Sounds like a plan to me. Can you meet me at my house around noon?"

Chloe agreed, and they got off the phone. Lyric placed the phone back on the cradle and got out of bed. She wrapped her long silk robe around her slender five foot five frame and went into the master-bath. Marble floors and countertops, mahogany vanities on both walls with plush covered stools, a matching round table in the center that displayed a purple floral arrangement, two oversized prayer plants on the floor, a TV housed in the wall, Jacuzzi bathtub, separate shower, a bidet, and a walk-in closet completed a bathroom to rival any spa setting.

She brushed her teeth and washed her face. Tucking her hair underneath a plastic cap, she disrobed before taking a quick shower. While standing underneath the running water, she thought about Michael. She wished they could spend more quality time together. At times, she longed to be with him; she missed him so much. She felt as though their relationship had reached a stale point, and she didn't know

how to fix it. They used to laugh and have fun.
Now their life seemed boring, predictable, and
routine. Fire. Passion. Excitement. That's what
she wanted. Lyric craved adventure. She wanted
Michael to romance her and sweep her off her
feet. She didn't expect flowers every day, but
sometimes would be nice. Once in awhile she'd
like a romantic candlelight dinner, just the two
of them. And foreplay. When they were newly
married, they were young. Neither one of them
understood the concept of making love to one
another's mind. Now that Lyric had matured,
she wanted the complete package. Her desires
had remained faithfully unto her husband, but
she wanted him to explore every part of her body,
not just the obvious spots. Not being able to have
another baby only added to her dissatisfaction.

Lyric snapped out of her reflective state. She
turned off the water and retrieved a bottle of
baby oil from the shelf. She slathered oil on her
moist skin before gently drying with a towel.
Then she tiptoed to the mirror and studied her
reflection. She removed the cap, then ran her
fingers through her tousled, highlighted hair,
which fell past her shoulders.

Her skin appeared smooth and even. Main-
taining her looks and health were important to
Lyric. Five days a week she alternated between

Pilates, Yoga, aerobics, and weight training. Her body was toned and lean. She even gave herself weekly facials, which made her face appear youthful. Admittedly, she hated her nose. The tip of her nose looked as though an invisible finger was holding it down. She had considered rhinoplasty, but Michael had talked her out of it, claiming that nobody was perfect. As for her diet, she didn't eat red meat or pork, and salt, sugar, and caffeine were used in moderation. Even with all that, she still couldn't conceive another child. With sadness in her eyes, she blinked away the tears.

"Snap out of it," she said to herself. She went into her custom designed closet and retrieved a lace bra and panties set from the lingerie drawer in the island. While standing there, she looked around her organized space. She removed a pair of jeans from the hanger and selected a ruby red twin sweater set. The clothes were already ironed, so all she had to do was put them on. When she finished getting dressed, she selected a pair of matching high-heeled boots and a soft leather oversized handbag. She exited the closet and checked herself out in the mirror. Not bad, she thought.

After spraying some of the Calvin Klein fragrance, Euphoria, on her neck, she traced the bottom of her eyes with white liner. Just beneath her lower lashes, she applied a thin layer of black liquid liner. Her eyes looked radiant. For her lips, she coated them with dark red gloss. She pressed her lips together while transferring the contents from one of her purses to another, then headed downstairs.

As soon as she entered the kitchen, the sound of her heels clanking against the hardwood floor seemed so loud. She immediately spotted Michael and Autumn sitting at the mahogany wood and European tiled island. Autumn had changed into a pair of fitted jeans with a golden yellow top that complemented her bronze complexion. Michael was dressed in a T-shirt and boxers. His caramel colored eyes were carrying some serious baggage. He looked as if someone had doused his eyes with hot sauce.

"Morning, gorgeous," Michael said as he put down the morning paper.

Kissing her husband on the lips, Lyric said, "You don't look like you slept at all." Having fallen asleep around midnight, she wasn't sure what time Michael came home. She playfully pressed her finger in the adorable dimple on his chin.

Lyric brewed herself a fresh cup of blackberry tea. She stopped drinking coffee after learning that long-term coffee drinkers often had a toxic, congested liver and impure blood. Not to mention that coffee dehydrates the skin and slows down the metabolism. As far as Lyric was concerned, she wasn't interested in drinking anything that seemed to speed up the aging process.

Autumn finished slurping the last bit of milk from her cereal bowl and placed it in the sink.

"Autumn told me you two were going to hang out at the mall and go to the movies today. Don't put a hurtin' on the credit cards," he joked.

Lyric discarded the used tea bag. "I thought that the black card didn't have a limit." She raised a brow.

"That's not funny." He playfully smacked her on the backside.

Looking him in the eyes, she gave him a wink.

Autumn shook her head. "I'll be in my room until it's time to leave," she announced as she headed upstairs.

Lyric added lemon and artificial sweetener to her hot drink and stirred. "How was the game?"

"I didn't lose any money, if that's what you're asking." He squinted his eyes and squeezed the bridge of his nose.

Lyric could see how tired he was, so she offered to run him a bath.

"No, I'm too tired for that," he mumbled. "I'll probably just take a quick power shower. You were snoring by the time I got in the bed. I had a difficult time falling asleep, so I stayed up watching TV."

As he bit into the half-eaten muffin, Lyric lightly massaged his broad shoulders, and said, "The house should be pretty quiet with Autumn and me gone. Make sure you get some rest."

She tried to be considerate and not bother Michael whenever he had a late night. She and Autumn usually went out of their way to keep noise to a minimum, even if that meant unplugging the telephone in the master-suite. Michael was a light sleeper, and if anything or anyone interrupted his sleep, he had a hard time falling back asleep.

"You don't have to tell me twice." Michael stood up and wrapped his arms around Lyric's waist. "You smell good."

"Thanks," she said, hugging his waist and resting her head on his chest. "Chloe and Heavyn should be here in about an hour. We'll be quiet."

Bending down and kissing her on the forehead, Michael said, "Have fun. Love you."

He went upstairs, leaving Lyric alone in the kitchen. She sipped her tea, and then opened the mahogany wooden blinds positioned above the sink. The sun shone through the slits, making the room brighter. Then she fixed herself half of a flax seed bagel topped with strawberry whipped cream cheese.

Having finished her bagel and tea, she called Chloe to ask her not to ring the doorbell when she arrived. She explained that Michael had gotten in from a late night, and she didn't want to disturb him. Instead, Lyric requested that Chloe call her on her cell phone, and she and Autumn would meet them outside.

After Lyric got off the phone, she went upstairs to check on her family. Autumn was in her fairytale princess-styled bedroom on the computer checking her MySpace page. Since Lyric knew Autumn's password, and her page was set to private, she didn't have a problem with Autumn interacting with her friends on the social networking site. Besides, Michael and Lyric had already warned Autumn about the perils of Internet predators and giving out personal information to strangers. She hadn't given her parents any reason not to trust her, so Lyric waved and backed out of the room.

She noticed that the master-suite door was closed. She figured that Michael was either getting ready for bed, or was already in bed. Careful not to make a lot of noise, Lyric slowly opened the door before entering. To her surprise, Michael came out of the bathroom with a towel wrapped around his waist. His copper tone skin glistened from the moisture. She closed the door behind her as she felt her heartbeat quicken. He looked so good that she wanted to make love to him. Her eyes traveled the length of his rock hard body. She was glad that Michael worked out and kept his body in tip top condition. She loved the feel of his strong arms wrapped around her.

"I was just about to lie down," he said, removing a pair of briefs from the dresser and tossing his towel on the sofa.

The way his muscles flexed with each movement drove Lyric insane! She knew Michael said he was about to lie down, but she felt like getting down. She licked her lips. Her mind was filled with naughty thoughts. At that moment, she would've given anything to be in the romantic throes of ecstasy with her husband. To her, Michael was the sexiest man alive. She didn't care what *People* magazine had to say about their pick for the sexiest man alive; they hadn't seen her husband.

Without taking her eyes off his body, she said, "I came to get my purse and to see if you needed anything before we left." She hoped he would say, "I need to get with you before you leave" and take her in his arms and ravish her body. But she knew that was wishful thinking.

He covered his yawn with his hand. "I'm good."

Biting her lower lip, Lyric tossed her hair back. Her hormones were raging. She must have been ovulating, she figured. There was no denying the chemistry between her and Michael. His touch seemed electric. If he grazed her skin just the right way, the fine hairs on her arm tended to stand at attention.

A faint smile appeared on her face. She knew that Michael was too tired to satisfy her at that moment, so she snapped out of her trance. As Michael nestled underneath the covers, Lyric went into the closet and located her purse. She hugged herself and closed her eyes. Her therapist, Dr. Skyler Little, a psychoanalyst, had suggested she show herself some love whenever she felt a void.

She had met Dr. Little while they were both guests at a wedding a year and a half ago. Larry, the groom, owned a radio station and had purchased a house in Lyric's neighborhood. He would always speak whenever he saw Lyric. She was happy for Larry when he told her that he had reconnected with Monday, his childhood sweetheart and the mother of his only child. At the wedding reception, Lyric discovered that Monday was a former patient of Dr. Little's. Monday had publicly thanked Dr. Little for helping her work through her issues.

After conversing with Dr. Little, Lyric admired the way she had incorporated her Christianity into her counseling services. So when Lyric needed to sort through her issues, she felt comfortable entrusting them to Dr. Little.

Thinking about Dr. Little reminded Lyric that she needed to schedule an appointment. With Autumn getting older and being caught up in school activities, Lyric no longer felt needed. She wasn't sure of her value within her family. She needed to get herself together, and Dr. Little was just the person to help her.

Two

"Listen up, girls," Lyric said to Autumn and Heavyn as soon as they arrived at Lenox Square Mall. "Meet us in the food court in two hours." She held up two fingers to emphasize her point. "And you better not come back with any crazy-looking outfits either." She had a smile on her face, but her tone was serious. "We're trusting you to go shopping by yourself; don't disappoint us."

When it came to Autumn, Lyric didn't allow her to wear make-up, except for neutral colored lip gloss. She refused to buy her daughter clothing that fit too tightly or showed too much skin. Lyric believed that a child should look, talk, dress, and act like a child.

They synchronized their watches. Autumn and Heavyn darted into the mall talking and giggling while Lyric and Chloe went shoe shopping. Through a store window they saw some stylish shoes on display with discount signs posted, so they entered the store.

"Did you hear that Frank and Stella are getting divorced?" Chloe announced as she secured the strap of a rhinestone studded high heeled shoe that she was trying on.

Frank was a prominent surgeon who worked at the same hospital as both Lyric and Chloe's husbands. They had chaired numerous fundraisers with Stella and attended monthly teas and luncheons with her as well.

Lyric's heart sank. She hated hearing about divorce, especially among people she knew and liked. She immediately felt bad for Stella. She made a mental note to call her and offer her support. "No, I had no idea." Lyric paused for a moment. "That's unfortunate." She stood in front of the full-length mirror and modeled a pair of platform pumps. "I wasn't aware they were having problems. I've always thought they made a terrific couple."

Chloe sat up and placed her hand on her knee. "Apparently Stella did too. At least they waited until both of their children were out of the house."

"Huh?" Lyric turned around to face her. She was confused by Chloe's statement.

"I spoke with Stella, and she told me that she was blind-sided. Supposedly, Frank traded her in for a younger model."

Lyric hated when people compared women to cars. Why couldn't Chloe just say he traded her in for a younger woman? There was a brief silence.

Chloe continued. "They've been living apart for the past nine months. Now they've decided to make it official and file for divorce."

Lyric remained silent. Hearing about Stella's unfortunate situation made her realize that no matter how much a woman loved her man, marriage didn't come with any guarantees. And looking good was only beneficial when attracting a man, not keeping him. Tommy Lee's song, "Tired," summed it up best. She felt a tinge of sadness, because she really cared for and respected Stella. After twenty-four years of marriage, one would think there should be some level of security. The thought made Lyric feel sick to her stomach.

"Anyway," Chloe continued, interrupting her thoughts, "I asked Stella if she had ever stashed any cash for a rainy day, and do you know what she said?" She unloosed the strap, slid off the shoe, and placed it in the box.

Lyric shook her head and sat down next to her on the bench.

"She told me that she didn't even have a separate savings account."

Lyric snapped her neck around so fast that she almost got whiplash. "You've got to be kidding. She's obviously never read any of Suze Orman's books about women and finances."

They both laughed, trying to lighten the mood. Deep down, Lyric didn't think anything was funny about Stella's situation.

"Keith and I have been married for fourteen years," Chloe announced as she zipped her fur trimmed boots. "You and I didn't come from wealth." She motioned her hand between the two of them. "Neither did our husbands. I'm grateful to God for everything He has blessed us with." She rubbed her hand over her thigh. "I know what it feels like to be broke and to have more month than money." She paused. "I'm not even going to lie; I enjoy having money a whole lot better. Why?" She didn't wait for Lyric to respond. "Because I appreciate everything that I have. I'm grateful. I don't take any of it for granted, and I never, ever forget where I came from."

Lyric stared off into the distance. She wondered whether she had made a mistake by becoming a stay-at-home mom rather than becoming the career woman she always envisioned herself being. At the time, staying at home and raising her baby seemed like the right thing to do. She enjoyed being there to care for her child and experience all of her baby's firsts. She wouldn't change that for anything. Yet, a small part of her wondered if she should've gone to work after Autumn reached school age.

Without realizing it, Lyric verbalized one of her thoughts. "Do you ever regret not pursuing your dreams?"

"What do you mean?" Chloe crinkled her forehead. "I've always wanted a husband and a family. I like the prestige of being a doctor's wife. Not just the status, but the means to help people. When we do our fundraisers and charitable events, I feel good knowing we've made a difference in someone's life."

Lyric didn't mean to imply that their lives didn't have meaning. She knew that being a good wife and mother were important jobs. When it came to taking care of her home and family, Lyric was on top of her game. She ran her home like a business. Lyric made sure the bills were paid on time; she managed a calendar to keep up with her family's appointments and events; she cooked, cleaned, did laundry, helped Autumn with her homework, and still found time to satisfy her husband's desires.

Lyric loved Autumn and Michael more than words could ever express. What she was talking about was having it all . . . husband, children, and a meaningful career.

Lyric chose her words carefully. Although Chloe wasn't the type to be easily offended, she still didn't want to risk putting her on the defense. "We're both college educated women." Lyric looked her in the eyes. "Sometimes I feel like I should be doing more for myself; do you understand what I mean?"

She hoped that Chloe understood where she was coming from. Lyric wanted to be more independent. Although Michael never put restrictions on her in terms of what she needed financially to run the household, Lyric still felt as though the money was his because he went to work outside of the home and earned a paycheck. In spite of Michael's assurances that his money was their money, she still couldn't shake that feeling. Because of that, she shopped on a budget and rarely bought things that weren't on sale. She didn't want anyone to think she was taking advantage of Michael's generous nature.

Chloe stood up and smoothed out her lime green sweater that beautifully accentuated her chocolate complexion. "The volunteer work that we do has meaning. The fact that we are involved in our daughters' lives is priceless. Do you have any idea how many women wish they didn't have to worry about how they were going to pay their bills, or how many of them wish they were able to raise their children without daycare? We're fortunate, Lyric. I don't take that for granted, and you shouldn't either."

Lyric felt like snapping on Chloe. She hated when Chloe acted like she didn't understand where she was coming from. "I'm not complaining," Lyric clarified. She tried not to sound as frustrated as she felt. She stacked the three boxes of marked down shoes and handed them to the sales clerk. "I'll take these," she said to the associate before turning her attention back to Chloe. "Michael has a rewarding career as a surgeon. He knows his purpose and answered his life's calling. And then there's Autumn. She's young, but the truth is, she'll be leaving home sooner rather than later. Where will that leave me? Everyone has a life plan except for me, and it has nothing to do with money. This is about feeling fulfilled at the end of the day."

Chloe patted her on the back. "I understand where you're coming from." Her warm eyes could liquefy concrete. Lyric finally felt as though she had gotten through to her friend. Chloe checked her watch. "Let's pay for our shoes and meet up with the girls. We can finish this discussion later."

Lyric gave her a sincere smile, and they went to the counter to purchase their items. They gathered their bags and walked to the crowded food court. From where they were standing, the smell of freshly baked cinnamon rolls teased their nostrils. Lyric's mouth began to water. She had a weakness for those sweet sticky buns, but she refused to give in to temptation. A moment on the lips, forever on the hips. She knew exactly how many calories each tasty treat contained and how long she'd have to exercise to burn them off.

"Lyric," a woman said while tapping her on the shoulder, causing Lyric to flinch.

Turning around, she stood face-to-face with Dr. Little. She was happy to see her. Lyric also recognized the good-looking man with dread-locks standing next to her from a photo on Dr. Little's desk as her husband. He was pushing a baby stroller.

"Hi, Dr. Little," Lyric said with a wide, toothy smile. "I must've thought you up this morning."

They hugged.

"Nice to see you, Lyric. You look terrific, as usual." Dr. Little turned around and said, "This is my husband, Donovan." He smiled and waved. "And that's our baby daughter, Nia." She pronounced the name as Ni-yah. The baby began to babble.

Lyric bent down to peek inside of the stroller and got a whiff of Nia's creamy baby oil scent. The fragrance reminded her of that new baby smell. Nia appeared to be no more than six months old. She was chubby and had a head full of dark, curly hair.

"Ooh, she's beautiful," Lyric said, feeling a tinge of sadness for the baby she longed to have.

When Lyric stood back up, she introduced Chloe to Dr. Little and Donovan.

"Pleasure to meet you," Chloe said, shaking both their hands. "And yes, your daughter is gorgeous. How old is she?" She smiled.

Beaming with pride, Donovan answered, "Six months today."

"You look incredible," Chloe said to Dr. Little. "It took me at least a full year to get my body back after having my daughter."

"Thank you," Dr. Little responded. Patting her stomach, she said, "Well, I'm not all the way back. I still have about ten pounds to go. Thank God for spandex." She turned to face Lyric. "So you were thinking about me? Is everything all right?"

Lyric sighed and said, "We haven't had a session since you had the baby. I was thinking about resuming our sessions."

Dr. Little reached down in her purse and retrieved a business card. "Here." She handed her the card. "Call my assistant, Yahkie, and schedule an appointment. Okay?"

Lyric accepted the card and nodded her head. "You'll hear from me soon."

"Great," Dr. Little said as she smiled and winked. "Enjoy the rest of your day."

"You too," Lyric and Chloe replied in unison.

As soon as Dr. Little and her family were outside of earshot, Chloe said, "That's a beautiful family."

"I know, and she was rockin' that sweater dress," Lyric complimented.

"O-kay," she said in an exaggerated tone and chuckled.

"I'm so glad that everything worked out for her," Lyric said, searching the area for their daughters.

Chloe had a strange expression on her face. "What are you talking about?"

"Don't you remember?" She stared at her, waiting for a response.

Chloe shrugged her shoulders.

"About two years ago, Dr. Little was attacked by a stalker. The *Atlanta Journal-Constitution* wrote a feature about it. It even made the news. I can't believe you don't recall that story about the high profile Atlanta based psychoanalyst. I remember talking to you about it, especially after I met her at Larry and Monday's wedding. Anyway, the stalker got off on a technicality. Does that jog your memory?"

"Vaguely." She scratched her scalp. As soon as she spotted a table being freed up by three teenage girls, she said, "My puppies are barking; let's go sit down while we wait for the girls."

Chloe led the way to the table, and they both sat down. They placed their shopping bags on the floor between their feet. Lyric glanced at her watch and realized that the girls should be arriving at any moment. The chatter coming from every direction sounded like bees buzzing. Lyric looked around and noticed that the majority of the people at the mall were young adults. Most of the girls were scantily clad, revealing belly-rings and tattoos; whereas nearly all of the guys wore oversized T-shirts and saggy jeans. She massaged her temple, hoping that Autumn wouldn't go that route.

"We should get tattoos," Chloe said seriously.

Lyric touched her forehead. "You don't feel feverish."

This reminded Lyric of the time she and Chloe were on vacation in Florida, and Chloe suggested they get their belly buttons pierced. Feeling adventuresome, Lyric went along with it. When Michael saw the piercing, he had a fit. She hadn't had the piercing a full week before losing a piece of the belly ring. She removed the jewelry, hoping to get a replacement. Well, she left it out too long. The hole immediately closed. She was upset, but not enough to get it re-pierced. Now Chloe was trying to talk her into getting a tattoo. This time, Lyric was turning a deaf ear. She wasn't about to let Chloe convince her of that.

Chloe pretended to smack her hand away. "We wouldn't have to get anything big or elaborate."

"Are you going through a mid-life crisis or something?" she teased. Lyric knew Chloe wouldn't appreciate that statement. It made her sound old. Lyric said it to shut her down.

Chloe squinted at Lyric, pretending to give her the evil eye. The look on her face let Lyric know that she was about to receive a tongue-lashing. Before Chloe could say a word, Heavyn and Autumn headed in their direction carrying small bags and eating soft parmesan pretzels.

Lyric welcomed the distraction. "Hello, ladies. What did you buy?"

The girls exchanged glances and smiled. Autumn wrapped her pretzel in paper and set it on the table.

"We bought some cute little shirts and ear-rings," Autumn said as she removed three shirts with different phrases printed on each.

Lyric and Chloe nodded their heads in approval.

"Let's see yours," Chloe instructed as Heavyn continued stuffing her face.

Heavyn handed her bags to Chloe for inspection. As Chloe pulled out the clothing, she held up the shirts for Lyric to see. They were both pleased.

"You two did good," Lyric said with a smile. She announced that they should take their bags to the car before the girls went to see the Disney Movie, *The Princess and the Frog*.

After securing their bags in the trunk, they purchased tickets for the girls. Autumn and Heavyn went inside the theatre, and Lyric and Chloe went to grab a bite to eat at The Clubhouse Restaurant. Once inside, the ladies were immediately seated at a booth. Lyric had eaten there on a few occasions. She really liked the décor, which consisted of draped white table cloths and fine china on the tables. She looked around and admired the extensive art collection covering the walls.

Lyric appreciated fine art. She had been collecting original artwork for several years. She had a rare painting from Africa that had thick leather ropes hanging like nooses. It was her favorite painting. She prominently displayed it over her balcony. Just the mounting alone cost her thousands of dollars.

The waiter filled their water glasses and took their orders. Lyric ordered the pomegranate chicken salad, and Chloe selected the lobster and rock shrimp risotto. As the waiter left with their menus, Chloe brought up the tattoo subject again; explaining that they should each get a butterfly on their foot or inner ankle. That way, it wouldn't be too obvious. Lyric reminded her about the disaster with the belly button piercing. They both chuckled at that one. After that, Chloe dropped the subject about the tattoos.

In the midst of their laughter, Lyric saw a handsome and distinguished looking gentleman walk past them. He appeared to be around forty-ish, six feet six inches tall, and slender with a hint of grey at his temples. She found herself turning around and looking at him. To her surprise, they locked eyes, and he flashed her a brilliant smile. Feeling embarrassed, Lyric turned around, only to discover Chloe giving her a disapproving look.

Lyric didn't acknowledge Chloe's watchful eye. Instead, she sipped on her ice water and used her fingers to wipe away the water drops clinging to the glass. When she couldn't take Chloe's staring anymore, she decided to go to the restroom and wash her hands before eating. As she walked past the attractive stranger, she gave him a closed mouth grin as her eyes looked away. By Lyric's definition, not showing any teeth was her friendly but not flirtatious smile.

On her way back to the table, the mystery man gestured for her to stop. Her heart raced, but she tried to play it cool.

"I couldn't help but notice you," he said in a suave and confident manner. "You're the most beautiful woman I've seen in a long time. I'm Richard Fredericks." He extended his hand to her, and Lyric shook it.

She was flattered. "Why, thank you. I'm Lyric Stokes."

"That's a nice name." His smile reminded Lyric of a toothpaste, teeth whitening, and fresh breath gum commercial all rolled into one. "Are you married, Lyric?"

"Actually I am." She remarked with a pleasant smile on her face.

"Some men get all the luck." He seemed disappointed. He shifted in his seat so that he could retrieve his wallet from his back pocket. "I'm an art dealer, and I own an art gallery." He pulled out a business card and handed it to her. "Call me anytime."

Lyric accepted his card and studied it briefly. She didn't have any art dealers in her circle of friends. He most certainly could come in handy, especially since she enjoyed collecting original art. She decided not to throw away his card. Lyric explained that she needed to leave; the waiter was at her table with her food. No sooner than she sat down did Chloe berate her for entertaining the stranger.

"I don't know what's going on with you, Mrs. Stokes, but you better reel yourself back in real quick," Chloe said seriously, emphasizing Mrs. "You mark my words," she looked from side to side, "if you get involved with that man, you will live to regret it. You can't mess with fire and expect not to get burned."

Lyric felt as if she were five years old being chastised by her mother. Deep down inside she knew Chloe was right. Still, there was something within her that liked the attention. Although she was committed to her marriage and wasn't interested in having an affair, she didn't think there was anything wrong with having a new associate.

Three

It was Sunday morning, and Lyric rolled over and felt the warmth of Michael's body lying next to her. He looked peaceful as his chest heaved with every breath. His lips were lightly parted. Lyric felt like sticking her finger in the dimple in his chin, but she resisted the urge.

Not wanting to disturb him, Lyric eased her body out of the bed and made her way into the bathroom. While in there, she emptied her bladder, washed her face, and brushed her teeth. Then she went into Autumn's room to check on her. No matter how old Autumn was, Lyric still checked to see if she were breathing, just like she did when she was a baby. A smile spread across Lyric's face when she saw her daughter sound asleep.

Lyric made her way downstairs and into the kitchen to cook breakfast. She enjoyed having her entire family at home. Times like this, she appreciated the quiet time to gather her thoughts.

When she ran into Dr. Little at the mall, she felt their encounter had been fate. She couldn't wait to call and schedule an appointment.

In preparation for her omelets, she went into the refrigerator to gather red, yellow, and green bell peppers, mushrooms, shredded cheese, and egg whites. She set the ingredients on the island before picking up the peppers and placing them under the running faucet water. She retrieved two plates from the cabinet, a knife from the drawer, and diced the peppers on a wooden cutting board. She went into the food pantry to pick out an onion and diced it as well. After mixing the vegetables, Lyric sprayed a small round skillet with a butter flavored cooking spray and placed it over medium heat. As soon as the pan became hot, she poured in the egg whites and added a dash of salt and pepper.

"Good morning, Mom," Autumn said as she entered the kitchen.

"Hey, sweetie," she said as she scraped the veggies into the omelet and sprinkled cheese on top. "You're right on time to toast the English muffins." She smiled.

"Are we going to church today?" Autumn rubbed sleep from her eyes.

"Of course. Hopefully Daddy will feel up to going with us." Using a spatula, she folded the omelet in half before sliding it onto a plate and repeating the process all over again.

Autumn washed her hands in the sink and dried them on a dish towel. "Okay. I'll call Heavyn and tell her to meet me in youth church." She removed one muffin, because she and her mother usually only ate half. "Is Daddy coming down for breakfast?"

Lyric sighed as she flipped the eggs. She wondered whether she should wake him up. She knew how cranky Michael could get when his sleep was interrupted, yet she didn't want the food to get cold. "He's got to eat, right?"

"Mom, do you ever get tired of doing everything by yourself?" She stared at Lyric.

Lyric blinked quickly. She wondered when her daughter had become so mature. Turning off the stove and dabbing her forehead with her arm, Lyric was astonished by her daughter's analysis. "What are you talking about, sweetie?" She tried to play it off.

Placing the muffin in the toaster, Autumn said, "Sometimes when we're out, and you see a family, you get this sad look in your eyes."

Lyric brushed Autumn's cheek with the back of her hand and assured her that she was imagining things. She didn't want her daughter to think she was unhappy. As a parent, Lyric felt it was her responsibility to protect Autumn from adult issues. The last thing she wanted was for Autumn to be worrying about her.

Autumn turned her face away and said, "You always tell me that I can talk to you about anything. I'm not a little kid anymore, Mom; you can tell me if something is wrong." Lyric felt a stinging in her eyes, and she turned her back to Autumn. "Mommy, I'm sorry. I didn't mean to hurt your feelings." She wrapped her arm around Lyric's waist.

Grabbing a napkin from one of the drawers, Lyric dabbed the corners of her eyes and turned around. She hated when she got all sensitive. Hearing Autumn talk like such a young lady, even sounding almost like a friend, caught Lyric off guard. It tugged at her heartstrings.

"Listen, Autumn. I love my family very much. Your father works extremely hard to provide us with a comfortable and lavish lifestyle. Just look around you." She made a sweeping motion with her arm. "I wouldn't be telling you the truth if I said I don't wish we could spend more time together as a family. But," she held up a finger, "nothing is perfect; there's always a trade off. Your father has paid his dues, and now we're reaping the benefits. He's a surgeon, so he needs plenty of rest. So," she cupped Autumn's face in

her hands, "my job is to take good care of you."
She chuckled. "That includes being active at your
school, attending all of your events, and teaching
you how to be a proper young lady. Got it?" She
kissed her on the nose.

"Got it," Autumn said as she removed the
toasted muffins from the toaster and spread
butter on top. "Miss Momma," she pointed at the
omelets, "you may want to make another omelet
for Daddy."

Lyric realized that she had become so ac-
customed to cooking breakfast for two that she
hadn't made an omelet for Michael. On the weekends, Michael typically left early in the morning
to go fishing, golfing, or play racquetball. During
the week, Michael usually had a protein shake.
Therefore, Lyric didn't have to prepare anything
for him. She started laughing uncontrollably,
and Autumn joined in on the banter.

"What's all the commotion?" Michael asked as
he walked in.

Startled, Lyric said, "Oh, nothing." She hoped
that Michael hadn't overheard her conversation
with Autumn. She went on to prepare another
omelet.

Michael kissed her on the cheek. "Smells good
in here."

"Thanks. I've already fixed plates for you and Autumn. If you're hungry, you can go sit at the table and eat."

He walked toward Autumn and gave her a hug. "We'll wait for you," Michael said to Lyric as he grabbed both plates and went into the breakfast area. He sat at the wooden table that sat six.

Autumn followed behind him with a plate of muffins and a jar of raspberry All Fruit. Not long afterward, Lyric joined them. She asked Michael to bless the food. They bowed their heads as Michael said grace.

Lyric excused herself from the table so that she could bring back a pitcher of orange juice and a glass. Seeing that her hands were full, Autumn went into the kitchen and got two more juice glasses and returned to the table. She kept one for herself and handed the other to her father.

"So tell me what's going on with school," Michael said to his daughter as he took a bite of his omelet and chewed.

Smiling, Autumn said, "My teachers love me; what else can I say?" She poured herself a glass of juice.

They all laughed. Lyric looked at her daughter with pride. She was happy that Autumn had been such an academic achiever. Ever since she had been in school, she'd excelled in all subjects. Whenever Lyric met with Autumn's teachers, they always had great things to say about her.

"Okay, okay," Michael relented. "What about your extracurricular activities?" He seemed to be making a genuine effort to connect with his daughter. Lyric liked that.

Autumn rolled her eyes upward and placed her fork near her mouth. Then she looked at her dad and said, "Cheerleading is fun. Heavyn and I are co-captains. I'm still taking piano lessons." She sipped her citrus drink.

Lyric added that she and Autumn were also taking private tennis lessons. She looked at Michael and asked, "Do you want to attend church with us?"

Lyric could tell by the look on Michael's face that he was surprised by her question.

"I hadn't planned on it," he replied, biting into his English muffin.

Although Michael believed in God, he didn't believe in organized religion. He felt that being spiritual was more important than being religious. As far as he was concerned, he had a relationship with God and didn't need to attend church to prove it. When Michael was a child, his family attended church regularly. His then-pastor had an extramarital affair, resulting in an illegitimate child. The scandal disrupted the church. Membership dwindled. That's when Michael learned that if people place their faith in man instead of God, they can be led astray. He realized *it is better to put trust in the Lord than to put confidence in man.*

Lyric pretended to pout. "It would really mean a lot to me and Autumn." She batted her eyelashes, hoping to sway Michael's decision.

Michael's eyes ping-ponged between Lyric and Autumn until finally he changed his mind. "I'll go."

Both mother and daughter cheered. Lyric felt good that Michael was going to church with them. She didn't really like attending church without her husband every Sunday. It made her feel as though he wasn't setting a good example for Autumn. She didn't argue with him about it, though. She had voiced her feelings once and that was enough. After that, she prayed about it and turned it over to God. She knew that if Michael went to church to appease her, it would only be temporary. If the Lord placed it in his heart to go, then the change would be lasting.

"After services we should go out to dinner," Autumn suggested, eyeing both her parents.

Michael agreed to take his girls out to eat. They finished eating breakfast and cleared the dishes from the table. Lyric immediately called Chloe to tell her the news. She could tell that Chloe was disappointed since they usually attended worship services together and took the girls out to eat afterward. It had become their routine. Still, Chloe said that she understood and encouraged her friend to enjoy spending some quality time with her husband. Especially since Chloe's husband was a CME; he only attended church on Christmas, Mother's Day, and Easter.

They got dressed, and Michael drove the family to church in his black 7 Series BMW. Walking into the church on the arm of her husband felt better to Lyric than buying a brand new Prada bag. Autumn went to youth church, and Michael and Lyric entered the main sanctuary. Lyric scoped out the room looking for Chloe. She didn't see her, so she followed the usher's instruction. They were seated near the front.

A couple of minutes later, an associate minister led a lengthy prayer. Then the choir sang two selections before church announcements, which was followed by two more songs. Immediately following, the pastor came out to share the Word. The sermon was titled "Improving Your Family by Bettering Yourself." The minister referred to the biblical text Matthew 1:18-25.

According to the minister, there was dysfunction in all families. No family member was isolated or insulated from trials, tribulations, or troubles. For Lyric, hearing the message confirmed that she had told her daughter the right thing during their earlier conversation.

At the end of the service, they ran into Chloe while they were going to meet Autumn, and she was headed to get Heavyn. Lyric and Michael gave Chloe a hug.

"Nice to see you at church, Mike," Chloe said.

Michael grinned. "What did you think about the message?"

"Pastor was definitely on point," Michael said. "I especially liked the part when he talked about people either being in a storm, just coming out of a storm, or getting ready to go into a storm. That's so true."

They started walking together to get the girls.

"I wish Keith could've heard that message," Chloe said. "I guess I'll get him the recorded version."

When they arrived at youth church, gospel rap music blared in the background. The kids were talking and laughing. As soon as Autumn and Heavyn saw their parents, they hurried over. They greeted them with hugs.

"What did you learn?" Michael asked Autumn.

"The youth pastor talked about loving yourself instead of things," she explained. "He told us that things don't make you happy. True happiness comes from God."

Michael nodded his head. He seemed impressed. The girls chatted and giggled as they exited the church. Since they had parked so far apart, they hugged again before going their separate ways.

Chloe whispered in Lyric's ear, "Be good. Don't give way to the devil." She released Lyric and waved goodbye.

Lyric briefly thought about Chloe's words. She knew Chloe was referring to the incident where she had accepted Mr. Fredericks's business card while they were at lunch. She didn't know whether Chloe was giving her a warning or what. She appreciated Chloe's concern because she knew that Chloe had her best interest at heart. Lyric inserted her arm through Michael's and looked at his handsome face. Smiling, she mouthed the words, "I love you." She couldn't wait until after dinner to get home and show her husband just how much.

Four

The beeping sound of the alarm clock jolted Lyric from her sleep. She removed the satin eye mask, and at the same time, took her head scarf along with it. She set them on the nightstand and tapped the buzzer, causing the alarm to stop. As she stretched her arms over her head, a slow yawn manifested.

Tapping Michael on his bare chest, she said, "Time to wake up, sleepy head."

Michael smacked his lips, mouthed some inaudible words, and rolled over on his side. Giving him a blank stare, her initial reaction was to shake him, but she thought better of it and got out of bed. She brushed her teeth before going into Autumn's room to wake her up for school.

Lyric flicked on the light switch and said, "Good morning. Time to get up, sweetie." Autumn pulled the covers over her head and pleaded with her mom to turn off the light. Lyric flipped the switch to turn off the light. "You better get your butt out of the bed so that you won't be late for school." Lyric waited, but Autumn didn't make a move. She walked over and yanked off the comforter. "That means now," she said sternly, standing over her.

Stretching her body, all the while murmuring and complaining, Autumn finally got up and went into the bathroom. While Autumn got ready for school, Lyric went into the kitchen and prepared scrambled egg whites, grits, and bacon. When she finished, she went back upstairs.

As soon as Lyric rounded the corner, she nearly bumped into Autumn. Already dressed in a hoodie, jeans, and faux fur trimmed boots, Autumn stood in the hallway.

"Don't you look cute," Lyric said as she smoothed down a fly away strand of Autumn's hair. "Breakfast is ready."

As Autumn trotted downstairs, Lyric noticed that Michael was out of bed. She went into the bedroom and heard the faucet running in the bathroom. From where she was standing, she could see Michael leaning over the sink, brushing his teeth.

She made her way into the bathroom. "Hey." She rubbed his T-shirt covered back. "I made you some breakfast."

He rinsed, spit in the sink, and wiped his mouth with a hand towel. Then he grabbed Lyric by the waist and peck kissed her on the lips. Being so close to Michael made Lyric feel all warm and fuzzy inside.

Michael followed her downstairs where he fixed himself a plate and joined Autumn at the table. Lyric grabbed a cup of yogurt from the refrigerator and ate with her family. She savored the creamy taste. When they finished eating, Autumn gathered her backpack, kissed her parents goodbye, and walked to the bus stop.

Before Autumn was born, Lyric and Michael had agreed that unless their child had a learning disability, she would attend public school. Both Lyric and Michael had been products of the public school system, and they excelled academically. Autumn had exhibited those same outgoing, achiever qualities as her parents. She had been an honor roll student ever since kindergarten.

Autumn enjoyed learning different languages. She was fluent in French, German, and Spanish. Whenever the family took European vacations, Autumn liked showing off her skills. People were often surprised to discover that Autumn didn't attend an expensive private school, and that made her parents feel extremely proud. They were determined to give Autumn a balanced life. Although they lived a privileged lifestyle, they never wanted Autumn to feel entitled.

Not long after Autumn left, Michael and Lyric made love, leaving Lyric basking in the afterglow. As Michael freshened up, Lyric lay on the bed feeling satisfied. Once dressed, Michael kissed his wife on the forehead as he prepared to go to work. On his way out the door, he pulled the trash receptacles to the curb and headed to the hospital, leaving Lyric all alone. Realizing that she couldn't just lie in bed all day, Lyric pulled out her day planner and called Dr. Little's office to schedule an appointment. She was pleased that Yahkie was able to pencil her in the same week. As soon as she hung up the phone, she changed into her workout gear and hopped on the elliptical machine for forty-five minutes.

After working out, Lyric felt refreshed. She left her sweaty clothes in a pile on the bathroom floor before stepping into the shower. Everything was fine until she attempted to turn off the water. All of a sudden, the water wouldn't turn all the way off. Lyric kept fumbling with the knob, trying to turn it off. It didn't work. She slid the glass door open and got out. Then she closed the door behind her and wrapped her body in a towel. She was about to call Michael but figured he wouldn't appreciate being interrupted at work for a plumbing problem. Besides, he would most likely chastise her for not calling a plumber instead of him anyway.

Just as she was about to go online to search for a plumber, she remembered that she had recently met one while attending a meeting at Autumn's school. Hearing the water still slightly running prompted her to react immediately. She searched her purse and stumbled across quite a few business cards. The one that read N. Richard Fredericks caught her attention. She held that one in her hand. She continued to search until she retrieved the business card that read Carlos Miguel, certified plumber. She grabbed the cordless phone and dialed the cell phone number listed on the card. He answered on the second ring.

"Hi, Mr. Miguel," Lyric said. "This is Lyric Stokes." She told him where they had met.

"Yes, yes, I remember you." He laughed. "To what do I owe the pleasure?"

Lyric sighed. "Well, I was taking a shower, and now I can't turn off the water. I could really use your help." She sat down on the edge of her bed.

"You're in luck." She could hear the smile in his voice. "I happen to have an opening."

Lyric exhaled in relief. She gave him her address, and they ended the call. She planned to run some errands afterward, so she put on a sweater skirt set and swept her hair up into a French roll, allowing some strands of hair to frame her face.

While waiting for the plumber to arrive, Lyric decided to give Mr. Fredericks a call. When he answered, she was surprised. She had expected to get his answering machine. She found herself tripping over her words.

"Mr. Fredericks, this is Lyric. We met a few days ago at The Clubhouse Restaurant." She hoped that she didn't sound as nervous as she felt.

"What can I do for you, Lyric?" His tone was courteous.

"I have some artwork that I want to get appraised. Particularly, an original African piece," she explained.

"Would you like to come to my office or should I come out to you?" he asked.

She hesitated for a moment, thinking about all of Chloe's doom and gloom warnings. Then she thought about the African work of art. It was huge and securely mounted, so she asked him to come to her house. He agreed. He mentioned that he could come out later that morning. Lyric gave him the address, and they discontinued the call.

An hour had passed before the doorbell rang, and Lyric trudged downstairs to answer.

She smiled when she saw Carlos through the glass panes. "Thank you so much for getting here so fast," Lyric said as she opened the door.

"No problem." As he lugged his toolbox inside, he said, "I don't know if you're aware, but your garage door is open."

Lyric shrugged. "My husband probably forgot to close it on his way out this morning. He had to pull the trash to the curb. I'll get it later."

"Okay," he said. "Where's the problem?"

"Follow me," she instructed as she closed the door behind him. She led him up the stairs and into the master-bath.

Carlos set his box down on the counter. Walking over to the shower, he attempted to turn the knob and nothing happened. He removed a roll of duct tape and some tools from his box until he found a clay-looking substance. Then he loosened some screws on the knob, used the clay, and tightened the knob. Next thing Lyric knew, the dripping had ceased.

"Thank you so much," Lyric said, sounding relieved.

"You're welcome." He placed the tools back in the box and closed it.

She smoothed her dress with her hands. "How much do I owe you?"

"Don't worry about it. We're on the PTA together. I wouldn't feel right charging you."

"No, I have to pay you something," she insisted.

"Fine," he relented, holding his box. "Pay whatever you want. It was a simple job and didn't take much time."

Lyric grabbed a pen and her checkbook from her purse. "Whom should I make it out to?"

"Oh, you can make it payable to me."

She filled out the check, ripped it from her book, and handed it to him. She thanked him again, and he left. Since she had some time before her meeting with Mr. Fredericks, she straightened up around her house.

Two hours passed before Mr. Fredericks showed up at Lyric's doorstep. As soon as she opened the door and invited him inside, he flashed her that million watt smile.

"Your home is beautiful," he said, looking around the foyer.

Lyric showed him the art lining the wall going up the stairs. "What type of art do you buy?"

"I buy original, one of a kind pieces. A few years ago I purchased a Picasso for 1.9 million dollars, and sold it for 25 million dollars."

Lyric was impressed. She could tell by his diamond encrusted Rolex watch and Salvatore Ferragamo loafers that he was doing well. When they got to the top of the stairs, Lyric showed him her African masterpiece. Mr. Fredericks gasped when he saw it.

"This is incredible." He stared at the art. "Where did you get this?"

Lyric could tell by his reaction that the piece was probably more valuable than she had realized. She went on to explain how she procured such an exquisite piece of art.

"My husband and I took a trip to Africa a few years ago. When I saw this piece, I had to have it. I had never seen anything like this before." She pointed at the painting. "The woman in the painting was murdered by her jealous lover. The man in the painting hung himself. That's why there are strong leather ropes dangling at the bottom similar to the ones used to hang slaves from trees back in the day."

"That's quite a story." He continued studying the artwork. "Are you interested in selling it?"

Pausing for a moment, Lyric seemed reflective. She really liked that artwork. It was her favorite. She wasn't interested in selling it at this time. He'd have to entice her with a whole lot of zeros. "At this time I don't want to get rid of it. Just trying to get it back to the States was a feat. Not to mention nearly paying a mint to get it mounted." She smiled. "That thing is held up by a steel beam. It could withstand an earthquake and hold hundreds of pounds without falling down."

Mr. Fredericks nodded his head. "Based on what I've seen, you've got quite the collection." He looked over the balcony. "I'll need to take some pictures and take down some information about the pieces that you want appraised."

Lyric stood by and watched Mr. Fredericks take digital photos and jot down some notes.

When he finished taking the last picture, Lyric remembered that there was a Van Gogh in her bedroom that she wanted appraised too.

"There's one more painting that I want to show you." She led him up to her bedroom and showed him the painting.

"It's exquisite." He jotted down more notes.

Lyric asked, "When can I expect to hear from you?"

He handed her another business card. "Give me a few days. I'll call you."

"I'm just curious. What does the N on your business card stand for?" she asked while he snapped the picture.

He stared at her for a moment before hesitantly saying, "Nigel."

He seemed to await a response, only Lyric didn't give him one. Nigel Richard Fredericks. His name sounded familiar, but she couldn't place it.

"Hmmm" was all she said.

"I think using the initial makes me sound more distinguished." He chuckled.

She nodded her head. "I really appreciate you coming out here."

Lyric extended her hand so that she could shake his hand and see him out. Rather than taking her hand, he looked around and asked, "Where's your restroom?"

Lyric didn't like anyone other than her husband and daughter using her personal bathroom. An uneasy feeling crept up upon her. Her bathroom was the closest, and Autumn's bathroom was the second closest. She didn't want him using Autumn's bathroom either. She paused for a moment. She contemplated sending him downstairs, but she didn't want to appear rude. So she showed him to the master bathroom suite.

A couple of minutes later, the bathroom door opened.

"You even have art in your bathroom," Mr. Fredericks said, standing in the doorway. Lyric was sitting on the couch. "Would you please tell me about this picture?"

Lyric wasn't sure which picture he was referring to, so she got up to go into the bathroom and see. Just when he was about to enter the restroom, he yanked her toward him and ushered her inside. Before Lyric could scream, Mr. Fredericks covered her mouth with his and tried to force his tongue inside her mouth. She clenched her mouth shut. She struggled to pry herself away from him. His grip was as tight as a vice. Lyric couldn't escape. She felt as though she were trapped in a nightmare. If Lyric could've forced herself to faint, she would've. She didn't want to be mentally present for what she suspected was about to come.

Mr. Fredericks picked her up and slammed her on the sink, causing her to bump the back of her head on the mirror. Before she could even say, "Ouch," he hiked up her dress. While ripping off her panties, he gripped her around the neck. Feeling as though she were having an out of body experience, Lyric stared in shock. She heard him unbuckle his belt.

"Lord, help me," Lyric pleaded as she pressed the palm of her hand against his forehead, trying to push him back. With the flick of a wrist, she scratched him on the side of his neck.

"Ouch!" he squealed as he touched the laceration which was turning red with blood. With one hand, Mr. Fredericks grabbed both of Lyric's wrists and held them over her head.

After attempting to knee him in the groin, Mr. Fredericks slapped Lyric across her left cheek. Then he released her while he grabbed a roll of duct tape off the counter. Lyric thought that her heart was going to stop beating when she saw the tape left behind by the plumber.

With a look of surprise, Lyric attempted to plead with him. "Please, don't." She shook her head as she frantically searched the counter, looking for something to throw at him.

Before she was able to locate a makeshift weapon, Mr. Fredericks restrained her and taped her hands together over her head. He then ushered her out of the bathroom and into the bedroom where he instructed her to get on the bed.

Sobbing and begging him to leave, Lyric refused to comply with his request. Picking her up like a duffel bag and placing her on the bed, Mr. Fredericks took his hand and guided his way into her body. Lyric flinched when she felt him. She could not believe this was happening to her. Tears streamed down her cheeks. She whimpered like a hurt puppy.

Fifteen minutes later, Mr. Fredericks rolled his two hundred twenty pound frame off of her and pulled up his pants. As Lyric lay on the bed sobbing, Mr. Fredericks went into the bathroom to fill the tub with water. He asked for a pair of scissors. Lyric's heart nearly beat out of her chest. She silently prayed that he wasn't going to stab her. She wasn't ready to die, especially not in such a violent way. Her body trembled with fear. She clenched her jaw so tight that her teeth nearly cracked. She could hear him in the bathroom rummaging through the drawers. The idea of him plundering through her personal belongings made her feel violated all over again.

"Why do you need scissors?" she dared to ask, hoping he'd stop looking through her stuff.

He entered the bedroom. "So that I can untie you."

She studied his face for a moment before speaking again. She didn't feel as though he was going to try and kill her. "There's a pair in the nightstand." She tilted her head to the right.

Mr. Fredericks retrieved the shears. He cut the tape and snatched it off Lyric's wrists, causing her to wince.

"Come on," Mr. Fredericks said. "It's time for you to take a bath."

Lyric rubbed her wrists before tugging on her dress.

Her clothing had been hiked up over her face. She wrapped her arms around her shoulders as a source of comfort. It didn't work; she wasn't comforted. As she pressed her knees into her chest, she blinked away the tears.

"Your husband's a lucky man," Mr. Fredericks said with a grin plastered on his face.

She wasn't flattered by his statement. In fact, she felt repulsed. She slid off the bed and stood up. Lyric stared at him blankly as fluid leaked onto her inner thigh. She felt disgusting.

"That felt so good. We're going to have to do this again sometime." He buckled his belt and zipped his zipper.

She visualized herself clawing his eyes out. She wanted to kick him in the family jewels as hard as she could. Staring at the floor, she balled her fists and flared her nostrils.

Mr. Fredericks stroked the side of her face with the back of his hand. She jerked her head away. He leaned in so close that Lyric could feel the warmth of his breath on her cheek.

"You look so beautiful," he said.

His words startled her. "Why did you do this to me?" she demanded to know. Tears filled her eyes and rage wreaked havoc on her body. She felt like killing him. He was bigger and stronger. She knew he could hurt her even more than he already had. Helpless was how she felt.

"You were made for me." He sounded so arrogant. Lyric wondered how many others there had been before her. "There's a chemistry between us that won't be denied, no matter how hard you try."

Feeling her insides quiver, she could hardly contain her anger. "Something is wrong with you." The words flew out of her mouth so quickly she barely had time to register what she had just said. She cleared her throat. "I hardly even know you. How could you ever think that I would want to be . . . raped? I HATE you! You disgust me. Get out of my house!" The words burned a hole in her throat like hot lava.

He raised his hands in surrender. His mouth was twisted upward in a satisfied smirk. "Not until you take a bath. Get in the tub," he instructed. His tone was nonthreatening, yet stern. "Your body should be clean." Lyric felt panic. The last thing she wanted to do was to wash away the evidence, especially since he hadn't used a condom. Even in her distressed state, she knew

that she should not take a bath or shower. She
had to think quickly.

"So you like your women clean, huh? Maybe I
don't want to wash your scent off me," she lied.
She stared into his dark round eyes and felt as
though she were looking into the eyes of pure
evil, the devil. Immediately she darted her eyes
to her bedpost.

He looked smug. "Sorry, babe, it's not op-
tional."

Ushering her into the bathroom by her arm,
Mr. Fredericks watched as Lyric undressed and
stepped into the warm water. Her eyes glistened as
loose tears escaped down her cheeks and plopped
into the water. She felt like scrubbing the skin clean
off her body. No amount of soap or bath gels could
remove the filth staining her insides.

When she finished, Mr. Fredericks wrapped
her in a towel and dried her off. She couldn't
believe how meticulous her rapist was being. His
actions perplexed her. She had always thought
rape was more about control than sex. If she
didn't know better, she'd think this pervert cared
for her.

As Lyric got dressed, he went into the bedroom and removed the sheets from the bed. He
balled up the sheets in a pillowcase so that he
could take them with him.

"All right, I'm about to leave," Mr. Fredericks announced. He stood close to her. "You smell good." He licked his lips. "You taste good, and you look good. You're everything I've ever wanted in a woman." He used his finger to trail her cleavage, and she pushed his hand away. "You don't have to admit it now, but we're meant to be together. The way your body responded to mine . . ." He sighed.

Lyric's head began to ache. She couldn't believe what she was hearing. There was no part of her body that willingly cooperated with that assault.

He glanced into the mirror at the scratch on the side of his neck. "Let me get something for this scratch," he said, pointing at his neck.

Lyric looked at him like he had just asked to use her toothbrush. Without saying anything, she removed a cotton ball and a bottle of peroxide from the cabinet and handed it to him.

"Thanks." He tended to his abrasion and tucked the cotton in his pocket. Mr. Fredericks said in a chilling tone, "You better not call the police either. What happened between us was meant to happen. You don't have anything to feel guilty about. Don't try to ease your conscious by crying rape." His gaze met hers. "Even if you did, nobody would believe you. Your friend saw you talking to me at the restaurant. And lest we forget," he wagged his finger, "you invited me here." He tucked the sheets underneath his arm.

She wiped her wet face with the palm of her hand and sniffed. The taste of salty tears invaded her mouth. She thought about picking up the crystal vase sitting on the table and knocking him over the head with it. What good would that do? she reasoned. He had already violated her. Too little, too late.

She stood there with her mouth agape as Mr. Fredericks brushed past her. She didn't move until she heard the front door close. That's when she ran downstairs and looked out one of the glass panes next to the door. Seeing Mr. Fredericks get inside of his company van, she locked the door. A gut-wrenching scream made its way up from the pit of her stomach like bile and escaped from her lips. She screamed, cried, and jumped up and down. By the time she had finished, her throat felt as scratchy as sandpaper. Her voice was raspy and her hands ached. When she looked at her balled fists, the delicate skin on her knuckles was broken with blood seeping from the wounds. She paused for a moment as she stared at her appendages. She didn't even remember punching the door and hitting the floor.

With trembling hands, Lyric ran her extremities underneath the kitchen faucet. She flinched from the stinging. Then she went into the half-bath next to the kitchen and removed the peroxide from the cabinet. She poured the solution on her wounds and dried her hands on a small towel, leaving light red stains behind. There was a topical ointment nearby, so she applied a small amount on the cracked skin.

When she finished, she retrieved an icepack from the freezer and placed it on her puffy, red eyes. Leaning against a barstool, she wondered whether she should call the police and report the assault. Then she thought about what Mr. Fredericks had said. How would this make her look? She was married. Yes, she had accepted Mr. Frederick's business card. She understood that was wrong. Yes, she had invited him over to her house. That was only because he was an art dealer, and she had art that she wanted appraised. Was she sexually attracted to him? No, she resolved. Never in her wildest dreams, or nightmares, had she imagined Mr. Fredericks would have been such a beast. And not in a good way. She was convinced that Mr. Fredericks was the devil! How would she explain the attack to her husband? She was afraid that Michael would blame her. What if Michael thought she deserved it? How would she handle that? What about Autumn?

Sighing, Lyric worried about the embarrassment this whole ordeal would bring upon her family. As the wife of a prominent surgeon, she had certain standards to which she was expected to adhere. The last thing she wanted to do was disgrace her husband.

The throbbing in her temples seemed to be getting worse, so she set the icepack on the counter and went upstairs into the bathroom to retrieve a bottle of pain medication. She removed two gel-tabs and popped them in her mouth. She filled a glass with filtered tap water and washed down the pills.

When she looked up, Lyric stared at her reflection in the mirror. She felt worthless. Her hair was disheveled. Tear streaks stained her face. Images of Mr. Fredericks attacking her replayed in her mind. Even closing her eyes didn't stop the images. She felt like throwing the glass and shattering the mirror. Instead, she set the glass next to the sink.

A feeling of disgust crept up and overtook her body. She ran out of the bathroom and into her bedroom where she plopped down on the couch and pressed her knees into her chest. She closed her eyes as the tears raced each other down her cheeks.

Five minutes later, she got up and scurried into the bathroom to splash cold water on her face. In spite of the fact that she had already taken a bath, she still felt dirty and had an overwhelming desire to cleanse her body.

She went into Autumn's bathroom and turned on the shower. Steam immediately formed, leaving its residue on the glass shower door and mirror. Stepping inside the shower, Lyric closed her eyes as the hot water ran down her face, neck, and traveled the rest of her body. Just as the water went down the drain, Lyric wished that she, too, could magically disappear down the drain. She bit her lower lip, angry at herself for letting this happen. She pleaded with God to help her. Removing a bar of soap from its tray, she scrubbed her entire body, including her face.

As she stood underneath the shower head, her hair became soaked. She didn't care. She used some of Autumn's shampoo and washed it. Ordinarily, she would've gone to the hairdresser to get her hair washed. This was no ordinary time.

Twenty minutes had passed before Lyric emerged from the shower. She wrapped a towel around her head like a turbine, and then cloaked another around her body. She trekked across the floor and back into her bedroom where she put on a long housedress. She glanced at the clock, and it read 11:00 A.M. This was normally the time that she would watch *The View*.

She never missed that show. Today, though, Lyric didn't even have the desire to TiVo the program. Then she thought about Autumn. She would be home in a few hours, and Lyric hadn't watched television, left the house, nor started dinner. The fact that Mr. Fredericks had disrupted her life so much angered her all the more. In spite of the fact that the Bible states: *Vengeance is mine; I will repay, saith the Lord,* that didn't stop Lyric from wishing Mr. Fredericks would get run over by a Mack truck. Until now, she could honestly say that she had never hated any man, or woman for that matter.

All sorts of thoughts came flooding to Lyric's mind. What if Mr. Fredericks was HIV positive? What if he had herpes or some other sexually transmitted disease? Dear God, she thought. In the midst of her anguish, she collapsed to her knees and pleaded with God.

"Father, I don't know why this happened today. If I've done anything to bring this on, please forgive me. I'm sorry. I beg you," she cried. "Please don't let me have contracted a disease. Help me not to become bitter or depressed. You command us to forgive one another and to pray for our enemies." She paused. "Father, I would be lying if I said I forgive that monster for what he's done. The truth of the matter is that I don't even want you to forgive him. I'm not ready yet. Soften my heart so that I can get to a place of forgiveness. Protect my husband and my daughter from his destruction. Help me, Father, to get past this."

She stood to her feet and removed the towel covering her hair. She tousled her mane with her fingers and allowed it to air dry. Inside she struggled as to whether or not she should report the crime. She realized that rape was hard to prove. Oftentimes, the victims ended up being the ones on trial. She didn't like the thought of having her character assassinated, but the thought of Mr. Fredericks harming another woman because of her selfishness was more than she could bear. Ultimately, her sense of obligation won out. She didn't want another woman to suffer the same fate she had. She changed out of her housedress and into a jogging suit before calling the police.

Fifteen minutes had passed before two uniformed police officers arrived at her doorstep. As soon as Lyric heard the doorbell ring, her heartbeat sped up. She knew there was no turning back now. She asked the Lord to give her strength. Hurriedly, she answered the door and let the officers in.

A male and female cop introduced themselves and showed their badges before entering Lyric's home. She escorted them into the living room where she told them about her initial encounter with Mr. Fredericks, and then his visit to her home. Her hands trembled and her eyes welled with tears as she recalled the events. Per the officer's request, Lyric handed the female officer Mr. Frederick's business card.

The short, stocky, female officer advised that the rape would be harder to prove with most of the physical evidence being gone. By changing clothes and bathing, viable evidence had been destroyed. Lyric knew that, but hearing it made her feel even worse. The officer commented that Mr. Fredericks must've done this sort of thing before. How else would he have known to force her to take a bath and take the sheets with him?

Lyric felt so overwhelmed by what the officer had said that she felt as if her insides were going to explode. She felt like screaming, throwing something against the wall. Just seeing something shatter, besides her dreams, would make her feel better. The thought of Mr. Fredericks getting away with this crime sickened her.

The taller policeman placed his hand on Lyric's shoulder, and she jumped. He apologized and explained that she was experiencing post-traumatic stress disorder. He offered to take her to the hospital for a psych evaluation and rape kit. Lyric agreed, but insisted that she drive herself. Riding in the police car would make her feel like a criminal. So she put on her sneakers and grabbed her purse.

"We're going to put out an APB on," the male cop looked at his report, "Mr. Fredericks. He shouldn't be too difficult to find considering he's a business owner. We'll bring him in for questioning and take it from there. Okay?" He looked her in the eyes.

Lyric nodded her understanding. The officers exited the house and Lyric activated the high tech security system and locked the door. She went into the garage and backed her cream colored Saab convertible out of the driveway. She followed the cop car to Dekalb Medical Hospital.

Once at the hospital, Lyric spoke with a female rape counselor. The counselor explained that Lyric would experience a range of emotions, and all of that was normal. She encouraged Lyric to lean on her family during this difficult time and not to blame herself. Easier said than done; Lyric already blamed herself. The counselor handed

Lyric her business card, and Lyric stuck it in her purse. Accepting a business card was what got her in this situation, Lyric thought.

Afterward, Lyric consented to a rape kit and HIV test. A female physician's assistant performed the procedures. Lyric couldn't believe that this was really happening to her. She was a married woman; she shouldn't have to be concerned about contracting a venereal disease. She had only seen this type of stuff happen in the movies. While every inch of Lyric's body seemed to be on display, she cried silently. The collection process took a few hours, and Lyric was relieved when it was finally completed. She wanted to call Michael for support, but she was scared. All sorts of thoughts went through her mind. She wondered whether he would blame her. What if he didn't believe her; how would she handle that? she thought. She wasn't ready to deal with the "what ifs."

"Do you want me to administer you the Morning-After Pill?" the PA asked.

The Morning-After Pill is an emergency form of birth control used to prevent pregnancy. It's a large dose of estrogen taken orally within 24 to 72 hours after intercourse.

"No, thank you." Lyric shook her head. After so many failed attempts at getting pregnant,

Lyric didn't think it was necessary to endure the possible side effects, no matter how slight, of nausea, vomiting, breast tenderness, dizziness, headaches, fluid retention, and irregular bleeding when the odds of her getting pregnant weren't in her favor.

When Lyric finished with the testing, she checked her watch. It was almost 4:00 P.M. Good thing Autumn had cheerleading practice and wouldn't be home for two more hours. She hurried home.

Once Lyric got home, she moved around slowly. She felt like a foreigner in a strange land. Her house no longer felt like her home. She didn't feel like doing anything. She just wanted to be alone. While sitting on the couch, she thought about Dr. Little and what she'd advise Lyric to do. She figured that Dr. Little would tell her not to wallow in self pity. After giving herself a pep talk, just as Lyric was about to go into the kitchen to prepare dinner, her phone rang, stopping her in her tracks. Sighing, she really didn't feel like talking to anyone. She checked the caller ID anyway and noticed that it was Chloe. After a brief hesitation, she picked up.

Clearing her throat, Lyric said, "Hello."

"Hey," Chloe answered. "Why didn't you call me today?"

She paused for a moment to contemplate her answer. A part of her wanted to tell Chloe everything. Although Chloe was her best friend, she wasn't in the mood to hear, "I told you so." After all, Chloe had warned her. Over and over again. Now, she was suffering the consequences of her actions. Lyric felt stupid enough; she didn't need to cast a spotlight on the depths of her stupidity.

"I had a lot going on," Lyric finally replied. She walked into the kitchen.

"Are we still on for tennis at the club this week?"

Lyric set the phone on the island and pressed the speaker button. She went to the refrigerator and pulled out a large pack of shrimp, red pepper, jalapeno, and lettuce and placed them on the island. "I hadn't really thought about it," she admitted, trying not to cry.

"What's going on with you? You don't sound like yourself." Chloe's voice was dripping with concern.

Realizing that she was behaving suspiciously, Lyric tried to play it off. She fought back the tears. "I'm just trying to fix dinner." Her tone was as flat as a tire. "Don't pay me any attention. I'm a little tired. Of course, I'll meet you at the club. That's our weekly ritual."

"Okay." Unconvinced, Chloe asked, "You sure there's nothing else?"

Knowing full well that if she stayed on the phone any longer, Lyric would end up telling Chloe everything. She made up a flimsy excuse to get off the phone.

"I'm fine. I'm about to make a spicy grilled shrimp salad for dinner, so let me go. I'll talk to you later." Without waiting for Chloe to say, "Bye," she pressed the OFF button on the phone.

Lyric tried to focus on preparing dinner, but her thoughts kept nagging away at her. She kept second guessing herself. She wondered whether she had made a mistake by calling the police and reporting the rape.

Lyric felt jittery and on-edge. She needed to calm her nerves. She was tempted to call Dr. Little and ask her to prescribe an anti-anxiety medication, but she didn't want to go that route. She was determined to work though her problems without relying on prescription drugs. Since she and Michael were non-smokers, there weren't any cigarettes in the house. Doing drugs wasn't an option. The only other thing she could think of was a glass of wine. She and Michael only served cocktails at dinner parties or had an occasional glass with dinner; they weren't regular drinkers.

Leaving the food on the countertop, she went downstairs into the wine cellar and pulled out a bottle of red wine. They had a wine cellar because some of their friends were wine connoisseurs. It made for interesting conversation. She carried the bottle into the kitchen where she popped the cork and poured herself a glass.

Holding up the glass, she looked at the color and clarity, and she swirled the vintage to give it some air. Then she smelled the beverage and sipped. She savored the flavor, getting the full sensation on all of her taste buds and throughout her palate.

By the time she finished her second glass, dinner was ready. Feeling slightly buzzed, Lyric re-corked the bottle and stored it upright in the refrigerator. She washed her hands before going into the sitting room and dozing off.

"Mom," Autumn said, standing in front of Lyric and shaking her shoulders. "Wake up."

Lyric was startled. She wondered how long she had been sleeping. "Huh?" Lyric replied, trying to get her bearings. She yawned and wiped the saliva that had made its way to a spot on the side of her face.

"Are you all right?" Autumn seemed concerned.

Lyric rose slowly to her feet and braced herself against the couch. "Sweetie, I'm fine." She offered a smile before reaching for Autumn and giving her a tight hug. Being around her daughter gave her the strength she needed to go on. As she released her, Lyric asked, "How was school?"

"Fine," was Autumn's usual response.

They went into the kitchen and Autumn removed some grapes from the refrigerator and rinsed them off in the sink. She dried them off on a paper towel before placing them in a bowl.

"Go do your homework. I'll go over it with you in about an hour and a half." Lyric held out her hand and waited for Autumn to pluck a few grapes from the vine and hand them to her. When she did, Lyric popped them in her mouth and chewed.

Nodding her head in agreement, Autumn went to her room to finish her schoolwork. For a brief moment, Lyric contemplated getting another glass of wine. She quickly admonished the thought and said a silent prayer. Her father had been an alcoholic for most of his adult life. He had warned her about the perils of alcoholism. Although he had been sober for the last twenty years, she had heard that he still struggled with his addiction every day.

Lyric ran her fingers through her hair. She would have to find another way to handle her problem. Alcohol wasn't it.

Five

For the past two nights after the rape, sleep had come in fitful spurts for Lyric. Constant nightmares about the rape would awaken her with beads of sweat on her forehead and satin sheets clinging to her body like a wet T-shirt. Oftentimes the bad dreams were accompanied by terrifying bellows and Lyric throwing blows. In her dreams, she fought the way she wished she had in real life. When Michael tried to comfort her, she lied and assured him that everything was fine. She was not ready to tell him about the attack. She was too afraid of how he would react. Her emotions were still too raw. She had been praying that God would help her find a way to tell Michael. She hated keeping something so important from her husband. The guilt was eating her up inside.

Now afraid of the dark, because that's when the panic and anxiety attacks seemed to occur, the illumination from the flat-screen television provided Lyric with just enough light for her to close her eyes without experiencing an attack.

When morning finally rolled around, Lyric had only slept two hours. The bags under her eyes told the tale. After Michael and Autumn left the house, Lyric found herself feeling lonely and paranoid. She couldn't stop checking the doors and windows to make sure the premises were secured.

While upstairs getting dressed in a sporting outfit, she activated the alarm. Living in a low crime neighborhood, Lyric didn't usually feel the need to turn on the security system during the daytime. She had a nagging feeling, though, that she had not seen the last of Mr. Fredericks. When she finished getting dressed, she grabbed her gym bag, which included a tennis racquet, tennis balls, and two chilled bottles of water, and went to the country club to meet Chloe.

Once she arrived at the club, Lyric parked her car and adjusted her sunglasses. She stood outside and breathed a lung full of air and exhaled. People were walking by, smiling and saying hello. She smiled back, trying to conceal her pain.

Lyric looked around at the perfectly manicured golf course and marveled at its beauty. Although she had been to the club countless times, never before had she paid such close attention to the green grass. Looking up at the sky, Lyric noticed that the sky seemed more vibrant. With only a slight breeze in the air, the weather was ideal for tennis. In fact, it felt like a summer day instead of what one would expect in December.

She lugged her bag over her shoulder and entered the club. The concierge greeted Lyric as she went into the dining room to meet Chloe for a light breakfast. As soon as she set foot on the royal blue carpet, Chloe waved her over. Hair pulled back in a loose ponytail with a sun visor and dressed in a racer back tennis dress, Chloe looked athletic and fit. Her bright white smile was a startling contrast to the dimly lit room.

"Good morning to you," Chloe said as she hugged Lyric by the shoulders and kissed the air.

Lyric took off her sunglasses, and they both sat down at the round table draped in a white linen tablecloth. The waitress came over and filled their crystal glasses with ice water. They both ordered egg whites, meatless bacon, wheat toast, and orange juice.

"What's going on with you?" Chloe wanted to know. "Have you been crying?" she said in a hushed tone as she leaned closer to Lyric.

Feeling her eyes fill with water, Lyric unfolded the linen napkin and removed the silverware.

After spreading the serviette across her lap, she lined the flatware next to the plate. "Nothing is going on." She glanced at Chloe out of the corner of her eyes. Judging by the smirk on Chloe's face, Lyric knew that she didn't believe her. "Fine," Lyric relented. "I still want to get pregnant, and it hasn't happened. I'm frustrated, okay?" She opened her eyes wide; hoping that some of the air conditioned air would dry up her misty eyes.

"If you say so." Chloe sounded skeptical. She turned her head in the direction of the entrance. Giving a slight nod, she said, "There's Stella."

"Really?" Lyric turned around in her seat. "We should invite her over." She was glad to get Chloe off her back. She thought Chloe should've been a reporter the way she asked questions and dug her heels into a story.

Chloe stood and summoned Stella over. Stella commanded attention as she walked over to them dressed in a fuchsia colored Vienna tank and matching teorema skirt.

"Hello, ladies," Stella greeted with a warm smile, showing off her bleached white teeth.

"Stella, you look amazing," Chloe said as she kissed her on the cheek.

"Thank you." She turned around and greeted Lyric with a hug. "May I join you?"

"Of course, you can," Lyric said, motioning toward one of the two vacant chairs at the table.

The waitress returned with their food and asked if they needed anything else. Stella requested a bran muffin, a side of mixed fruit, and a cup of decaffeinated coffee. The waitress nodded her understanding and left.

"What have you been doing with yourself?" Chloe inquired of Stella as if she were waiting for her to reveal a juicy secret.

Giggling, Stella said, "What haven't I been doing?" She tossed her head back. "For starters, I hired a personal trainer and lost thirty pounds."

"I can tell. Your thighs are so tight and toned," Lyric complimented.

"That's not the only thing that's tight," Stella said with a naughty grin.

Chloe and Lyric both dropped their jaws. "You had the rejuvenation surgery?" they said in sync.

Stella nodded her head. "It's like being fifteen all over again." She laughed. Then her tone sounded serious. "After Frank left, I became depressed. I stopped socializing with my friends because I was so embarrassed. My life seemed to be falling apart. I felt like giving up. Truthfully, I didn't care if I lived or died." She smoothed some hair behind her ear. "My kids were grown and my marriage was over. So much of my identity had been tied into Frank and my kids. Without them, I felt like nothing." Lyric patted Stella's

hand; she understood better than she cared to
admit. "I started overeating to pacify my feelings. My weight gain made me feel even worse.
Then one morning I woke up, and it was as if the
good Lord Himself told me to snap out of it. Life
is for the living, so I needed to live my life. Just
because Frank didn't want me, so what, life goes
on. So I slowly started getting back out little by
little." She paused. "Now you know that I'm not
a traditional beauty." She laughed again. "I've
always had to rely on my personality and smarts
to get by. Well, my daughter convinced me to get
a makeover." She pointed at her breasts. "I got a
breast lift. Then I went to a dermatologist, and
he helped to shave ten years off of my appearance, thanks to chemical peels and Botox." She
tilted her head to the side. "I even lightened my
hair color." She wrapped a loose strand around
her finger and smiled. "Whitened my teeth too;
you like?"

They both nodded in agreement.

Chloe bit a piece of her toast. "You look amazing. If I didn't know you were forty-four, I'd
think you were in your early thirties."

"Thank you." Stella blushed. "I feel like a
new woman. Not only did I make a physical
transformation, I made a mental one too." She
paused for a moment and looked at Lyric. "I've

been going to see Dr. Skyler Little. I remembered that you spoke so highly of her. She's everything you said and more. She's helped me a lot. Now I feel like I'm whole and complete. I'm sorry that I didn't return your calls. I know that you were worried about me, and I truly appreciate it. I just wasn't in a good place mentally."

Lyric gave her a perceptive smile. "I understand."

The waitress set Stella's food and java in front of her. She asked the ladies if they needed anything else, and they all replied, "No."

"Besides looking good," Chloe pretended to sniff around, "do I smell a man on the horizon? You have a glow about you."

They all laughed.

Lightly clapping her hands, Stella replied, "And you know this."

"I want details," Lyric chimed in.

"Well," Stella licked her glossy lips, "I went to visit my sister in New York. While I was there, her husband introduced me to one of his friends." She rubbed her hands together. "Brad is attractive. He's got a little pot belly and receding hairline, but that's all right. He's really nice and accomplished. He's a hedge fund manager."

"Stop playing, Stella," Lyric teased. "You did not find a single, decent-looking, rich as all get up and go, black man in New York." She chuckled before placing a forkful of scrambled egg whites into her mouth.

"I know, right?" Stella admitted. She even sounded as if it were hard to believe. "He's been divorced for two years." Her eyes bounced between Lyric and Chloe like a ping pong ball. "He's only been married once. He has three grown children. At first I thought he was too good to be true. Just like you, I thought he was either the serial marrying guy, or a bonafide player. He's neither."

Chloe and Lyric eyed her intently.

Holding out her wrist to reveal a ten-carat diamond tennis bracelet, Stella said, "He got me this."

Chloe and Lyric were both impressed with the size, clarity, and cut of the diamonds. They complimented her accordingly.

Stella placed her hands on her lap. "We've only been seeing each other for three months, but things are getting pretty serious."

"How so?" Lyric asked, taking a sip of orange juice.

"I told him that lobster was my favorite dish." She giggled. "He's such a romantic that he chartered his private jet to fly me to Maine for a seafood dinner."

"Awww," Lyric and Chloe replied in unison.

Although Lyric was happy for Stella, a part of her wished that Michael was more romantic. She would love for him to whisk her away on a romantic excursion just because.

Unable to contain her enthusiasm, Stella said, "He also asked me to move into his New Jersey mansion." She covered her mouth to stifle a squeal. "And I said yes."

"Wow! Things really are moving fast," Lyric said. "I'm happy to hear that you're getting on with your life." She had a concerned look on her face. "I don't mean to be a killjoy, because I'm not. I care about you and don't want to see you get hurt again." She looked her in the eyes. "Brad sounds like an incredible guy. Before you pack up and leave your friends and family, make sure you know his intentions. You shouldn't live with him without being married. What do your kids think?"

"She's right," Chloe said in a serious tone. "The relationship is exciting now, because it's new. You know better than anyone how controlling rich men can be. If he's serious about you, he shouldn't have any problem proposing. You're not just some flavor of the month." She smiled.

"I can tell that you two really are concerned about me, and I appreciate it. But don't worry,

my eyes are wide open. Brad has already told me
that he wants a committed relationship. I want
that too. I've never been into that whole dating
scene." Stella sipped her coffee. "In fact, he told
me not to squabble over a divorce settlement,
because he is able to give me more than I would
ever receive from Frank." She raised a brow. "I'm
not stupid." She laughed. "If it came down to it,
he agreed to put his intentions in writing. He's
also planning a holiday so that we can meet each
other's family. As for my children, they just want
me to be happy. They're grown.

They're already living their lives. It's time for
me to do the same."

Lyric and Chloe both seemed pleased with
Stella's response. They continued to talk about
Brad, their children, Stella's pending divorce,
and upcoming move. Lyric welcomed the distraction; anything to keep her mind off of Mr.
Fredericks. Now that they were engaged in
Stella's business, Lyric was confident that Chloe
wouldn't interrogate her any further . . . at least
not that day.

Six

Lyric's palms felt clammy as she sat in her car trying to get the courage she needed to walk into Dr. Little's office. Although her appointment had been scheduled prior to her rape, Lyric's reason for needing to speak to the psychoanalyst had changed dramatically. She flexed her wrist to check her watch, and the time read 9:55 A.M. She had five minutes to get herself together.

"You can do this," she coached herself.

Retrieving a tissue from her purse, Lyric wiped the moisture from her hands. Then she clutched her purse and went inside of the building where she took the elevator to the fifteenth floor. As she stepped off the elevator, she saw the signage for Dr. Little's office on the right and followed. When she stepped inside, Yahkie greeted her with a warm smile.

"Good morning, Mrs. Stokes," Yahkie said in a singsong tone. He seemed to be in a good mood. He looked handsome dressed in a chocolate colored suit and an ecru shirt. "Please sign in, and I'll let boss lady know you're here." He pointed to the clipboard on the center of his desk.

While Lyric complied with Yahkie's request, Yahkie pressed the intercom button and announced that Dr. Little's ten o'clock appointment had arrived.

"Can I get you a cup of coffee or some tea?" Yahkie asked.

Lyric cleared her throat and swallowed. "Sure, a cup of tea would be nice. Any flavor you have is fine." She finished filling out the sheet and set it on Yahkie's desk.

Yahkie left the room and came back a couple of minutes later holding a Styrofoam cup and a container filled with packets of sugar and sugar substitutes. "I love Red Zinger tea. It's my favorite. Here you are." He handed her the hot drink and various sweeteners.

"Thank you." A reluctant smile spread across her face as she accepted the contents from his hands.

After they successfully made the exchange, Dr. Little emerged from her office.

"Nice to see you, Lyric. Come on in," Dr. Little said with a grin.

Lyric emptied a couple of packets into the cup and tossed the trash in the wastebasket next to

Yahkie's desk. She left the container on the desk and followed Dr. Little into her office. Dr. Little closed the door behind them as Lyric lowered her body on the gray couch. She glanced around the office and didn't see any major changes since the last time she had been there. The suite consisted of a wooden bookcase lined with hardcover books, solid oak desk with pictures of Dr. Little's family and a computer monitor housed on top, a leather chair behind the desk, various animal printed chairs around the office, and art by African-American artists hanging on the walls.

Dr. Little pulled up a chaise decorated in black and beige African design motif and sat next to Lyric. "Before we get started," she extended her hands to Lyric, "let's pray."

Grabbing Dr. Little's hands, Lyric closed her eyes as Dr. Little led them in prayer.

"Heavenly Father, thank you for this day. We come humbly before you asking that you direct our paths and order our steps. We invite your presence into this session. Give us insight, wisdom, knowledge, and revelation. I ask that I may decrease so that you can increase. Thank you, Father, for being such a loving and caring God. We love you, and we praise you. In Jesus' name, we pray. Amen."

They released each other's hands and opened their eyes.

"How have you been?" Dr. Little asked.

Before Lyric could even open her mouth to speak, the tears broke free like the levees had in New Orleans. Dr. Little's almond-shaped eyes opened wide with surprise.

"Here," Dr. Little said, handing her a box of Kleenex. She didn't say anything for the entire five minutes Lyric sat crying on the sofa.

After a final sniffle, Lyric blew her nose, dabbed her eyes, and discarded the tissue. "Sorry about that."

Shaking her head, Dr. Little said, "There's no need to apologize. You ready to talk about what's got you so upset?"

Lyric nodded her head and confided in Dr. Little about how she met Mr. Fredericks, why she called him over to her house, and how he had violated her.

When Lyric finished talking, Dr. Little stood up and paced the floor. She paused, folded her arms across her chest, and tapped her foot.

Lyric had never seen Dr. Little upset before. She was usually professional and composed no matter what.

"Dr. Little, are you all right?" she asked, feeling concerned.

Dr. Little took a seat next to her on the couch and said, "No, I'm not all right. What happened to you was all my fault."

"What?" Lyric had no idea what Dr. Little meant by that, and her facial expression reflected it.

"Let me explain." She patted Lyric's hand. "A couple of years ago, I was stalked. The guy would leave trinkets at my office and my home. I didn't really take the situation seriously until he attacked me at my birthday party." She recalled the incident in detail.

Dr. Little walked outside to get some fresh air. Large crowds tended to generate heat, and the atmosphere inside was stifling. The night air felt soothing against her bare arms and back.

"Skyler, you look radiant tonight," a male voice had whispered in Dr. Little's ear, startling her.

She turned around immediately. She didn't like that guy being so close to her that she could smell his lunch.

"What are you doing creeping up on me like that? Scaring me half to death," Dr. Little had quipped.

The mysterious stranger stood approximately six feet six inches tall. He didn't appear to be a guest at the party, as he was dressed in baggy jeans and a hoodie.

"I'm Nigel." He extended his hand to Dr. Little, and she hesitantly shook it.

As soon as Lyric heard the name Nigel, the fine hairs on her arm stood on end. She felt like interrupting Dr. Little, but she decided against it. Instead, she listened intently as Dr. Little continued with the story.

Not wanting to appear rude, Dr. Little plastered a slight smile on her face. "Nice to meet you, Nigel. How did you know my name?"

"I've been watching you for months."

Her smile faded. She felt as if she were trapped in a horror movie. "Excuse me?"

"Happy birthday, Skyler. Did you like your gift?"

"The . . . the lingerie was from you?" she had stuttered.

"You got it. I would've delivered it in person, but I wasn't invited to the party." He chuckled, but at the same time seemed hurt.

Dr. Little felt like running back inside, but she knew he'd grab her. So she had said, "Thanks for the present. It's starting to get chilly." She rubbed her arms. "I don't have a shawl. I'm going back inside. It was nice meeting you."

Dr. Little walked backward toward the door, never taking her eyes off Nigel. As she reached for the door, he had said, "Why are you walking away from me? I love you."

She attempted to run, but he lunged for her. "I've waited all these months to be with you, and this is how you treat me?"

Dr. Little screamed, and he covered her mouth. She bit his hand and tried to claw at his face. He picked her up by the waist, and she kicked him with all her might. He released Dr. Little, and she ran. He sprinted after her like a linebacker, shoulder down, gaze affixed on his target, ready to topple. He hit Dr. Little squarely, and she fell to the ground. She slammed her knees and palms on the gravel. There was a large hole in her pantyhose, revealing the bloody scrape on her knee. Pain radiated through Dr. Little's leg.

She turned over, trying to crawl backward. "Please, let me go," she had pleaded as he jumped on top of her.

"Stop fighting me."

He pinned Dr. Little to the ground and attempted to kiss her on the mouth. She turned her face away from him.

"What's wrong with you? Why are you fighting me?" he had asked with a hint of disappointment and disbelief.

Dr. Little spat in his face and shoved him as hard as she could. He toppled off of her. She scurried off the ground before running inside of the building, yelling and screaming.

"What's wrong?" Donovan had hollered as he ran toward his wife.

"There's a man outside dressed in baggy jeans and a hoodie. He tried to kidnap me."

Donovan, their friend Kevin, and a few other men from the party ran outside. They searched the premises. Dr. Little's best friend, Gabriella, retrieved her cell phone from her purse and called the police. Dr. Little was scared and thankful to be alive. She could get over the bruises.

About thirty minutes later, the men returned with the culprit. Dr. Little cringed when she saw Nigel again. In the light, she could clearly see the crevices in his forehead and deep laugh lines around his mouth. Blood oozed from the scratch she had given him. His round eyes narrowed in on Dr. Little, sending frightening chills throughout her body. She felt as though she was looking into the eyes of the devil. Dr. Little turned away in fear.

"We found him hiding underneath a car in the parking lot," Donovan had said as he held Dr. Little in his arms. "You're safe now."

She cried. Not long afterward, the police arrived and took Dr. Little's statement. She was glad when they took Nigel away in handcuffs.

When Dr. Little was finished telling her story, she looked at Lyric. "Due to a technicality, he was released."

"I remember hearing about that on the news," Lyric said, massaging her forehead with her fingers. "I'm sorry that happened to you."

"Me too." She took a deep breath and exhaled. "There's more. The monster who assaulted me was Nigel Richard Fredericks."

Lyric turned as pale as a sheet of paper. Dr. Little had finally confirmed what she suspected as soon as she heard the name of Dr. Little's stalker. Her first instinct was to deny that it was the same man. Her eyes filled with water again as she shook her head vehemently and screamed, "No! No! No! That can't be!" Now Lyric paced the floor. "I knew his name sounded familiar, but I couldn't figure out why. He initially introduced himself as Richard. It wasn't until he was already in my home that he mentioned the name Nigel." She looked at Dr. Little. "And when you said he introduced himself to you as Nigel, red flags went up in my head. I had an eerie feeling, but I was hoping it was merely a coincidence and not the same guy."

Dr. Little went to her desk drawer and retrieved an old newspaper clipping. "Here's a photo of Nigel." She stood in front of her and placed her hands on her shoulders to stop her from pacing. Then she shoved the article at Lyric, forcing her to look at it.

Lips pressed together, Lyric studied the black and white photo. Although in the picture Nigel had a full-beard and looked like a bum, indeed, it was the same man. He didn't look exactly the same now, because he had a haircut and was clean shaven. However, his eyes spoke volumes. There was no mistaking those soulless windows. She nodded her head and handed the paper back to Dr. Little.

"Listen to me," Dr. Little pleaded. "You've got to keep a cool head in this situation. Nigel is a dangerous man. I'm glad that you reported the rape to the authorities." In an attempt to soothe her, Dr. Little patted her on the back. She then looked her in the eyes and gave a reassuring smile. "I'm going to be honest with you; I don't think the meeting at the restaurant was the first time Nigel ever saw you."

"What? Why do you say that?" Lyric raised a brow and took a step backward. Just hearing that sent chills up her spine.

"He's a stalker. Most stalkers stake out their prey long before the victims ever realize it."

"Oh, God. I think I'm going to be sick," Lyric said as she ran over to Dr. Little's trash receptacle and upchucked the contents of her stomach.

"I know this isn't what you want to do, but you've got to tell your husband," Dr. Little said sympathetically.

"No," Lyric sobbed as she grabbed a couple of tissues from the box sitting on Dr. Little's desk and wiped her mouth.

Dr. Little grabbed a disposable cup from the dispenser, filled it with water from the three-gallon bottle, and gave it to Lyric. She took a sip.

"Listen to me, Lyric." Dr. Little had a pleading look in her eyes. "Now is not the time to lose your wits. You've already proven that you know how to handle a crisis. Now you need protection. Your family can help you. I'll help you through this too."

Lyric nibbled on her lower lip. "I'm scared," she admitted as she set the cup on the desk.

Dr. Little placed her hands on Lyric's arms. "I understand."

"How did you handle the situation when Nigel stalked you?" Lyric searched her face for understanding.

"Let's sit back down," Dr. Little instructed. They took their seats on the couch. "After the incident with Nigel, my lawyer got a court order to have Nigel's psychiatric records admitted in to evidence. Unfortunately, my lawyer didn't review the files in time for the hearing." She shook her head. "That's another story. Anyway, I took a selfdefense course. My husband wanted me to get a gun to protect myself, but I refused. I wasn't comfortable with that. Instead, I started carrying other weapons like pepper spray, a pocket knife, and a whistle."

"A whistle?" Lyric had a confused look on her face.

"Yes. A whistle is a good attention grabber," she explained. "I also learned how to turn the objects in my purse, like keys, an ink pen, and a fingernail file into weapons."

Lyric nodded her understanding.

"Being stalked is a terrifying experience. It changed my life forever. Because of that experience, I'm much more aware of my surroundings. I pay attention to the people and things around me. I try not to go out alone, especially at night. Whenever I do go out, I always let someone know where I'll be and how long I'll be gone. I even got OnStar for my car."

"Did Richard, I mean Nigel," Lyric corrected, "stop stalking you after his arrest?"

Dr. Little smirked. "Humph. Not at first. He would stay just far enough away so that I could see him, yet not close enough to violate the restraining order. He did that for six months. My husband wanted to pounce on Nigel, but I wouldn't let him. The police wouldn't arrest him, because he wasn't breaking any laws. Apparently, it's not against the law for people to insinuate themselves into the lives of others as long as they don't get physical." She sighed. "Then one day Nigel was gone. I didn't see or hear from him anymore. I figured that something, or someone else, captured his interest."

Lyric held her head down. "I feel like such a fool."

"Don't do that," Dr. Little admonished while lifting Lyric's chin and looking her in the eyes. "None of this was your fault. You didn't deserve to be violated. Nigel is a monster; he doesn't deserve to be called a human being.

There was no way you could've known what he had in store for you. You said yourself that he seemed like an attractive, classy, normal guy when you met him. He's a deceiver. Forgive yourself." Dr. Little released her chin.

Wiping away a lone tear, Lyric reached out and hugged her. "Pray for me, Dr. Little," she whispered in her ear.

They broke the embrace, and Dr. Little said a heartfelt prayer.

"Father, forgive us for where we have sinned and fallen short of the mark. We come before you in need of healing and deliverance right

now. Lyric has not only experienced a physical
violation, but an emotional and spiritual one as
well. Help her to forgive herself and not to be
bound by guilt. Touch the hearts and minds of
her family and anyone else who comes in contact
with her so that they will provide her with love,
support, encouragement, and understanding.
Give Lyric the strength she needs to make it
through this difficult time in her life. Father,
you gave us the power and ability to cast out
demons. Nigel is a demon, and we rebuke him in
the name of Jesus. Cast him out, Father, so that
he can't hurt anybody else. We plead the blood
of Jesus over Lyric; that she may be made whole
and complete in every way. In the mighty name
of Jesus, we pray. Amen."

Lyric squeezed her eyes shut and covered her
mouth with her hands as Dr. Little rubbed her
back.

"I'm ready," Lyric said as she opened her eyes
and placed her hands on her lap.

Dr. Little gave a faint smile and nodded her
head.

"I don't like that this happened to me, and
I don't fully understand it. But while you were
praying, I got a revelation."

"You did?" Dr. Little furrowed a brow.

"Yes," she said as she held in her hand the diamond encrusted crucifix that was resting on her chest. Lyric was raised as Catholic but became a Baptist while in college. Her college roommate was Baptist and had taken Lyric to church with her. Lyric enjoyed the music and shorter church services, so she converted. She still wore a crucifix as a reminder of God's sacrificial love. "Everyone has a cross to bear, and this is mine. I can either lie down in defeat, or trust God to see me through."

Looking into her eyes, Dr. Little said seriously, "Do you want me to write you a prescription for anxiety and depression medication?"

Past sessions had revealed that Lyric suffered from stress-related anxiety and depression. Whenever she felt overwhelmed, feelings of hopelessness tended to follow, which triggered panic and anxiety attacks.

"No," Lyric said, surprising Dr. Little. "As the axiom goes, 'What doesn't kill you makes you stronger.' Well, I'm not dead."

Seven

Lyric waited until Autumn went to Heavyn's house for a sleepover before preparing to tell Michael about the assault. She had prayed about it, and the Lord finally gave her peace. The Holy Spirit had ministered to her and told her not to be afraid to tell Michael; he would understand and not leave her.

Lyric had everything planned. Michael was off for the holidays, so the timing was right. The only thing she was unsure about was when exactly she should spring the news on him. Should she begin the discussion before or after dinner? If she told him before, neither one of them would be hungry. If she told him after, he'd most likely be full and tired. She just decided to play it by ear.

It was 6:30 P.M. when Michael arrived home, and Lyric sat quietly in the family room waiting for him. She had prepared a fish and vegetable dish that was in the oven. The sound of smooth jazz played softly in the background. When

Michael entered the room, she greeted him with a hug and kiss.

"Where's Autumn?" he asked.

"She's spending the night with Heavyn. Dinner's in the oven."

Turning on a lamp, Michael asked, "Everything all right? Why is it so dark in here?"

She grabbed his hand and led him to the couch. "There's something I need to talk to you about."

Sighing, he said, "Can it please wait until after dinner? I'm famished. Give me ten minutes, and I'm all yours."

"Sure," Lyric relented. She was a little disappointed. She didn't want to drag this out any longer than she had to.

While Michael fixed his plate and took a seat at the breakfast nook, Lyric said a silent prayer. She prayed that the Lord would give her the right words to say and to strengthen her marriage.

She thought about how she and Michael had met and how they beat the odds and stayed together. They met through a mutual friend. Lyric had been a sophomore at Spelman College, and Michael was a third year medical student at Morehouse School of Medicine. The chemistry between the two of them was undeniable. Michael had a rock hard body from weight-lifting, and a face so handsome it looked as though it had been chiseled from stone.

After only six months of dating—and to the disapproval of their family and friends—Michael and Lyric eloped. Although they relied on student loans, grants, and Lyric's part-time job for support, their love was strong. Michael promised that one day they would be rich and that his wife wouldn't have to want for anything; Lyric believed him.

Michael graduated with honors and immediately began his internship. With their full schedules, they had very little time for partying, or each other. Neither one of them complained, because they realized that success required sacrifice. Not long after graduating, Lyric became pregnant with Autumn. Michael was elated. He was in residency and earned enough to support his family, provided they kept expenses to a minimum. After giving birth, Lyric stopped working and had been a stay-at-home mom ever since.

For their ten year wedding anniversary, they renewed their vows in grand style with 150 guests. They had an elaborate ceremony at Cascade Mansion and Gardens in Atlanta, complete with doves and a horse drawn carriage ride. Lyric wished she was in a carriage now. One that would take her away from her thoughts, her pain, and *this* conversation with her husband. The weight of Michael's body as he plopped on the couch pulled her back to the present. She snuggled up to him and prayed he would understand.

Placing his arm on her shoulders, Michael said, "Talk to me, baby girl."

Fiddling nervously with her fingers, Lyric took a deep breath and slowly exhaled. Trying to muster up the courage to speak, she sucked her bottom lip and blinked her eyelids shut. As her heartbeat quickened, she felt tears welling in her eyes. She shifted in her seat and faced her husband. She placed her thumb on top of the dimple in his chin and peck kissed his succulent lips. Looking into Michael's caramel brown eyes, Lyric told him everything about her encounter with Nigel—*cringe*—starting with how she'd met him at the restaurant—*cringe, flinch, recoil.*

When she finished, she was in tears. She expected Michael to take her in his arms and console her. Instead, she was blindsided.

Michael stood up and squeezed the bridge of his nose. His eyes darted to his wife like daggers. "Let me make sure I got this correct." He pressed his hands together as if he were about to pray. "You met a man at a restaurant and took his business card. Then a few days later you call him to take a look at some artwork, right?"

Lyric was confused by his response. The way he was speaking to her was chilling. She questioned whether she had really heard from the Holy Spirit or if that had been her own wishful thinking. "Yes," she stuttered.

Clenching his jaw, Lyric noticed that Michael's right eye had a slight twitch. Michael only did that when he was angry.

"What kind of a fool do you think I am?" He stared at her, scratching the brow above his twitching right eye.

"What? Why are you saying that?" The words stammered from her mouth.

He remained incensed, gazing out of the living room window, to the aqua blue waters of the backyard swimming pool. "I work hard to provide a comfortable life for us." His voice elevated an octave. "I pay all of the bills, and you still have access to every dime I make." His nostrils flared.

Lyric wondered where all of Michael's anger was coming from. Just as she had feared, he blamed her. Shaking her head, Lyric said, "What does that have to do with anything?"

"Let me finish." He backed up and sat on the sofa where Lyric was not sitting. Hanging his head, Michael said, "You're a gorgeous woman,

Lyric. I get that. Men are attracted to you." He swallowed the lump in his throat and lowered his voice. "Why did you accept his card? Why can't you just be happy being my wife and Autumn's mother?"

Lyric walked over to Michael and touched the back of his bowed head. "Michael, I love you," she said sincerely. "I have loved you since the first moment I laid eyes on you. I don't want any other man." She hoped and prayed that he believed her. She didn't know what she'd do if he left her. It would break her heart.

He looked up. "You still haven't told me why you took his card."

Kneeling down at his feet, Lyric stared at a spot on the glass coffee table. She had no excuse. She had already repented and asked God to forgive her. Now she needed her husband's forgiveness too. She hated to lie, so she decided to tell Michael the truth. "I guess I was flattered."

Michael stood up so fast that he accidentally bumped into Lyric, causing her to fall on the floor. She hurried to her feet and chased behind Michael. He was headed upstairs.

"Michael, wait," she called.

He didn't answer.

Catching up to him, Lyric tugged on his shirt. She pleaded, "Please don't. I didn't ask for this. I didn't want to be raped! Please forgive me."

Stopping in his tracks, Michael turned to face his wife. Tears streamed down her cheeks. Hanging his head, Michael grabbed Lyric and held her close. He could tell that she was in pain, but so was he.

Stroking her hair, Michael said, "I apologize that I didn't handle this the way that you wanted me to. When you first told me that another man had touched you, I wanted to rip out his throat with my bare hands." He exhaled. "And then I felt betrayed."

Lyric gently pushed away from his grasp and looked him in the eyes. "Betrayed?" She could understand him feeling hurt and angry, but not betrayed. She didn't have an affair. Why was he feeling betrayed? she wondered.

"Look, I'm feeling a lot of stuff right about now, and I'm having a hard time putting it into words. I just need to be alone for a while."

"But what about what I need?" Lyric blurted out. The tears flowed harder. She desperately wanted Michael to hold her in his arms and tell her that everything was all right. She needed his assurance that she was still the woman he loved and not damaged goods.

Clasping his hands together, Michael said, "I can't do it right now. I'm having a hard time understanding how all of this went down. You told me that you were raped, yet you waited to tell me. That doesn't make sense to me."

Lyric bit her lower lip. She then wiped her wet face with the palm of her hand. "I waited to tell you because I was in shock. I couldn't believe it happened to me. I also didn't want you to blame me like you're doing right now." She grabbed him by the crook of his arm. "I'll admit that I shouldn't have taken his card. I'm sorry for that." She shook her head. "I promise you that the only reason I called him was because I wanted him to appraise my artwork, especially the piece from Africa. I remembered that he was an art dealer, and he owned a gallery. That's it, as God is my witness."

She released his arm. He went back into the family room and sat down on the loveseat.

"I want to believe that what you're telling me is true," he said, staring at the carpeted floor.

Sliding her toned frame next to his, Lyric rested her arm on his shoulders and squeezed. "You can believe me. I have always loved you. Never once have I been unfaithful. I promise you that. You are the love of my life."

Michael gritted his teeth. "Not even in my wildest dreams would I have thought we would've been dealing with something like this."

He turned his head to look at her. He searched her eyes, looking for some indication that she was telling the truth. He touched the side of her face.

"What?" she questioned, removing her arm from his shoulders.

"I believe you."

She pressed her eyes shut. "Thank God."

Wrapping his arms around her, Michael planted soft kisses on her forehead. "I'm sorry I doubted you. I love you. I promise I'll do a better job protecting you."

Eight

How dare Lyric go running to the good doctor, Skyler Little, like she was her savior or some crap, Nigel seethed, sitting on the bed in his one-bedroom condo. He had been laying low since his encounter with Lyric. For the past five days, he hadn't gone into the gallery or on a single work-related appointment. Instead, his manager handled it. For two nights after the incident with Lyric, he stayed at a friend's house. He had made up some lie about having an extermination problem. As luck would have it, his cousin took a trip to the Big Apple and asked Nigel to house-sit for three days, which he gladly agreed to do.

Nigel cracked his knuckles. Lyric and Skyler ought to know better than to mess with him. He was far more cunning and clever than the two of them could ever be. Nigel picked up a photo album dedicated to Skyler. He opened the book and flipped through the pictures. He ran his hand over the plastic covering and remembered the exact day, time, and place he first laid eyes on Skyler.

It was a Friday morning, and Skyler was rushing into her office. Nigel had been visiting a client in her office complex. At the time, he worked for a prominent financier and art collector based out of New York that was interested in expanding into Atlanta. The way she looked in those slacks gave new meaning to "Georgia Peach." She brushed past him, leaving her sexy scent lingering in the air. Euphoria: that was the fragrance she wore. He licked his lips at the mere thought of Skyler. When they locked eyes for that brief moment, he knew he had to have her. He felt a spark. The moment she parted those glossy lips and said, "Good morning," he felt as though his heart was going to explode out of his chest. Not only was she beautiful, she was sweet.

For months, Nigel watched Skyler from a distance. When he found out that she was a psychoanalyst, he became even more intrigued. During his early years, he was forced to see a psychiatrist for his behavioral issues. He wondered why Skyler had become a mental health professional. He learned everything he could about her, including where she shopped and what she liked to eat. He knew her schedule as well as he knew his own. Wanting to wait until the right moment before he introduced himself to her, Nigel began sending trinkets to Skyler just so that she would know he was thinking about her.

When Skyler's birthday rolled around, Nigel wanted to do something extra special. He bought her some lingerie and mailed it to her home. He had hoped that while everyone else was attending Skyler's surprise birthday party, he would whisk her away. His plan included taking her back to her house and seeing the lingerie up close and personal. Things didn't go according to plan.

In Nigel's mind, he envisioned Skyler being ecstatic to learn that he was her secret admirer. He expected her to leap into his arms and admit that she was attracted to him too. Instead, she became fearful and tried to run away. Surprised and confused by Skyler's actions, Nigel attempted to stop her. He wanted to calm her down by telling her that he loved her. Why did she feel the need to fight? She made him tackle her to the ground. That was the last thing he wanted to do. He never would've hurt the woman he loved.

Spitting in his face and pushing him away, Skyler scurried into the building, yelling and screaming. Terrified, Nigel ran away. Before he could make his escape, he heard angry voices explode from the building. People were looking for him. In an effort to dodge any bullets, he hid underneath a car in the parking lot. Didn't matter, though; those men were relentless in their pursuit. They didn't stop looking until they found him.

The angry mob pulled and tugged on Nigel. No sooner than Nigel stood to his feet, he heard a loud cracking noise. It was Skyler's husband Donovan's fist connecting with his left eye. Knocked him off balance. He hadn't seen that coming. It took two men to restrain Donovan. That brother had fire in his eyes, which let Nigel know that he was prepared to fight for "their" woman.

Nigel gave a wicked grin. He wanted to make it clear that he was not a punk. There was no fear in his heart. If need be, he was ready to throw down for his woman. In Nigel's mind, it was just a matter of time before he and Skyler would be together. Donovan was just a minor inconvenience. He was prepared to take him out if it came down to that.

Just as Nigel was about to swing back at Donovan, one of the men in the crowd grabbed his raised fist and stopped him. A couple of the wannabe security guards apprehended him.

They detained him until the police arrived and took him away in handcuffs.

The media jumped all over that story. Even still, Nigel pleaded not guilty to the charges. When the prosecutor asked to have Nigel's psychiatric records admitted into evidence, Nigel invoked his patient-client privilege to block the prosecutor from obtaining the records. During the trial, the prosecutor used his discretion to dismiss the case due to lack of evidence.

Nigel took that as a sign. It confirmed what he already knew; he and Skyler were meant to be together. After the scandal died down, Nigel opened the art gallery in Atlanta and started going by his middle name, Richard.

Nigel closed up the photo album and set it on the floor. He then picked up one of many framed photos that he had of Lyric and kissed the glass. After months of continuing to observe Skyler, this fine honey named Lyric stepped into the equation. Nigel was not looking for somebody new, but there was something about Lyric. She would meet with Skyler weekly. When he started following her home, he discovered that she lived in an upscale neighborhood, was married to a doctor, and had a young daughter.

At first, Nigel thought that Lyric was just another rich woman creating problems.

"Oh I'm so lonely," he would imagine her saying.

What in the world did she have to be unhappy about? She didn't look miserable on the surface. But if she were going to a therapist, she must've had something going on that was making her less than happy, he figured. He had a hard time feeling sorry for a woman who had everything and still wasn't fulfilled. Thinking about Lyric was like eating a piece of Sour Patch Kids candy. Sweet; then sour.

Still holding Lyric's image in his hand, he walked over to the shrine he had dedicated to his mother.

"I need to get you some fresh flowers," Nigel said, referring to the withered up carnations resting in front of his mom's black and white photo.

Lyric reminded him of his mother. They both had restless spirits. His mother, Rachel, had been somewhat of a wild child. She used to run the streets, sleep around, and take drugs. When she was fifteen, she got knocked up with Nigel. She pinned the pregnancy on a drug dealer named Marcus. Marcus used to take good care of Nigel and Rachel. They had plenty of money and lived in a nice apartment. That lasted for about five years before Marcus went to prison for trafficking.

After Marcus left, Nigel's life started to un-ravel. His mom had developed a serious drug habit. Things got so bad that Rachel would have sex with strangers for money just to support her addiction.

Once, Rachel got a hold of some bad LSD. She was trippin' so bad that she swore she heard voices telling her to hurt Nigel. Rather than obeying the voices in her head, Rachel tried to protect Nigel by locking him in a closet for two days without food or water. When she finally came down from her trip, she took Nigel to live with his grandmother.

Having his mother reject him scarred Nigel emotionally. He developed some behavioral problems and had a very bad temper. He was diagnosed with attention deficit/ hyperactivity disorder (ADHD). While in school, he would fight at the drop of a hat. Kids were afraid of him, and Nigel liked that. He didn't take any stuff off of anybody. No matter whom it was, man, woman or child, Nigel had no fear.

All the while, Rachel continued moving around and hanging with shady characters. She would do anything to get a quick buck, come crook or hook. She was the first person that Nigel hated.

When Nigel turned eighteen, just two months before Marcus was supposed to be released from prison, Rachel dropped a bombshell on Nigel. She confessed that Marcus was not his father, and she had no idea who was. The only thing Nigel could see was red. It took everything within him not to knock the daylights out of her. Like an angel sitting on his shoulder, he kept hearing the voice of his grandmother telling him, "Don't ever hit a girl. They are weaker than you, and you could really hurt them."

"You're dead to me" was the last thing Nigel ever said to his mother.

Later that night, Nigel and his grandmother received a phone call telling them that Rachel had hung herself. Nigel did not shed a tear. He was relieved that she was finally dead and out of his life for good.

As for Marcus, Nigel wrote him off too. He had no respect for a man weak enough to try and turn a whore into a housewife. He then took every letter that Marcus had ever written him and burned them. Whenever Marcus called, Nigel refused his calls. Eventually, Marcus stopped calling. That was fine with Nigel. He had no love for him anyway.

Still holding Lyric's photo, Nigel gathered the dead flowers and tossed them in the trash. He picked up the box containing his mother's hair and fingernails and took them to bed with him. He had stolen them from her corpse after the viewing of her body. Nigel had convinced his grandmother that he wanted to spend some alone time with his deceased mother. He decided that he wanted something to remember her by. So he cut off a strand of her hair and plucked the nails from her left hand. Having such personal parts of her made him feel closer to her.

He leaned back on his unmade bed. Staring at Lyric's picture, he ran his finger over her lips. "Can I trust you, Lyric?"

When it came to women, Nigel didn't trust any woman further than he could see her. The only exception was his grandmother. She was old school and part of a dying breed. He was convinced that the rest of the women only wanted money or sex. They didn't care about love or family. That's why he never married or had children.

During the time that he used to date, he encountered women who were just as broken as he was. How could he help them when he was still trying to help himself? He noticed that the women who had daddy-issues were usually insecure and promiscuous. A lot of them had babies with different daddies. He didn't have time for that.

The women who had strained relationships with their mothers usually had anger management issues. Those women either had a bunch of kids because they were trying to be a better mother than their mom, or they didn't want kids at all. He wasn't feeling that either.

On rare occasions when he met women from two-parent households, he usually had to deal with their idealistic views about men and relationships. They wanted a man to take care of them just as good, or better, than their daddy had. They also liked being in control. Since Nigel wasn't the type of man to let anybody, especially not a woman, control him, that wasn't going to work for him. Nigel wasn't anybody's sucker.

Enough was enough. Rather than being actively involved in the dating scene, Nigel became a watcher of women. He could put up with them from afar. The relationships were on his terms, and he was in complete control. That's the way he preferred it. There was something about being incognito, or in-cog-negro, as Nigel liked to say, that gave him a rush. A thrill.

Just from watching, Nigel learned so much about women. Sometimes he watched women he already knew, like ex-girlfriends. They proved everything he ever thought about women: That they were untrustworthy sluts.

On a few occasions, like with Skyler and Lyric, Nigel would see an interesting woman, and he insinuated himself into her life. Rarely would he make his presence known to them. With Skyler and Lyric, he couldn't resist. They were different.

Not only was Skyler fine, she was a good woman. She was the type of woman he could marry. Never had he caught her doing dirt. As a psychoanalyst, she helped people. He admired that. She was also a devout Christian. He was not big on religion, because he had seen so many hypocrites. Being a Christian didn't get any points with him. If anything, it may have been a strike against her as far as he was concerned. However, from everything his grandmother had ever taught him about being a Christian, Skyler lived up to it.

"I'll give you what you need, Lyric. Just give me a chance." Nigel closed his eyes. He couldn't stop thinking about the object of his desire. He wanted her so bad that he could taste her skin.

When it came to Lyric, she was far needier than Skyler. Something about her vulnerabilities attracted him to her. She was the damsel in distress, and he wanted to rescue her. Her husband was too out of touch to do it.

Becoming concerned after Lyric stopped going to her weekly counseling sessions, Nigel spent more time observing her. She didn't seem to be doing any better. Why had Sklyer not been able to help her? he wondered.

The first time he made his presence known was at the restaurant. He decided to introduce himself to her because he thought she could use a friend, someone in her corner. He could tell by the intense look on her face while she was conversing with her girlfriend. Her country club, spa-filled, luncheon, and fundraising existence seemed superficial to him. Something was missing. He wanted to know why she wasn't happy. The only way he could truly find out was by befriending her.

Lyric probably didn't even realize that she throws off vibes. The way she looked at him told him everything he needed to know. Something was obviously lacking in her relationship, and her eyes told the tale. Whether intentional or not, Lyric was throwing up smoke signals, and he was receiving them. That let him know he was in with no problem. Therefore, he wasn't the least bit surprised when she called him. If anything, he would've been shocked if she hadn't. Although things were going according to plan, he had no intention of having sex with her that day. The way she batted her long lashes at him and swayed her hips when she walked turned the tides. That was all he needed to take their relationship to the next level.

Nigel had no regrets about the passion he had shared with Lyric. With all of the good lovin' she had put on him, she was wifey material. He just hoped that she wouldn't allow her guilt to get in the way of their relationship. He wondered whether she had tried to save face by crying rape and reporting their sexcapade to the po-po. What had she told Skyler? He needed to find out.

Nine

Christmas had come and gone. Lyric hadn't felt much like celebrating. After sleepless nights and nightmares, Lyric and Michael discussed numerous options to help alleviate some of her stress. Michael had even suggested they hire a bodyguard or security, but Lyric wouldn't hear of it. Instead, they made the mutual decision to rid the house of the mattress she had been violated on and get a new one. Funny how small changes could make big differences. Lyric's family spent the holiday at Chloe and Keith's house. Since they had spent Thanksgiving at Michael's mom's house in California, they decided not to go back for Christmas.

She received word that the police finally tracked down Nigel at his home the day after Christmas. They took him in for questioning. So much of the physical evidence had been compromised. Without a confession, they didn't have enough evidence to hold him. Although the rape kit confirmed that sexual contact had occurred, it wasn't enough. The authorities simply warned Nigel that they would be watching him.

After the authorities notified Lyric, she was livid. The only good news was that she had gotten her test results back, and she didn't have any STDs. She thanked God for that.

Feeling the need to vent, she called Chloe and invited her over for tea. She had been wrestling with the idea of whether or not she should even tell Chloe about the rape. Besides Michael, Chloe was the closest person to her. She trusted Chloe like the sister she never had. She didn't feel right keeping such a secret from her best friend. She lifted up the matter in prayer and felt at peace about her decision to tell Chloe.

When Chloe arrived, she carried a small platter filled with mini-muffins and miniature sandwiches.

"What's going on, lady?" Chloe said in her usual upbeat tone as she entered the house and placed the tray on the kitchen counter.

Lyric rubbed her hands on her denim covered thighs. "I have something to tell you."

"You sound serious." Chloe removed the plastic wrap covering from the tray and popped a poppy seed muffin in her mouth.

Lyric filled two cups with Jasmine tea and honey and handed a cup to Chloe. She took a sip before confiding in Chloe about the rape. When she finished sharing the sordid details, she stopped talking and waited for Chloe to say something. She hoped that Chloe's silence didn't mean that she was judging her or getting ready to give her a lecture. She wasn't in the mood to listen to Chloe preach to the choir or say "I told you so."

Chloe set her cup on the marble countertop and hugged her. "You poor thing. I wish you would've told me sooner. You didn't have to go through this alone."

"I was so ashamed and embarrassed," Lyric admitted.

"You had nothing to be ashamed or embarrassed about.

None of that was your fault. What can I do to help you?" Chloe released her and looked her in the eyes.

At that moment Lyric understood why Chloe was her best friend. Chloe wasn't afraid to confront Lyric when she was wrong. Yet, when she needed a listening ear or shoulder to cry on, Chloe always came through.

Lyric wiped away a tear. "Just knowing that you're here for me is enough. There's really nothing any of us can do, except pray."

"I hate to think that buzzard got away with this. He deserves to fry for what he did," Chloe seethed. "What did Michael say?"

Lyric explained Michael's initial response, and then went on to explain that he had since been very supportive.

Chloe nodded her understanding. "Did you ask Dr. Little to give you a prescription?"

"I don't need one," Lyric said confidently.

Resting her hand on Lyric's shoulder, Chloe said, "Look, Lyric, I know you're trying to be strong, but there's no need to suffer in the process. We both know that you suffer from stress-related anxiety and mild depression. There's no shame in getting help."

"I'm fine. I've been taking Black Cohosh and St. John's Wort every day. They have helped to stabilize my mood. I'm trying to go with natural herbs instead."

Chloe removed her hand from Lyric's shoulder and exhaled. "Okay."

"You don't seem convinced."

Tracing the brim of her cup with her finger, Chloe said, "I'm worried about you. I hate to even bring this up, but I feel I have to. You told me yourself that when you were pregnant with Autumn, you felt overwhelmed and anxious. That was the first time that a medical professional ever diagnosed you with anxiety and depression. When you were seven months pregnant, you thought about cutting the baby out of your stomach and shared that with your doctor. Because of that, you had to be institutionalized. It was only when Michael convinced the doctors that you weren't a threat to yourself or your unborn baby that they released you and prescribed an anti-depressant to stabilize your mood. Even then, someone had to watch you around the clock for the rest of your pregnancy."

"Don't you think I know that?" Lyric snapped. "I'm not some nutcase. My hormones had a lot to do with that. It was my first pregnancy, and I was nervous about my baby. Although I was excited, there was a lot that I didn't understand. That was scary for me. After I had Autumn, I no longer needed the medication. I was fine."

"Yes, you were." Chloe grabbed her hand and led her into the family room. They sat on opposite ends of the couch. "You and I are the children of alcoholics." Her tone sounded serious. Lyric wondered where Chloe was going with this. Chloe continued. "That's one of the things that bind us. We have discussed our childhoods, and we both took on the roles of being responsible 'parents' within our families and amongst friends. We coped with our parents' alcoholism by being controlled, successful overachievers in school even though we were emotionally isolated from our peers and teachers." She let out a sigh. "Our emotional problems didn't really surface until we became adults.

"I remember when my brother became terminally ill with cancer." Chloe's eyes became wet. "That shook me to the core of my being and almost killed me. After my brother died, I turned to alcohol. I didn't care whether I lived or died. He had been the one stabilizing force in my life, and he had been taken away from me. I went on a downward spiral for almost a year before Keith forced me to go to rehab. He had threatened to divorce me and take Heavyn away from me, if I didn't get my act together." A lone tear escaped and rolled down her cheek. "I had truly become my mother's child. Heavyn was only three years old at the time, and I couldn't imagine my life without her. I knew that if Keith had taken her away, I would've died for sure. That's when I made the decision to stop drinking. While I was in rehab, I became more spiritual. I developed a relationship with the Lord and got saved. I haven't had a drink since."

Lyric nodded her head. Clearing her throat, she said, "I had a few drinks after the rape."

"Oh God," Chloe said. There was a look of sheer horror etched on her face.

"No," Lyric held up her hands, "I stopped myself before I got drunk. I refused to go down that path."

Chloe let out a sigh of relief. "Thank God!"

"I'm scared," Lyric blurted out.

"Of what?"

"Sometimes I feel so . . . . crazy. When I started going to Dr. Little, I explained to her that I'm only normal for two weeks out of the month. The week before my cycle, I'm moody, emotional, and pretty sad. The week of my cycle, I'm able to have some normalcy. The week after that, I'm usually stable for the most part. If I'm going to be happy, that's about the time I feel some semblance of happiness. After that, it's right back to the vicious cycle. She suggested that I may have premenstrual dysphoric disorder and for me to consult with my primary care physician. I did, and Dr. Little was right. "

"Did your doctor prescribe you any mood stabilizers?"

"Yes, but I didn't take them. I didn't want to risk developing a dependency, so I started using herbal remedies. That's been working for me. It's when I don't take the herbs that the moodiness and irritability tend to surface. Before I got help, that's when Michael and I would have our worst arguments. Nothing he could say or do would sit right with me." She seemed reflective for a moment. "But that's not all."

Chloe stared at her without saying a word.

"Sometimes I get tired of life." She glanced at Chloe. "Remember when we went to see the movie, *The Secret Life of Bees?*"

She nodded.

"I could relate to Sophie Okonedo's character, May Boatwright. I'm not mentally challenged like the character, but I feel deeply the way that she did. Whenever something bad happens or someone dies, it unnerves me in ways that I can't even explain. I can remember times when someone that I cared about died, and I would lose sleep for days. I wouldn't be able to be alone without looking over my shoulder. It was almost like I expected them to pay me a visit from the other side. At times my feelings would overwhelm me to the point where I couldn't stand the dark."

Chloe grabbed her hand. "I understand how you feel. It's like we've had problems connecting with people all of our lives, and when we finally do and something bad happens, it's hard for us to handle."

"Right." Lyric allowed the tears to flow freely onto her lap. "God hasn't given us the spirit of fear. I knew it was an attack of the enemy trying to take over my mind. I went to Dr. Little because I wanted help. Prayer helped with some of my issues, but it seemed like whenever I conquered one fear, another one popped up. Between premenstrual dysphoric disorder, stress, anxiety, and bouts with depression, I couldn't focus. It was hard for me to be truly happy. I believe God worked through Dr. Little to help me."

"I believe He did," Chloe assured.

They sat quietly as they finished drinking their tea. They were all talked out, but found solace from being in the presence of one another.

Ten

Michael Stokes's lips were pressed so tightly together that they formed a thin line. He sat at the noisy bar at Fox Sports Grill in Atlantic Station nursing a Corona, surrounded by flat screen TVs. After the police told him and his wife that they didn't have enough evidence to hold Nigel, he wanted to strangle the life out of that . . . He could think of a slew of names to call Nigel and none of them were nice.

Sitting on the bar stool, Michael couldn't stop thinking about Nigel and what he had done to Lyric. He imagined Nigel's filthy hands touching her. In slow motion, like a scene from a movie, Michael envisioned Nigel raping the love of his life, his wife, the mother of his only child. His temple began to throb. He took a swig of his beer and set the bottle back on the mirrored countertop.

"Excuse me," Michael heard a feminine voice say.

He turned to face the young woman dressed in a form-fitted short dress.

"Is someone sitting in the seat next to you?" She flashed a smile.

Michael shook his head and the woman slid her slender frame onto the stool. He returned to his thoughts. The first time he had ever laid eyes on Lyric, he knew that she was the one. There was something about her warm smile that seemed infectious. When she smiled, other people smiled with her. The one thing that truly endeared him to Lyric was her willingness to sacrifice for her family. She was a modern woman with old-fashioned values.

When Michael was coming up, both his parents worked. He secretly resented his mother for working outside of the home while having young children. Some of his friends had stay-at-home moms, and he wanted that for himself. He wished that his mom would've been at home when he got home from school. He wanted home cooked meals and after school snacks waiting for him when he came through the door. The fact that Lyric put her family's needs ahead of her own carved out a permanent place in Michael's heart that belonged exclusively to her.

Then anger overtook him again. He was angry with himself for the way he had handled the situation with his wife. When he had searched Lyric's eyes the day she told him about her attack, he was looking for some indication that she was telling the truth. After seeing the warmth and sadness in her eyes, his heart softened. He immediately knew that she wasn't lying to him.

He tried to rationalize his behavior, but couldn't. After fifteen years of marriage, Lyric had never given him a reason to doubt her fidelity. He couldn't have asked for a more loving and considerate spouse. Whenever Lyric went out, she had no problem telling him where she was going, who she was with, or when she'd be back. Even if he called her on her cell phone, she usually answered. If she didn't answer, she called back not long afterward.

Michael wondered what his actions said about him as a man. Was he paranoid? Insecure? Then it occurred to him.

He knew a lot of divorced couples. Most of the time, one or both spouses had cheated. He realized that men and women tended to have different views of their relationships. If a man thought his relationship wasn't that bad, then the woman likely thought the relationship was on the verge of a breakup.

He downed some more of his beer. Michael thought about the state of his marital relationship. Although he was faithful to his wife and was a good provider, he had fallen short. He had sacrificed spending quality time with his family for a successful career and financial stability. It was no wonder Lyric felt vulnerable enough to accept a business card from another man. He blamed himself for neglecting her emotional needs. He wasn't there to protect her. How could he ever make this up to her?

Twisting the platinum wedding band on his left ring finger, Michael heard the woman sitting next to him say, "You want some company? You seem sad."

He glanced at her and said, "No, thanks. I'm all right."

"What's your name?" the woman insisted.

Michael had been around long enough to know that this lady was trying to push up on him. Without finishing his drink, Michael stood and placed a twenty dollar bill on the counter. The bartender came over.

"That's for mine and hers," Michael said.

He had been raised to believe that a man should provide for a woman, especially his woman. His father always worked and took care of his family. As a young boy, Michael watched his dad open doors for ladies and pull out chairs. He grew up treating women with the same consideration. He never understood why some men felt that buying a woman a drink or a meal entitled them to something more. To Michael, treating a woman special was the right thing to do. If a woman was with him, she didn't have to pull out her purse for anything.

As a wealthy black man, Michael knew that he was a hot commodity, but he never tried to capitalize on that with the women. He had too much respect for them and himself. When he made a kind gesture to a woman, there was no hidden agenda on his part.

The woman seemed impressed and batted her eyes at him. "Thank you."

"Have a good one," he said before leaving the bar alone.

Once back in his BMW, his mind was consumed with thoughts of Lyric. He loved her deeply. He could not, nor did he want to, imagine his life without her. He knew that she had some emotional problems, but he could handle that. As far as he was concerned, he understood her. That made him feel needed. She loved him, and he knew that. Her love helped fuel him to succeed. She brought out the best in him.

Michael placed the key in the ignition and drove out of the parking deck. He wondered how he could make things better with Lyric. He realized that he had become like every other rich man he knew, minus the mistresses on the side. Without realizing it, money had become like a god to him. He never meant for that to happen.

Becoming a doctor had been a lifelong dream of his. Having a loving, supportive wife and beautiful daughter were the icing on the cake. He had everything he wanted. He thought that by giving Lyric the luxuries in life, she would be happy too. Now he realized that his wife needed balance, and so did he. Not having to worry about money was great, but Lyric and Autumn needed him to be present in their lives, not sleeping or participating in activities that didn't involve them. He made up his mind that he was going to take his girls on bi-annual family vacations and his wife on at least one mini-vacation every quarter. He knew that he had been slacking in the romance department, so he made a mental note to stop off and pick up a bouquet of flowers on his way home.

While driving on I-75 going south, Michael still felt unsettled. He entertained the thought of buying a gun again to protect his family from Nigel, but he knew Lyric would never go for that. Regardless, he was the head of his household. The decision was ultimately his, and he wanted the firearm.

Lyric had told Michael about Nigel's stalker past, so he was more convinced than ever that he needed to take a proactive stance when it came to his family. No one was going to come up in his home and mess with his wife ever again. Michael was so determined to protect what was his that he seriously considered hiring a private investigator to track down Nigel. Instead of waiting for him to make a move, Michael thought about confronting him and giving him a strong warning about messing with another man's wife.

At that moment, he heard a gentle, yet comforting voice tell him, "Don't do it."

Michael furrowed his brows and wondered if that was the Holy Spirit ministering to him. He knew that he needed to pray, but he was too angry to do so. He wanted Nigel to pay for what he had done to his wife. Choosing to ignore the voice, Michael continued exploring his options for getting back at Nigel. Michael devised a plan of how he was going to make Nigel pay for what he had done.

Eleven

Nigel lit a candle and placed two roses at his mother's shrine. He let out a wicked laugh as he thought about how dumb the police were. They had brought him in for questioning knowing that the only evidence they had was circumstantial. He was proud of himself for not breaking a sweat.

He sat on the butter colored leather couch in his living room and stared at the blank screen of his plasma TV. He had been very careful that day at Lyric's house to ensure he hadn't left any incriminating evidence behind. He made her take a bath because he simply wanted her to be clean. Lyric was his ideal woman, and he didn't want to ruin the fantasy. The fact that the bath washed away evidence was just extra. Taking the sheets off the bed, now that was brilliant, Nigel had to admit. He was no dummy. If the police were looking for those sheets, good luck. He had long since burned them and spread the ashes all over

Lake Lanier. As for that tiny scratch on his neck, he lied and said that he had cut himself shaving. It's not like Lyric had his skin underneath her nails. He made sure of that.

Nigel prided himself on staying two steps ahead of the police. Not to mention that he had access to some of the best legal representation that money could buy. Some of his patrons were successful attorneys. He rubbed his hands together and leaned back on the couch, thinking back to the interrogation at the police station.

The authorities had waited until the evening hours before knocking forcefully on Nigel's door. He wasn't intimidated by them, so he let them in. The uniformed officers explained that he was a rape suspect and needed to go to the station. They allowed him to change from his T-shirt and boxers into sweats and sneakers before hauling him into the back of the squad car and subsequently into the precinct.

Once at the station, they took Nigel into the interrogation room. He was as cool as a polar bear's toenails. When asked how he had met Mrs. Stokes, Nigel replied, "Who is this, uh," he tapped his temple with two fingers as if trying to recall the name, "Mrs. Stokes that you keep mentioning?"

The officer ignored him and asked, "Why were you at her house?"

Grinning, he said, "How do you know I was at her house?"

The officer slammed his hand on the desk and inched his way toward Nigel. Finger wagging in Nigel's face, the officer said, "Don't play games with me. We have video footage from the Stokeses' home security system showing you at the residence. You spent a few minutes in the garage before ringing the front doorbell."

With a smug look on his face, Nigel relaxed in the chair.

The officer removed his hand from Nigel's face and stood up. "You're feeling real arrogant right about now, huh? Don't think just because you got away with being a stalker that you're going to get away with rape. You can forget about that." Bits of spittle escaped from the officer's mouth. "If it's the last thing I do, I'm going to put your crazy self behind bars." Nigel just stared at him. "Why did you rape that woman, Nigel?"

"If you didn't see me do it, then how you know I did?"

The officer bit the corner of his lip and shook his head. "If I could knock that smug expression off your face, I would." He turned the empty chair around and straddled it. "So what happened? I've seen Mrs. Stokes, and I'm not going to lie; she's hot." He chuckled. In an even tone, he continued. "Tell me what happened. Did you make an advance, and she rejected you?"

Nigel yawned and covered it with his hand. He then leaned into the table and said, "Look, we both know you don't have any evidence linking me to such a crime." His gaze penetrated the officer's.

The officer seemed to become frustrated. He went on to tell Nigel that Mrs. Stokes had already identified him as the man she had met while dining at a restaurant with a friend. He further explained that according to Mrs. Stokes's statement, the only reason she had called him over to her house was because she wanted to get some artwork appraised. The officer gave Nigel an opportunity to fill in the rest, but Nigel refused to cooperate.

When asked to provide a voluntary DNA sample, Nigel flatly denied that request. He knew that without his DNA, the cops didn't have enough evidence to charge him. The only thing Nigel confirmed was that he had indeed met Mrs. Stokes at a restaurant and that he had received a call from her. He deliberately left the conversation open ended just in case he had to come back later and cover his tracks. If it came down to it, he would say that he and Mrs. Stokes were having an extramarital affair. In the meantime, he didn't want to give too much information.

Nigel's experience had taught him that when dealing with the law, less was best.

Two hours later, they released Nigel due to lack of evidence. That didn't stop the officer from giving Nigel a stern warning.

"I'm going to be on you like stank on chitlins," the officer warned. "You better not even spit on the sidewalk, because I'm going to get you. One way or the other, you best believe you will get got."

Nigel smirked and left. The officer's threats hadn't fazed him in the least bit. With all of the crime happening on the streets of Atlanta, he wasn't worried about the cops sweating him.

Nigel's thoughts shifted back to the present. He got off the couch and went to the refrigerator to retrieve a Jamaican ginger beer. He twisted the cap and threw it in the garbage can. Taking a sip, he wondered what Lyric was doing. He finished his carbonated soft drink and tossed the empty glass bottle into the trash. His keys were hanging on a key hook on the side of the refrigerator. He grabbed them and hopped in his black Ford Mustang.

Twenty minutes had passed as he drove from Stone Mountain to Lithonia. Nigel turned off his headlights as he parked across the street from Lyric's house. The lights in her bedroom were on. Besides the outside lights, the rest of the house was dark. He imagined her getting ready for bed and licked his lips. She had the softest skin he had ever felt. And she smelled delicate, like a flower. He couldn't wait to see her again.

He wondered whether her husband was at home. It didn't really matter. It's not like he was going to break into their house. He needed some time for things to cool off before he did something so bold. He was simply curious.

He fantasized about being intimate with Lyric again. He was convinced that she wanted to be with him too. If it weren't for her husband, Nigel was certain they'd be able to explore their love. He resented her husband, because he stood in the way of their blossoming relationship. He had to find a way to convince Lyric to be with him. Either that or he would have to get rid of his competition.

Twelve

Lyric turned off her bedroom light and took off her satin robe. She placed the robe at the foot of the bed and climbed onto the mattress next to her husband. She rested her head on his chest as he planted soft kisses on top of her head.

"The roses are beautiful," she said. "That was really sweet of you to pick up flowers on your way home." She had displayed the fuchsia colored flowers in a crystal vase next to the bed. She preferred brightly colored flowers.

"I love you, baby. We're going to get through this."

Closing her eyes, Lyric took a deep breath and exhaled. Tears began to sting her eyes. Feeling wetness on his chest and hearing his wife's sniffles, Michael held her close.

"I didn't mean to cry," she explained. "It's just that I feel so angry and overwhelmed. I can't believe that Nigel is going to get away with what he did to me." She sat up and removed a couple of tissues from the box on the night-stand. She wiped her eyes and blew her nose.

Michael propped a pillow behind his back. "Regardless of whether the law prosecutes him or not, he won't get away with anything."

Lyric stopped crying and searched Michael's light colored eyes. Although she wanted Nigel to pay for his crime, she did not believe in vigilante justice. "Honey, I know you want to protect me, and I love you for that. Let me make something perfectly clear." She held up a manicured finger. "I don't want you to do something that could land you in jail, or worse."

Michael shifted his body and pulled the sheets above his waist. "Baby, stop talking like that. Just let me be the man."

Lyric seemed taken aback by his statement. "I can't believe you said that. Let you be the man?" She tilted her head to the side. "That's all I ever do. I respect you as the head of this household, and I have honored you as such. I don't nag you or tear you down."

"I know, and I appreciate it." His expression softened.

She pulled her hair back with her hands and released it. "All I'm saying is that I don't want you going after this guy. We both know he did a very bad thing. Even still, it's not worth you jeopardizing your livelihood over. He's not worth it. Think about your career. You've worked too hard to get where you are." She looked him in the eyes. "Think about Autumn. She adores you. If something happened to you, it would devastate her." Cupping the side of his face with her hand, she said, "And I need you. You know how much I love you."

Michael nodded his head, and Lyric kissed him on the lips. They began to get more intimate. When images of Nigel flashed on the screen of Lyric's mind, she stopped Michael from going any further.

"I'm sorry, honey," she said in a hushed tone. "I can't do this right now."

Catching a glimpse of the pained expression on her husband's face, Lyric got out of bed and went into the bathroom to splash cold water on her eyes. She realized that she must be suffering from posttraumatic stress. That was the only thing that made sense. She patted her eyes with a hand towel before going back out to talk with her husband. She explained to him that no matter how much she desired to be with him, she needed more time before resuming their normal activities.

His voice filled with understanding and compassion, Michael said, "I think you should either go back to seeing Dr. Little regularly or join a support group for rape survivors."

Lyric's eyes became misty. "I probably should go back to Dr. Little. I don't feel comfortable talking to a bunch of strangers."

He put his arm around her and squeezed her. That night, Michael held his wife as she cried and released her pain. He continued to hold her until she fell asleep in his arms.

The next morning, Michael got up with Autumn while Lyric slept. When she finally awoke, she was surprised that the clock read 10:00 A.M. She didn't usually sleep that late, but she figured that her body must've needed the extra rest. She got out of bed and went into the bathroom. When she saw her puffy eyes in the mirror, she frowned at her reflection. She washed her face and brushed her teeth before taking a hot shower.

When she finished showering, she read the Bible and prayed. Then she called Dr. Little's office and scheduled a same day appointment. After she hung up the phone, she put on her make-up, trying to lessen the appearance of her swollen eyes, and slipped into a purple wrap dress with a pair of open-toed purple suede heels. As she rubbed lotion into her hands, Michael walked in and said, "Where are you going looking all good?"

She removed her wedding rings from her jewelry box and slid them on her left ring finger. She preferred not to sleep in jewelry. "I have an appointment with Dr. Little."

"Oh." He gave her a hug and kissed her on the forehead. "Do you want me to go with you? I don't have any patients until later today."

"No, I'm all right. Thanks for letting me sleep in this morning. What did you tell Autumn?"

"Just that you stayed up late and needed some rest. She understood." He released her. "Want to go out to dinner tonight?"

"That would be nice." She smiled at him. "It's Friday, so Autumn's spending the night at Heavyn's house." She inserted some dangling earrings into her lobes. "I need to get going. See you in a few." She kissed him on the cheek, grabbed her designer handbag, and left.

She hopped on I-20 West to I-75 North. By the time she got off on the Tenth/Fourteenth Street exit, her stomach was grumbling, so she pulled into the Einstein Bros. Bagels parking lot. She went inside and ordered a cranberry bagel topped with honey almond cream cheese and a cup of chai latte. Then she headed to Dr. Little's office.

Lyric finished eating her breakfast in the car and carried the spiced milk tea into the building with her. When she arrived, she was relieved that she didn't have to wait. Yahkie, dressed in an olive green suit, greeted her and took her straight into Dr. Little's office. The ladies embraced before Dr. Little opened the session with a prayer.

After finishing the prayer, Dr. Little asked, "How are things going?"

Lyric recalled what happened when she told Michael about the rape. She then went on to explain that Nigel had been questioned by the police, but they didn't have enough evidence to hold him.

Dr. Little nodded her understanding. "The last time you were here we didn't get a chance to discuss treatment options. With the stress you've been under lately, have you been experiencing an increase in panic and anxiety attacks?"

"Yes," she admitted. "Especially at bedtime when all of the lights are out. The darkness seems to trigger the irrational thoughts. I have to sleep with the TV on." She sipped her beverage. "It also happens when I'm alone."

"That's not uncommon." Dr. Little scribbled something on her legal pad. "Today we're going to focus more on the healing process. I'm going to teach you some relaxation techniques. You'll learn to control your fear reactions via exercises designed to reduce physiological sensations. One of the methods is called progressive muscle relaxation and the other is diaphragmatic breathing."

Lyric listened attentively as Dr. Little explained that the process of progressive muscle relaxation was simply isolating one muscle group, creating tension for 8-10 seconds, and then letting the muscle relax and the tension go for 15 seconds.

"Take your right hand and make a fist," Dr. Little said as she balled her right hand into a fist to demonstrate. Lyric did as she was told. "Can you feel the muscle tension increase in your hand and forearm the longer you hold it?"

"Yes."

"After awhile it doesn't feel so good, right?"

"Right." Lyric's arm was beginning to hurt. She wondered how much longer she'd have to hold that position.

They kept their fists balled for 15 seconds, which felt like 10 minutes to Lyric. Suddenly Dr. Little said, "Relax and let it go." Her hand flopped down into her lap. Lyric's did the same. "Notice a difference?"

"Big time," Lyric said, breathing a sigh of relief.

Smiling, Dr. Little said, "Now let's go through the rest of the body. When you're at home, you'll need to sit in a comfortable chair. No tight clothes, don't wear any shoes, and don't cross your legs."

Dr. Little went on to explain the breathing technique of taking a deep breath and releasing it slowly, repeatedly. She told Lyric that she should concentrate on the feel of the muscles, specifically the contrast between tension and relaxation.

When she finished explaining, Dr. Little took off her shoes and demonstrated the techniques for 10 to 15 seconds each. She started with her hand by making a fist, and then extending the fingers. She then tensed and relaxed her biceps and triceps. After that, she pulled her shoulders back, relaxed them, and hunched her shoulders forward, then relaxed. She did lateral and forward moves with her neck.

Next she opened her mouth and extended her tongue as far as she could and let it sit at the bottom of her mouth. Lyric couldn't help but laugh. That didn't stop Dr. Little. She brought her tongue back into her throat as far as possible, and then relaxed. She dug her tongue into the roof of her mouth and relaxed. Dug it into the bottom of her mouth and relaxed.

She stopped for a moment and said, "It looks silly, but it feels really good. I'm halfway done, and then I want you to do it."

Dr. Little resumed with the relaxation exercises. She opened her eyes as wide as she could and relaxed. Then she squinted and relaxed. Next she took a deep breath and drew in a little more. She let it out and resumed her normal breathing for 15 seconds. She appeared to let all of the air in her lungs out, and then a little more before inhaling and breathing normally again.

With shoulders resting on the back of the chair, Dr. Little pushed her body forward, causing her back to arch and relaxed. Then she tensed her bottom and raised her pelvis slightly off the chair and relaxed.

She extended her legs and raised her feet a few inches off the floor, then relaxed. She dug her heels into the carpet, and relaxed. She sucked in her stomach, relaxed, then pushed out her stomach, and relaxed.

She pointed her toes without raising her legs and relaxed. With her legs relaxed, Dr. Little dug her toes into the floor and relaxed.

"I'm done," Dr. Little said with a smile. "Your turn."

She stood up and instructed Lyric to take her seat. They switched places, and Dr. Little talked Lyric through the relaxation process.

When they finished, Lyric admitted that she felt more relaxed. Dr. Little told her to do the entire sequence once a day until she was able to identify her tension areas and eliminate some of the steps.

"Do you still do Yoga?" Dr. Little asked.

"I do, but I have not really felt like working out since . . ." She paused, thinking about the attack. "Well, you know."

"Start back doing Yoga and other exercise routines right away. Resuming your normal activities will help relieve some of your stress and get your mind focused on more positive things." She scribbled on her notepad. "Since you do Yoga, I know you're familiar with diaphragmatic breathing."

Lyric nodded her head and said, "Yes, I am."

"Good. Remember to breathe deeply every day." Dr. Little checked her watch. "It's time for us to wrap up our session, but I want you to schedule a follow-up appointment with Yahkie on your way out."

Lyric agreed, and Dr. Little ended the session with a prayer. They hugged, and Lyric left, feeling as though she had done the right thing by coming.

Thirteen

The atmosphere in Sambuca Jazz Café in Buckhead was quite romantic on New Year's Eve. Lyric and Michael had gone to six o'clock prayer service and decided to go out to dinner afterward. They wanted to be back at home before midnight rather than returning to church for Watch Night services.

Lyric enjoyed listening to the jazz music as she and Michael sat at a cozy table with a flickering candle between them. She was elated that she and her husband were out on a date, alone. They usually went out with other couples or to social networking events.

Michael slid his chair closer to his wife's and whispered in her ear. "You look good." He nibbled on her earlobe.

She smiled and tilted her head back. Michael had a way of making her feel as though she was the sexiest woman alive. Looking around the establishment, she noticed other couples dressed in casual chic. Some of them were eating, others were chatting, and a few were laughing. She looked at the Baby Grand Piano sitting on the stage and wondered whether someone would perform while they were there.

She felt Michael grab her hand and lightly squeeze. She appreciated the gesture and let him know by peck kissing his lips. They stared lovingly into each other's eyes until the waitress arrived and they were forced to break their gaze. The waitress seemed pleasant as she set down two glasses of water and took their food and drink orders. For starters, they ordered calamari and two iced teas with lemon. As entreés, Lyric selected the blackened tilapia étoufée, and Michael chose crab-stuffed salmon.

When the waitress left them alone, Lyric told Michael about her session with Dr. Little and the relaxation techniques she had shown her. Michael had a serious look on his face.

"I haven't been completely honest with you," he admitted, using his straw to swirl the ice water around in the glass.

Lyric felt her pulse quickening. She hoped that Michael wasn't about to make some earth shattering confession, like he was having an affair, he really liked men, or he wanted a divorce. She didn't say anything; she simply held her breath, hoping to lessen the impact.

"You know how I always told you that having another baby really wasn't a big deal for me?" He glanced in her direction.

Lyric allowed herself to breathe, a little. She nodded her understanding.

"I never told you, but I always wanted to have three children." He leaned in closer to her. "We've been trying to get pregnant for years without success. At first I wasn't too concerned about it since we were both fairly young and healthy. Now that we're getting older, we need to hurry up and do this. When I saw how difficult it was for us to have more children, I tried to convince myself that it didn't matter. Besides that, I saw the toll it was taking on you. I didn't want to make you feel worse, so I told you it didn't matter to me." He smiled at her. "I think we should go to a fertility specialist."

Shocked, Lyric let out a breath. "Why now?"

Michael traced the brim of his water glass with his finger. "I know how badly you want another baby. As do I. I think it would be good for us."

She raised a brow. "Are you serious?"

"Very."

"That means a lot to me, Michael." She touched the side of his face.

The waitress returned with their drinks and let them know that their appetizer would be out shortly. Then she left.

All sorts of thoughts were going through Lyric's mind. She wondered whether the problem was with her or her husband. Would she need an egg donor? In vitro fertilization? What if she had a multiple birth?

Michael placed his hand on top of hers. "I can tell by the look on your face that you have a lot of questions. I'll get a referral for a specialist, and we can take it from there."

She put on a happy expression before sipping her tea through a straw and grooving to the music. After the waitress set their appetizer before them and left, they held hands and bowed their hands while Michael blessed the delicious smelling food.

A few minutes later, the waitress returned with their meals and took away the half-eaten appetizer. As Lyric enjoyed her spread, she caught a glimpse of a man who resembled Nigel sitting at the bar. She dropped her fork. Her hands began to tremble. She hoped and prayed that her eyes were playing tricks on her.

"You all right, baby?" Michael asked, looking at her.

"Um, don't flip out, but I think Nigel is sitting at the bar."

"What?" He snatched the linen napkin from his lap and threw it on the table. He stood up.

Grabbing his arm, Lyric pleaded, "Please don't cause a scene. I'm not even sure if it's him. With the dim lighting it's hard to tell. Besides, even if it is him, he probably wants us to cause a commotion. Let's not give him the satisfaction of seeing us upset."

Michael gritted his teeth. Lyric could tell by the fire in his eyes that he wanted to knock Nigel out. Honestly, she would've loved to have seen that happen, but she couldn't risk her husband injuring himself or catching a case behind some psycho. In all of the years she had known him, she had never seen him raise a hand in anger. He wasn't the violent type.

"Honey," Lyric said. "Let's just go."

Sitting back down, Michael said, "No." His eyes stared in the direction of the bar. "We aren't going anywhere. Nobody's going to run us from out of here."

Lyric's throat felt dry, so she drank some tea. The waitress stopped by to check on them, and Lyric asked for a clean fork. Not taking her eyes off the guy at the bar, Lyric noticed that he paid his tab and headed toward the exit. Only able to see his side profile, she never got a clear view of his face.

Not long afterward, the waitress returned with flatware and a bottle of expensive champagne.

She set two flute glasses on the table and said, "There was a guy at the bar who wanted me to give this to you after he left."

Lyric and Michael exchanged glances. "Do you know his name?" Michael asked.

"No, he didn't say. He just told me to tell you thanks for giving him the time of his life."

"Excuse me," Michael said as he bolted from the table and went outdoors.

Lyric saw Michael through the window walk up and down the sidewalk looking for Nigel. She asked the waitress to take the bottle away because they didn't want it. Then she asked for to-go boxes and the bill of fare.

The waitress seemed visibly shaken and apologized. Lyric assured the young woman that they didn't blame her.

When Michael returned to the table, he released a barrage of cuss words. "The nerve of that guy."

"Calm down, honey." Even though her heart was racing and hands trembling, Lyric tried to keep her emotions in check. Michael was upset enough for the both of them.

Without sitting down, he retrieved his wallet from his back pocket and paid the bill in cash, along with a generous tip. The waitress picked it up and thanked them.

Lyric grabbed her purse and stood up. Carrying the doggy bag, Michael ushered his wife out of the restaurant. During the ride home, the tension in the air was as thick as London fog. Neither one of them spoke. Michael drove, and Lyric stared out of the window at passing cars and lit office buildings.

Lost in her thoughts, Lyric tried to figure out what she should do next. She thought that Nigel had been bold to send over the bottle of bubbly. A part of her wished that Michael had caught up to him outside of the restaurant and snatched him up. Besides being angry, she felt disrespected, again. Something had to give. She kicked off her heels and discreetly practiced the relaxation techniques.

When Lyric finished, she looked at Michael and said, "I want to report this incident to the police and get a restraining order."

"I think that's best. We need to keep a paper trail."

Lyric stared out the car window. She felt disgusted at Nigel's nerve.

Fourteen

After signing in at the receptionist's window, Lyric sat in the waiting room of the doctor's office and flipped through a magazine. A month had passed since Lyric's assault. She had been nervous and jittery ever since seeing Nigel at the restaurant. She did get a restraining order. That still didn't make her feel any more secure. She found herself constantly looking over her shoulder to the point of paranoia. Fortunately for her, she had not seen or heard a word from Nigel. That made her even more concerned. She often found herself consumed with thoughts of him. What was he up to? she wondered. Where was he hiding?

Lyric felt so emotionally and physically drained that all she wanted to do was sleep. She found herself napping throughout the day. She was concerned. It's not like she felt sad. If she were depressed, she would've known. This was different. She felt fatigued. Since she and

Michael were about to begin seeing a fertility specialist, she made an appointment with her family practitioner for a physical. If there was something wrong, she wanted to know about it right away.

When her name was called, she put down the publication and followed the nurse to the back where the nurse took her vitals.

"You're here for a physical, right?" the nurse said as she flipped through the pages on the clipboard.

"Yes," she replied. Anticipating the nurse's next question, Lyric volunteered the information. "I've been feeling kind of sluggish lately, so I need to have some blood work done."

The nurse nodded her head. She took Lyric to one of the examining rooms. She handed Lyric an exam gown and asked her to change into it. "Dr. Hart will be right in," she said before leaving and closing the door behind her.

Lyric took off her clothes and put on the thin, loose gown. She scooted her body back on the exam table and tried to relax. She prayed that nothing was wrong.

When Lyric heard a knock on the door, she turned her head in that direction. The doctor immediately entered and shook Lyric's hand.

"Nice to see you again, Mrs. Stokes," Dr. Hart greeted. She sat down on the stool. "The nurse said that you've been feeling a bit sluggish. Tell me about that."

Lyric confided in Dr. Hart that she had been sexually assaulted. Although she didn't think that she was depressed, Lyric admitted that it was possible. Why else would she be so tired all the time? She went on to explain that she and her husband wanted to have another child and would begin seeing a specialist.

Dr. Hart offered a few words of sympathy and encouragement before going into the examination. Once done with all the poking and prodding, the doctor left and the nurse came in to draw a few vials of blood.

"The doctor will run some tests, and she'll be back to discuss the results," the nurse said.

Lyric nodded and waited for the doctor's return. A few minutes later, Dr. Hart returned with the nurse. She closed the door behind them.

"Mrs. Stokes, I've got your results. I know why you've been so tired," Dr. Hart explained.

Lyric's heartbeat sped up. "What's wrong?" She sounded serious.

"You're pregnant." The doctor offered a warm smile.

Lyric felt as if her heart were about to beat out of her chest. Her jaw dropped. All she could do was stare at a crack in the tiled floor.

"I know you're surprised." Dr. Hart patted her hand. "I'd say you're about four weeks along."

Lyric wanted to speak, but her tongue wouldn't cooperate. Every time she attempted to say something, she stuttered. After a couple of tries, her tongue became untied and regained functionality. "There must be a mistake," she insisted. "Run the test again."

"I figured you'd say that, so I took the liberty of running the test three times. The results came back the same every time."

Lyric's eyes filled with tears. She felt as though a cruel joke had been played on her. She struggled to get her mind to absorb the fact that she was one month pregnant. Why couldn't she be five, six, or more weeks? she wondered. No, that would be too good to be true, she figured. Besides, that wouldn't be her life. In her life, things either started out as a battle or struggle. Not too much ever went easy for her. This wasn't the time for a pity party, though. Lyric understood that the hardships helped to shape her character and make her stronger.

She blinked and tears streamed down her cheeks. She had never felt so conflicted in her life. Lord knew how badly she wanted to have another baby. As impossible as it was for Lyric to wrap her mind around the fact that she may very well be carrying her rapist's baby instead of her husband's, she knew in her spirit that she had to trust God.

She felt Dr. Hart hug her and the nurse rubbed her back. They both told her that everything would be okay.

"Under the circumstances," said Dr. Hart, "we brought you some pamphlets discussing your options." She released Lyric and retrieved two thin booklets from her coat pocket.

Lyric's brows knitted together. "What options?" she asked.

The doctor handed her a pamphlet about abortion and another about adoption. "Since you were a victim of rape, it would be understandable if you didn't want to keep the baby."

The nurse stopped rubbing her back and stepped into a corner.

Closing her eyes and taking a deep breath, she blew the air out of her mouth. Dr. Hart handed her a tissue, and she wiped her face. "I need to make something perfectly clear," Lyric said, balling up the tissue. She spoke very deliberate. "I'm a Christian. An abortion is not an option for me. Yes, I was raped," her lips formed a tight line, "but I also had sex with my husband that same morning. There's a chance that this baby could be my husband's." Lyric had a faraway look in her eyes. "Even if I hadn't slept with my husband, it still wouldn't matter. This baby is innocent." She glanced at the adoption booklet and said, "Adoption is definitely out of the question. I have a husband and a daughter. There's no way I could go through an entire pregnancy and give up the baby. That would be too painful."

"Oh, I understand," Dr. Hart said. "In that case, congratulations." She gave a warm smile. "I'll write you a prescription for prenatal vitamins and iron pills. You're slightly anemic." Her eyes were filled with warmth and compassion. "You'll need to make a follow up appointment with your OB/GYN. Let me know if there's anything I can do to help." There was a pregnant pause. "A child is a gift from God. I admire you for having such faith."

Lyric hoped that she had as much faith as Dr. Hart seemed to think she had. The doctor and the nurse left her alone while she changed back into her street clothes. She felt numb as she thought about what that meant. What if the baby really was Nigel's? How would that affect her family? Would Michael be able to accept a baby that wasn't biologically his? She wondered whether she would be able to bond with a child that was a constant reminder of a traumatic experience in her life. What would she tell Autumn? How could she make her understand? She started to cry again.

Lyric remained in the examination room a while longer while she composed herself. She heard a knock at the door, and the nurse announced herself. After telling her to come in, the nurse entered and handed her a piece of paper with the prescriptions written on it. Lyric thanked her and left.

On the way to the pharmacy, Lyric's mind was on everything except driving. She ran a red light and nearly got into an accident. She didn't trust herself to leave and come back to pick up her prescriptions, so she waited until they were filled.

When she got home, she dialed Michael's number and hung up. What if he were consulting with a patient? she wondered. She didn't want to worry him, so she made the difficult decision to wait until he got home to tell him the news.

She needed to talk to someone, though. She was tempted to call Chloe, but she decided against it. Although that was her best friend, and she knew she could trust her, she thought that the first person she should tell about her condition was Michael.

The thought to take a drink crossed her mind. She dismissed that notion. She didn't want to do anything that could harm her unborn child. Instead, she went into her bedroom and removed her Bible from the nightstand and began reading from the book of Psalms. She read two passages before kneeling next to her bed to pray. Her eyelids felt heavy, and she was having a hard time keeping her eyes open . . . let alone finishing her prayer. She climbed on top of the bed and nestled underneath the covers before drifting into a sleeping bliss.

Two hours later, she awoke, feeling hungry. She went into the kitchen and fixed herself a turkey and provolone panini. She was so hungry that she almost bit her fingers. Her purse rested on the counter, reminding her that she needed to take her pills. She still couldn't believe that she was pregnant. She patted her belly. Although there was no baby bump yet, she still felt surreal.

Removing the vials from her purse, she twisted the lids. Then she popped the horse pills and downed them with bottled water.

"What are you taking?" Michael asked as he came through the garage door entrance.

Startled, Lyric dropped her water and spilled it on the floor. "You scared me," Lyric said as she tore a few paper towels from the holder to soak up the water off the floor. She wished she had a magical towel that could soak up the mess that had become her life.

Michael walked over to the wall pad and keyed in the code to deactivate the beeping alarm. Lyric had the alarm set to "home." That way if anyone came in from outside, the alarm would beep.

"I'm surprised you didn't hear me come in," he said.

She threw the wet towels in the trash and dried her hands on a kitchen cloth. "I had a lot on my mind."

He approached her and hugged her. "What's going on?"

She buried her face in his chest. "I'm pregnant," she mumbled.

An invisible vacuum seemed to suck the air out of the room. He released her and took a step back. Unable to look him in the eyes, she hung her head and repeated herself.

Michael covered his mouth with his hand and slid it down his neatly trimmed goatee. "Are you sure?" He seemed taken aback.

She nodded her head. "I went to the doctor, and she confirmed it." She picked up the bottle of prenatal vitamins to show him.

"I'll be . . ." A smile spread across his face. He bent over and kissed her on the lips. "How far along are we?"

She bit the corner of her lip. Looking him in the eyes, she said, "Four weeks." His smile faded. He stroked his goatee again. The disappointed look in his eyes pulled at Lyric's heartstrings. She couldn't stop the tears. "I'm so sorry, honey."

In an attempt to console his wife, Michael pulled her into him and held her close. "Listen to me. I love you, baby. You're my wife, and we're having a baby. That little girl or boy that you're carrying is a part of you. That's all that matters. Because of that I will love him or her no matter what. I'm not going anywhere. I'm that child's father."

"I love you so much, Michael." She sniffled, wiping her nose with the back of her hand.

She freed herself from his embrace. Lyric used to wonder whether she was lucky or unlucky. Now she knew the answer. Neither. She was blessed. She breathed a sigh of relief that Michael had been so supportive. She didn't think it was possible for her to fall any deeper in love with her husband, but she had. When she looked into his eyes, she saw her college sweetheart. The man she had fallen in love with all those years ago.

"You need to take it easy for the next few weeks, at least until you get out of the first trimester," Michael said, sounding like a doctor.

He leaned against the island. "How would you feel about my mom coming to stay with us for a few months to help out around here?"

Lyric shunned the thought. She couldn't stand her mother-in-law, Erica. If morning sickness didn't make her sick, being around Michael's mother surely would. "Michael, before we go into that, there's something I need to get off my chest." She folded her arms across her bosom.

He raised a brow.

"Heaven forbid if this baby turns out not to be yours." He turned his face away from hers. "I would be devastated. No matter what you say, I know that you would be too. I thank God that you're willing to stand by me and claim this baby as your own. I have to keep it real with you. I'm scared to death. The thought of carrying Nigel's seed gives me the creeps. If that turns out to be the case, what will we tell Autumn? Our family? Better yet, what will we tell this baby?"

He looked at her. His eyes were watery, but no tears fell. Michael was not the type of man to shed tears. Out of all the years she'd known him, she had only seen him cry once, and that was at his father's funeral. Even then he was composed.

He spoke deliberately. "The paternity of this baby doesn't matter. I'm the father. I don't see why we need to tell anyone about it. This is a

family matter. It's none of anyone's business."
He paused for a brief moment. "As for Autumn,
she's too young to deal with that right now. If
need be, we'll wait until she's much older."

Sadness crept into her eyes. "And what about
Nigel? He's been low-key since the restaurant
incident, but I know he's lurking around. What
if he tries to come after me, or worse, what if he
hurts the baby?"

He let out a deep breath. "I wasn't going to say
anything, because I didn't want to upset you."
She braced herself. "I bought a gun."

"You did what?" Her tone elevated.

He held up his hands. "Before you start going
off, let me explain." She gave him an icy glare. "I
got the gun for our protection. If Nigel wants to
act crazy, I'll show him the definition of crazy.
Nobody is going to violate my family."

Although she didn't approve of guns, because
she hated violence, she understood Michael's
sentiments. Nigel was unpredictable, and she
hated living in constant fear. Deep down she
appreciated the fact that Michael was willing to
go through such extreme measures to protect
her. He had proven to be her "knight in shining
armor."

"So where is it?" she asked.

He pursed his lips. "It's locked in a gun safe at the top of my closet." He noticed the concerned look on her face. "Don't worry; it's not loaded. I even got a trigger lock. And the ammunition is locked up in a separate location too." He went on to explain that he had applied for a firearm permit so that he could carry a concealed weapon. That could take up to three months to get. In the meantime, he could only keep the gun in the house or car.

He seemed to have taken all of the appropriate precautions. That made Lyric feel better. She relaxed her shoulders. They went into the living room, and Michael gave her a foot rub. They talked about baby names and going to Lyric's next doctor's appointment together. She thanked God for Michael's unconditional love and support. Because of him, she allowed herself to get excited about the baby. Her baby.

Fifteen

After a long day full of appointments, Nigel scarfed down a sub sandwich and cherry flavored soda. He took off his suit and took a quick shower. Before turning in for the night, he logged on to his computer to check the real time GPS tracking device he had installed underneath Lyric's car. He had previously purchased the device and waited for the right opportunity to install it. The day that he had gotten the call from Lyric regarding her artwork, he was relieved that her garage door was open. That was all he needed. Prior to ringing her doorbell, he discreetly installed the gadget.

His previous routine included watching Lyric in between his appointments. Lyric made it easy. She didn't leave the house before 11:00 A.M., and she always returned by 4:00 P.M. He could set his watch by her. She rarely deviated from her schedule.

He had tested the tracker by showing up at Sambuca. True to the advertised guarantees, he really was able to track Lyric's whereabouts in real time. Thank goodness for modern day technology. Because of that, he knew her comings and goings with minimal effort. Even when his eyes weren't physically on her, his eyes were still on her. He felt that was worthy of a celebration. That's why he sent over the champagne.

While checking the report, he did an Internet search on an unfamiliar address. He discovered that Lyric had gone to a doctor's office. He wondered what that was about. Why had she gone to see a doctor? he wondered. Was she sick? Was it a routine physical? Not knowing really bothered him.

He logged off his computer and turned off the monitor. He decided that he needed to keep a closer eye on her. The fact that she had gotten a restraining order against him wasn't a deterrent. If anything, it made him more determined. Did she really think a piece of paper would stop him? He found her actions comical. He knew the law. Accused was not the same as convicted. So what if he allegedly raped her? Her word against his. She wouldn't be foolish enough to pursue those charges, he reasoned. And if she did, he was prepared to slander her. He'd show the world the real definition of a desperate housewife. He was convinced that there wasn't a jury in the world who would convict him of any wrongdoing. Especially since those trumped up stalker allegations weren't admissible. Since he had been cleared, it was as if none of it ever happened. Poof! Vanished like a cloud of smoke.

He paced the carpeted floor before picking up a framed photo of Lyric off his desk. He had personally taken numerous pictures of her doing day to day activities.

"You belong to me," he said as if Lyric were standing right there in the room with him. "I can tell by the way you look at me that you want me. I know you do." He stared at the picture and touched the glass. "I love you. If it weren't for your misplaced loyalty to your husband, you'd love me too. He doesn't deserve you. He doesn't appreciate you the way I do."

He set the picture down and sat on the edge of his bed. He thought about kidnapping Lyric, but figured that the police would be on him like wet on water. She had already cast him under a negative light, so he needed to be more careful. If she went missing, he'd be the prime suspect.

Then he thought about killing her neglectful husband. He grimaced. The image of him slowly squeezing the life out of Mr. Stokes while looking him in the eyes gave Nigel a twisted sense of pleasure. He marveled at that idea. He liked the idea of murdering him with his bare hands. That was far better than just shooting him, he figured. He wanted him to suffer and to know who was snuffing him out and why.

He convinced himself that if Mr. Stokes were out of the equation, Lyric would more freely come to him. They could be together without her feeling guilty.

Then it occurred to him that Lyric might feel responsible for her slain husband. How could he get around that? he wondered. What if he made it look like an accident? All sorts of thoughts flooded his mind. He toyed with the idea of cutting the brake line of Mr. Stoke's car. He'd have to research that, he concluded. Maybe he could hire a crack head to attack him. To the police and everyone else the incident would have to look like a random act of violence. Nigel's hands would appear to be clean. He liked that idea. He rubbed his hands together as he seriously considered that option. Mr. Stokes had better enjoy himself, Nigel thought. His days were numbered.

Sixteen

Lyric was relieved that she had made it out of the first trimester without any complications. She had been exercising, eating right, and getting plenty of rest. Now it was time to tell Autumn about the baby. Michael had taken a week off from work so that the family could spend Spring Break in Myrtle Beach, South Carolina. The timing couldn't be better, Lyric thought.

The bags were packed, and Michael was loading up the convertible. Lyric was in the kitchen filling the cooler with bottled water and fruit juices.

"What's the matter with you?" she asked Autumn, who had her lip poking out.

"Why can't Heavyn come with us?" She pouted.

Lyric reached for the Ezekiel bread and started making turkey and cheese sandwiches to pack in the picnic basket. "Daddy and I already told you that this is a family vacation." She emphasized the word family.

"Heavyn is like family," Autumn insisted.

"Give it a rest," she said seriously. "I'm not in the mood to debate with you. We don't spend enough time as a family as it is. You should be glad that we're getting this quality time, just the three of us," she scolded. "Now get the light mayo and mustard out of the fridge."

Autumn scrunched up her face and did as she was told. She placed the condiments inside of the cooler. She went inside the pantry and pulled out some snacks. "Mommy," she sounded whiny.

"Stop it. You're too old to act like a baby. All of the whining in the world isn't going to change a thing." She finished stuffing the basket with sandwiches. Then she selected fruit from the refrigerator and added them to the woven container.

Michael entered and said, "Everybody ready?" He was smiling and appeared to be in a good mood.

Autumn didn't answer. She sighed and continued to pout. Michael walked over to her and started tickling her.

Laughing, Autumn said, "Stop it, Daddy."

"No more attitude, right?" He tickled her some more.

Her body jerked from laughter. "Okay, okay. I promise; no more attitude."

He ceased with the tickling. "Let's go." He clapped his hands. "Let's put the food in the car and get this party started.

"Wait," Lyric said. "I forgot the chicken and potato salad." She grabbed the items from the fridge and added the chicken to the basket and the salad to the cooler. "Now I'm ready."

Michael grabbed both containers and put them in the backseat of the car. Autumn traipsed behind him, carrying a shopping bag filled with snacks. Doing a last minute sweep of the house, Lyric checked to make sure the doors were locked, automatic lights turned on, and appliances unplugged. She then grabbed her purse, locked the door behind her and waited until she was in the car before using the remote to activate the alarm.

After watching TV and munching on snacks for the first half of the ride, Autumn had dozed off and slept the rest of the way. Lyric tried her best to stay up and keep Michael company while he drove, but that only lasted a couple of hours before she was out like a light. The six-hour drive was pleasant and uneventful.

When they arrived in Myrtle Beach, Michael announced, "We're here." He parked the car in front of their beach-front rental property.

Lyric woke up yawning. Autumn rubbed her sleepy eyes. Looking out the window at the view of the ocean, Autumn perked up. "I can't wait to go to the beach," she said.

Michael glanced at her in the rearview mirror and smiled. They unloaded the car and headed up to their two-story vacation home. The house was immaculate and cozy—hardwood floors throughout and wicker furniture. They stocked the refrigerator with food. Autumn claimed her bedroom upstairs. Michael and Lyric stayed on the ground floor.

When they finished unpacking, they all took naps. Two hours later, they awoke. Feeling refreshed, they changed into their bathing suits and hit the beach. Lyric and Michael sat on beach chairs and watched with shaded eyes as Autumn splashed in the water. She seemed to be having fun.

Lyric tilted her brim hat to further shield her face from the sun.

Standing up and adjusting the large umbrella, Michael asked, "Is this better?"

"Much," she said. He sat back down and held her hand. "Think we should tell Autumn about the baby over dinner?"

"Yes, the sooner the better. How are you feeling?"

She laughed. "I've started craving hamburgers. You know; those big, juicy ones."

"Just like you did with Autumn. That just means you need more protein and iron. While you're pregnant you need to eat liver and steak." Lyric scrunched up her face. "Thick burgers are a good source of protein, but high in cholesterol, so don't overdo it."

She playfully tapped him on his arm. "You sound like a doctor," she joked.

"Do you want to take a walk on the beach, Mrs. Stokes?"

She loved it when he called her 'Mrs. Stokes.' Even after all these years she never got tired of hearing it. "I'd love to, Mr. Stokes."

They walked hand-in-hand toward the water and told Autumn that they were going for a stroll. She waved at them and continued playing with some kids she had just met. Lyric took off her thong sandals and held them in her left hand while holding hands with Michael with the other. She enjoyed the feel of the cool, wet sand squish between her toes. She especially liked leaving foot compressions in the sand, and then watching the water run over her feet and wash away the footprints.

Michael let go of her hand and wrapped his arm around her waist. "I want you to be happy, baby."

"What do you mean?" she wanted to know.

"I was just thinking about your many talents. I know I don't tell you very often, but I think you're a smart woman. You could do anything you put your mind to."

They continued walking as the waves lightly crashed against their feet.

She thought about what he had said. "I've often wondered what I should be doing with my life. I used to think that once we had money, everything would fall into place. The truth of the matter is that money doesn't make a person happy." He nodded his understanding. "In some of my previous sessions with Dr. Little, we talked about goal setting. I had actually made a list of things that I was good at. I made a separate list of things I would do even if I couldn't get paid." She leaned in closer to him. "What I came up with was that I enjoy interior decorating and wedding planning."

She had not pursued her passions because the timing never seemed to be right. After Autumn was born, she and Michael agreed that she would be a stay-at-home mom until Autumn was school age. Then she got caught up with the lifestyle of being a doctor's wife. She held various positions on different nonprofit boards. She was actively involved with fundraising and church activities.

Her social calendar was full even though she felt a void.

He stopped walking and faced the ocean. "I could see you doing that. Why don't you take some classes while you're pregnant and get a certificate?"

She looked at him. "Are you serious?"

He stared straight ahead. "Of course. You supported me while I pursued my dreams; now it's my turn to support you. Autumn is old enough to look after herself while you do your thing."

Sighing, she said, "Yeah, Autumn is, but what about the new baby?"

He turned toward her and said, "Don't stress about it. Get the training out of the way now. When the baby comes, I'll ask my mom to come live with us. I'm sure she would love watching the baby while you get your business off the ground."

There he was again, bringing up his mother. Lyric wished he would give that a rest. "I couldn't ask her to do that." She shook her head.

The thought of Michael's mother staying with them sent shivers down her spine. Lyric could tolerate her in small doses, but for an extended time, Lord, help her! And the feeling was mutual. Her mother-in-law never approved of her marriage to Michael. She had complained that they were too young. When Lyric became pregnant, Erica accused her of trying to trap her son. Called her a gold digger. Erica always felt that Lyric wasn't good enough for Michael.

Once, she even told Lyric that she should get a job and stop mooching off of Michael. Lyric couldn't believe her ears, much less Erica's nerve. The only reason she hadn't cussed Erica out was because she respected Michael. Out of consideration for him, she refused to disrespect his mother. Although she didn't feel right hiding behind Michael to fight her battles, because she was more than equipped to handle Erica on her own, she felt that since Erica was his mother, he should've been the one to put her in her place, not her.

At Lyric's urging, Michael had spoken to his mom and told her that he would not tolerate her disrespecting his wife. He had told her that if she didn't accept Lyric, then she wouldn't have a place in his life. Although Erica looked like she had swallowed a bitter pill every time she saw Lyric after that, she was civil.

"Baby, that's what family is for," Michael continued. "There's nothing wrong with asking for help when you need it."

They turned around and started walking back along the shoreline. On the inside, Lyric rejoiced at the thought of enrolling in a class to become a professional wedding planner. Her excitement was somewhat contained by the thought of Erica coming to live with them. She figured that Erica could stay in the in-law suite. At least she wouldn't technically be in the same house. Lyric hoped that if Erica saw her pursuing a career, she'd back off. She decided not to let Erica steal her joy. She allowed the excitement and optimism that she felt to surface by shouting, "Woo hoo" and pumping her fist in the air. Michael simply smiled at her.

Lyric couldn't wait to tell Chloe. Perhaps they could go into business together. She remembered that Chloe had an interest in flowers. Chloe had shown creativity when arranging blooms. She also had good color coordination.

When they made it back to their original spot, they signaled to Autumn that they were about to leave. While waiting for Autumn to get out of the water, they gathered their belongings. Bikini clad and dripping wet, Autumn ran toward her parents and into the wide open beach towel her father held for her. She wrapped her body, and they returned to the beach house where they showered and changed clothes. Lyric, nor Michael, felt like cooking, so they went to a nearby seafood restaurant and ate dinner.

At the restaurant, they sat near a window and admired the tranquil waters. They feasted on shrimp and crab legs. They talked about the wonderful time they were having.

When they returned to the house, they went into the living room to talk some more. They decided to tell Autumn about the baby in private. Michael and Lyric held hands as they sat on a loveseat. Autumn sat in a chair next to them.

"Your mom and I have something to tell you," Michael said. He sounded excited. "You're going to have a little brother or sister."

Lyric smiled. "How do you feel about that?"

"Wow!" Autumn responded. "A brother or a sister, huh? That's cool."

"We thought you'd be happy," Lyric said. "Especially since you've been talking about having a sibling since you were four years old." She grinned. "Just so you know, we're three and a half months along."

Autumn went and hugged her mom. "Congratulations."

"Thank you, sweetie."

She sat back down. "I can't believe it." She fiddled with her fingers. "I had pretty much given up on the idea of having a brother or sister. Heavyn is my play-play sister, but that's not the same thing." She paused for a moment. "Just don't ask me to change diapers or babysit," she joked.

They all laughed. They talked about possible baby names and themes for the nursery. Lyric wished that she could freeze that moment in time. She would give anything to preserve the feelings of love and happiness she felt at that instant, because soon enough, things would change.

The following day, Lyric went shopping while Autumn and Michael hung out at the beach. While browsing through the selections, Lyric caught a glimpse of a man who looked just like Nigel. Seeing the man spooked her out so bad that she had an anxiety attack. She thought she was going crazy. Feeling embarrassed, yet frightened by the episode, she left the store in a hurry.

As she drove back to the beach house, she felt paranoid. She kept checking her rearview mirror. If that really was Nigel, how did he know where to find her? she wondered. If it wasn't him, was she delusional? She hoped that she wasn't losing her mind.

Once at the villa, Lyric hurried inside and locked the door. She immediately began to close the blinds.

"What's the matter with you?" Michael questioned. He was sitting on the sofa reading a book.

Closing the last wooden blind, Lyric asked, "Where's Autumn?"

Michael closed the book and looked at his frantic wife. "She's taking a shower. What's going on?"

Hardly able to catch her breath, Lyric said, "Michael, I saw him." She could tell by the perplexed expression on Michael's face that he didn't have a clue as to whom she was talking about. "Nigel. He's here."

He stood up and hugged his wife. "Are you sure?"

Lyric felt herself become agitated. "I-I think it was him. I mean, the guy looked just like him."

"You need to calm down. Getting upset isn't good for you or the baby."

Before she realized it, she was crying. "I'm so scared, Michael. A part of me feels like I should check myself into a mental institution just so that the baby and I can be safe."

He lightly pushed her away from him and placed his hands on her shoulders. "Get that thought out of your mind. There's no way I'm going to let you get committed. Voluntary or otherwise."

She wondered how long Nigel had been in Myrtle Beach. Had he followed her there? Had he been watching her the entire time? Just thinking about it made her feel nauseated. She felt like a prisoner, only she hadn't committed any crime.

Nigel had followed Lyric to Myrtle Beach simply to be close to her. Because he didn't like the thought of Lyric going out of town and him not being able to see her beautiful face, he bought a plane ticket and rented a car. He had no intention of being seen, but he found himself staring just a little too long while Lyric was in the store. When she turned around and saw him, he hurried up and left before she could run after him. He'd have to be more careful next time.

Seventeen

The Stokeses had returned from their family vacation. Michael was back at work, and Autumn was at school. Lyric fluffed the pillow on the couch before taking a seat. She ate a bowl of mixed fruit and watched *The View* while she waited for Chloe to come over. Fifteen minutes into the programming, the doorbell rang. She chewed a sweet, tangy pineapple chunk and placed the empty bowl in the kitchen sink. Then she opened the door.

"Hey, lady," Chloe said as she entered, kissing Lyric on the cheek."

"Well, hello to you." Lyric grinned.

They went into the living room and sat next to each other on the sofa. Lyric picked up the remote and turned down the volume on the TV.

"So how was the vacation?" Chloe asked. She shifted on the couch so that she could face Lyric. "Look at you," she teased. "You're glowing."

Lyric blushed. "The vacation was incredible. Michael was so loving and attentive. It felt so good to have my family all together." She pulled a hanging eyelash and discarded it on the floor. "We hung out on the beach, went kayaking, scuba diving, even fishing."

"Fishing?" Chloe laughed. "That's so not you."

"I know, right?" She smiled. "It was Michael's idea, but Autumn and I really enjoyed it. It was so," she tried to think of the word, "relaxing." She rubbed her bare arm. "And of course we went shopping."

"Of course." She patted Lyric's hand. "Sounds like you had a wonderful time. I'm so glad to hear that."

Lyric didn't want to cast any negative light on the vacation by mentioning that she may have seen Nigel. Especially since she wasn't 100 percent sure it was him. "So how was your stay at your mom's house in Saint Petersburg? Did you and Heavyn have a good time?"

"Girl, you already know. The first day or two, everybody is happy to see each other. After that I'm ready to check into a hotel or hit the road." They both laughed. "I'm a grown woman with a husband and a child, and my mom still treats me like I'm six-years old." Lyric nodded her understanding. "Besides being bossy, Mom is doing fine. She's almost sixty and still getting around. Thank God for that."

Lyric placed her hand under her chin. "These days, sixty isn't that old. Did you get a chance to hit up the beach?"

Twisting the cap off the water bottle she had brought with her, Chloe took a swig. "Saint Pete Beach was lovely. I couldn't keep Heavyn away." She had a faraway look in her eye.

"You okay?" Lyric sounded concerned.

"Oh, yeah." She dismissed her with the wave of her hand. "It's just that after hearing about your family vacation, it made me remember an argument that Keith and I had during our trip."

"Anything you want to discuss?"

Sighing, Chloe said, "It was nothing major. I had purchased a two-piece bathing suit for Heavyn, and Keith flipped out when he saw it. He told me that she was too young and should only wear one-piece swimsuits. I thought he overreacted. It wasn't like the suit was too revealing. It was age appropriate."

Lyric patted Chloe's hand. "He's an overprotective dad. He's not ready for his little girl to grow up. Cut him some slack." Chloe grinned. Lyric tried to lighten the mood. "Guess what?"

"Why do you have that 'I got a secret' look on your face?" Chloe wanted to know.

"Because I do." She could hardly contain her excitement. "I'm pregnant!"

Chloe stared at her, speechless. She finally found her voice. "I wasn't expecting that." She cleared her throat. "Congratulations!" Chloe hugged her. "So how far along are you?"

Lyric told her when the baby was due and about what Michael had said about the pregnancy. She assured Chloe that she and Michael were both happy about the baby. Chloe reached out and hugged her again.

After their heartfelt bonding moment, Lyric went on to tell Chloe about her aspirations of becoming a wedding planner and how she could use her help as a florist. She explained that she and Michael were going to ask his mother to help with the baby.

"I think that's the perfect profession for you," Chloe said sincerely. "I would love for us to work together. It would be fun. I used to work in a flower shop part-time in college. That was a long time ago, but I'm sure I wouldn't have any problem brushing up on my skills."

Lyric breathed a sigh of relief. "I'm so glad to hear you say that."

"Yeah, yeah," she joked. "What in the world are you going to do with the original Mrs. Stokes living so close by?"

"Ugh!" Lyric dreaded the thought. "It's not about me; it's about the baby." She tried to convince herself.

Michael took an early lunch. He had a meeting with private investigator, Guy Williams, at a nearby sandwich shop. It was their second meeting. Some of Michael's colleagues had hired Guy whenever they wanted to get divorced and needed to prove infidelity. He came highly recommended.

Michael ordered a hot pastrami sandwich, chips, and soda and took a seat facing the door. He bit into his sandwich before putting on his reading glasses and reading *The New York Times* newspaper.

A few minutes later, a tall, dark-skinned, baldheaded man approached Michael's table. Michael glared at him over the rim of his glasses. He removed his eyewear and folded the newspaper.

"What's up, Guy?" Michael smiled. "Have a seat."

Guy sat across from him. They exchanged small talk before getting down to business.

Leaning into the table, Guy said, "I've been watching this Nigel character. For the most part he's been pretty quiet. He goes to work and comes home. No social life. No girlfriend or boyfriend. I'd say he's a loner." He handed

Michael a manila envelope. "That right there is his background information." He cracked his knuckles.

Michael skimmed through the contents. Nothing really stood out at him. "Look," his eyes darted around the room, "my wife is pregnant now. I need to make sure that Nigel doesn't come anywhere near her."

"I feel you." He looked him in the eyes. "Congratulations. He hasn't been following your wife." He sounded confident.

Michael stroked his face, trying to decide what he should do next. "All right."

"In my professional opinion, I think the cat has moved on." He paused. "To what, I don't know. I just think that if he were going to pounce, he would've done so by now." He shrugged.

Michael rested his hands on the table. "So you're saying I should fire you now?"

Guy chuckled. "Right now there's not enough going on with this cat to justify the expense."

Michael nodded his head. He appreciated Guy's honesty. He wanted to believe that Nigel had just moved on, but something didn't feel right about that. Without proof, he didn't have anything to go on.

"I'll take your word for it," he said.

He agreed to let Guy go. Maybe he'd pay Nigel a visit so that he could see for himself.

Eighteen

"Mother," Autumn said, waking Lyric up from a perfectly good sleep. Lyric sat up in bed and rubbed her weary eyes. "Don't forget that I have cheerleading practice today. It's your turn to pick up Heavyn and me. Okay?" She placed her backpack on her right shoulder.

Lyric assured her that she wouldn't forget.

Autumn walked over and kissed her on the cheek. "Good luck with your doctor's appointment," she said before turning to leave.

"Oh, thanks for reminding me, sweetie."

Her 4D ultrasound appointment had slipped her mind. She was twenty weeks pregnant, and today was the day that she and Michael would find out the sex of their baby, as well as triple screen testing to determine if their unborn child may suffer from birth defects or serious brain and spinal conditions like spina bifida, Down Syndrome or anencephaly.

After Autumn left for school, Lyric went back to sleep for an hour. When she got up, she showered and got ready for her appointment. She put on comfortable separates with flat thongs.

Feeling famished, she fixed herself a bowl of Special K cereal with strawberries and vanilla soy milk. She loved the way the strawberries flavored the milk, giving it a sweet taste. Then she downed a glass of water. She checked the clock on the microwave, and it read 10:45 A.M. She grabbed her keys and purse before heading out to meet Michael at the doctor's office.

It only took her ten minutes to get to Dekalb Medical Hillandale. She parked the car and entered the building. As she waited for the elevator, she saw Michael walk through the door. He smiled when he saw her. They exchanged pleasantries as they waited together. The doors opened and they stepped inside at the same time. Michael pressed the floor button. When the doors closed, he kissed her on the lips. The conveyor opened, and they exited holding hands.

In the physician's office, Lyric signed in with the receptionist while Michael took a seat. Moments later, she sat next to him. She read a parenting magazine while they waited.

A few minutes later, the nurse called Lyric's name, and they walked to the back. She took Lyric's vitals and weight. She had gained 15 pounds. Lyric was used to giving a urine sample, but this time she couldn't. The ultrasound required a full bladder. She uncomfortably joined her husband in the exam room. She then sat on a padded table.

"Are you nervous?" Michael asked as he rubbed her protruding belly.

A slight smile graced her face. "A little," she admitted. She was thirty-six, and her pregnancy was considered high risk. She prayed that the baby she was carrying was healthy. She was also concerned about developing gestational diabetes. Silently, she prayed.

The ultrasound technician entered and greeted them. She shook their hands before asking Lyric how she felt and if she had any concerns or complaints. Lyric explained that she had felt tired and nauseous in the beginning of her pregnancy, but she was much better now. The technician seemed glad to hear that.

Lyric lay back on the table and raised her shirt, exposing her midriff. The technician warned Lyric that the ultrasound gel she was about to place on her stomach would be cold. Lyric expected that, so she didn't flinch. The technician placed the transducer on top of the gooey gel. She moved it around until she detected the baby's heartbeat.

The technician smiled. "The baby's heartbeat is strong and normal."

"Thank God," Lyric said, breathing a sigh of relief. Michael lightly squeezed his wife's hand.

The technician turned the monitor so that the couple could have a full view. She moved the wand around continuously. She took measurements. "You see that?" She pointed at the screen. "Those are fingers." Lyric felt so emotional that she wanted to cry. The baby was moving around. The technician captured the toes and spine. The spine looked like a string of pearls. They even caught a glimpse of the baby's face. Lyric thought the face looked a little spooky, like a skull mask. That was until the technician switched from still photographs to video. At that moment, her bundle of joy looked like an adorable baby. Just when they were about to learn the sex of the baby, the technician said, "Oh my goodness."

"What's wrong?" Lyric and Michael said in unison. Lyric held her breath, bracing herself for bad news.

"I'm sorry," the technician apologized. "I didn't mean to alarm you. It's just that I found a separate amniotic sac." She stared at the screen. "There's a second fetus. I detected a second heartbeat."

"What?" they said at the same time. Both of them sounded shocked.

"It appears you're having fraternal twins, Mr. and Mrs. Stokes." She sounded happy to make that discovery.

Lyric was speechless.

"Are you sure?" Michael wanted to know. He furrowed a brow.

The specialist pointed to the monitor. "The second baby was hiding." A wide grin graced her face. "Congratulations."

Michael and Lyric exchanged glances. He leaned over and kissed her on the forehead. His sparkling eyes assured her that everything was going to be all right. Lyric's grandmother had a fraternal twin brother, and they were the only known twins in her family. Whenever someone got pregnant in the family, people would joke about the possibility of having twins.

"You ready to learn the sex of your babies?" the specialist asked.

Lyric nearly stuttered as she spouted out yes. She hoped and prayed that at least one of the babies was a boy.

The technician continued moving the wand. Pointing to the first baby, she said, "It's a boy."

Gasping, Lyric said, "Thank you, Jesus." Tears freely flowed from her eyes. She was finally giving Michael a son. Her heart was overjoyed as she felt a slight flutter in her belly.

Michael's chest was sticking out with pride. He couldn't stop smiling. They continued watching the screen, hoping that the second baby would reveal him—or herself to them. For a while, the fetus played hide and seek. At one point, the baby sucked its thumb. Lyric's heart melted when she saw that. After several minutes of playing coy, the second baby moved its leg and revealed its sex.

"You have two little boys," the technician proudly announced.

They burst into laughter. Tears flowed down Lyric's cheeks. Her heart felt full. So many thoughts went through her mind. Her prayers had been answered. She couldn't believe that she was having two sons. That was more than she had hoped for. Praise God! she thought.

Nigel forcefully threw his keys across his living room and they crashed against the wall, hitting the floor. One of his appointments had cancelled, so he decided to spy on Lyric. Nothing could've prepared him for what he saw. She was pregnant! He had seen her at least once a week since their intimate encounter; how could he have missed that? He replayed the tape in his mind, trying to recapture the previous times he had seen her. He realized that with the exception of this instance, every other time he had observed her, she wore flimsy dresses. He noticed that she had put on a few pounds, but he liked it. She looked good.

He grabbed a brew from the fridge and twisted off the cap. He envisioned Lyric in that maternity shirt. That blew his mind. He threw his head back and swallowed his drink.

"How could you keep this from me, Lyric?" he said out loud.

He had followed her to the doctor's office. There was no denying the obvious. Based on how Lyric looked, Nigel wondered if he were the baby's father.

He went into the living room and sat down. Setting the bottle on the floor, he thought long and hard about what he should do. He already had an ax to grind with Michael Stokes for sending that amateur private investigator to spy on him. He was still angry about that.

Nigel had known right away that someone was tailing him. He always checked his surroundings every time he left the house or drove his car. He constantly checked his rearview mirror, so the investigator stood out like someone wearing red at an all-white party.

Nigel got a kick out of outsmarting the private eye. Since he had a tracking device on Lyric's vehicle, he was already two steps ahead of the investigator. He didn't have to lurk, hoping to catch a glimpse of the object of his affections. Nigel was so slick that if Lyric went to the grocery store, he would arrive shortly thereafter. He knew that she liked to go aisle by aisle and browse. She usually shopped for at least an hour. All he cared about was seeing her. Most times after spotting her he'd buy a pack of gum and leave. The investigator never caught on.

He thought back to the baby and felt a sense of entitlement. Now that Lyric was carrying his child, he was entitled to be with her. A child needed a father, he reasoned, and he intended to be there for his baby and Lyric. There was no way she could deny him now.

He finished his malt liquor. His connection to Lyric seemed stronger than ever. The woman that he loved was having his baby. He tried to wrap his mind around that. The thought brought a smile to his face. He had an overwhelming desire to reach out to Lyric. Not only did he want to let her know that he knew about the baby, he wanted to give her a gift. A peace offering. He left and went to one of Lyric's favorite places . . . Lenox Mall.

Once at the mall, Nigel went to a jeweler and purchased a diamond tennis bracelet for Lyric. With her being the classy type, he thought she'd love it. He then went and bought the baby a sterling silver feeding set. Only the best for his baby. He wanted to remind Lyric that he had money too. Taking care of her and the baby wouldn't be a problem.

He got the presents professionally wrapped, filled out a tiny card, and left. He checked his portable device to see where Lyric was. She wasn't at home, so he went to a messenger service to have them deliver the package. He wanted to surprise her by leaving the gifts at her front door. As tempted as he was to hand-deliver the gifts, he didn't want to be detected by the security cameras monitoring the Stokeses' residence. He knew that her daughter would still be at school, and Mr. Stokes would either be with her or back at work. The coast was clear.

Nigel was pleased with himself after the delivery service notified him that the luxury items for his family had been delivered. He wished he could see the look on Lyric's face when she opened the box, but he had to get back to work. He had a client to see.

Lyric and Michael were elated after finding out about the twins. Michael treated her to lunch at Arizona's at Stonecrest Mall. He ordered the barbecue chicken grill, and Lyric chose the hickory grilled Atlantic salmon.

"This is so exciting, Michael," Lyric beamed. "I've been thinking of baby names ever since we left the doctor's office."

"Me too," he admitted. He looked her in the eyes. "What do you think about the name Logan, after my father?"

She smiled her pleasure. "I think that would be nice. Your father was a good man. He would be honored." She sipped her ice water. "I like the names Logan and Michael."

"You don't think that would cause friction between the boys when they get older if one of them is named after me?" He folded his hands on top of the table.

She pondered the thought. "I don't think so. Whichever one is born first would be Michael the second." She chuckled. "We don't want to call him Junior."

He joined in the banter. "Then I'd be senior. That just sounds so . . . old."

The waiter brought out a bread basket. Michael helped himself. Lyric looked around the Azteca designed establishment and admired the décor. They continued talking and decided to name the twins Landon and Logan instead. They talked about Autumn and how they thought she'd make a good big sister. They discussed having Chloe and her husband as godparents. Lyric loved that idea.

The waiter returned with their food. They said grace and ate. Lyric savored the taste of the tender, delicious fish. After lunch, they parted ways. Michael went back to work, and Lyric called Chloe before going over to her house for a visit.

Lyric pulled up in Chloe's driveway. The doorbell chimed when she pressed the button.

"Hey, lady," Chloe greeted. Her smile was as warm as the weather they were having.

Lyric stepped inside the foyer and waited for Chloe to lock the door behind her. They went into the kitchen and talked.

Sitting on a barstool, Lyric announced, "Michael and I just left my doctor's appointment."

"How'd it go? What are we having?" Chloe propped her elbows on the island and held her face in her hands.

"We," she pointed at the two of them, smiling, "are having fraternal twin boys."

Chloe sat up. "Get out of here." She burst into laughter. "You must be so excited." She smiled so hard that fine lines formed around the corners of her eyes.

"I am," she admitted. "And we want you and Keith to be the godparents."

"Are you serious?"

Lyric nodded her head like a bobble head figurine.

Chloe hugged her. "We'd be honored. Thank you," she whispered in Lyric's ear.

They made plans to go on a double date with their husbands to celebrate. Chloe mentioned throwing Lyric a baby shower, and she was open to the idea. She admitted that she hadn't done any shopping because she wanted to wait until she was at least seven months along. She wasn't superstitious; she was being cautious.

Two hours had passed, and Lyric announced that she had to leave to pick up Autumn and Heavyn from cheer-leading practice.

"I'll get the girls," Chloe volunteered. "You need to go home and get some rest."

Lyric stood up. "That's sweet of you. You don't have to get them."

Chloe grabbed Lyric's hands. "I know I don't have to; I want to," she insisted.

Lyric thanked her and gave her a hug. She left and went home. When she arrived, she first checked the mail before pulling all the way up the driveway. From a distance, she noticed a package at the front door. She waited until she parked the car in the garage before opening the front door and bringing the box inside. The parcel was addressed to her, but there was no return address. Lyric found that strange. She set the parcel on the island in the kitchen and opened it. She was surprised to discover a diamond tennis bracelet and silver feeding set.

When had Michael had time to order those gifts? she wondered. She absolutely loved them. She knew that Michael was excited about having twins, but she had not expected anything like this. That was so sweet and thoughtful.

She picked up the phone and called Michael. She had to wait a few moments before being connected with her husband. As soon as she heard Michael's voice, she said, "You are the sweetest husband a woman could ever ask for." Without taking a breath, she continued. "Thank you so much for the lovely gifts." She took the bracelet out of the velvety box and clasped it on her wrist.

"Baby, as much as I'd like to take credit for lavishing you with gifts, I can't do it this time."

The smile on Lyric's face faded. "Oh." She sounded surprised. She told him what she had received. Then she searched the box and found a card tucked inside. She read the card aloud. "Congratulations on the new baby. We've been given a second chance. With all my love, Nigel."

Lyric dropped the card on the floor. The color drained from her face. She thought she was going to be sick. She felt as if someone had stabbed her in the stomach.

"Lyric, Lyric," Michael called.

At first she was too choked up to speak. All she could do was cry. She finally found her voice. In a tone barely above a whisper, she said, "I'll call you back."

Why was this happening to her? she wondered. How had Nigel found out?

Lyric heard Chloe's car pull up, so she pressed the off button on the phone. She grabbed a paper towel and wiped away her tears. She walked outside and waved for Chloe to come inside. The girls giggled as they got out of the car.

"Hey, Mom," Autumn said as she gave her mom a hug. She rubbed Lyric's stomach and asked, "So am I having a little brother or sister?"

Lyric was still shaken up about Nigel's surprise. She ushered the girls into the house before saying, "We're having twin boys."

Autumn and Heavyn both squealed with delight. They held hands as they jumped up and down.

"Congratulations, Auntie Lyric," Heavyn said.

Lyric thanked her and gave her a quick hug.

"Okay, okay," Chloe said, closing the door behind her. She caught a glimpse of Lyric's sad eyes and said, "Girls, give us a few minutes to talk."

Autumn and Heavyn went into the kitchen to get snacks. Then they went upstairs to Autumn's bedroom. As soon as the girls were out of earshot, Lyric told Chloe about her delivery. She explained how she originally thought the gifts were from Michael. She showed Chloe the presents. Chloe's jaw dropped after reading the card.

"The nerve of him," Chloe seethed. "How did he even find out?"

Lyric checked the stairs to make sure the girls were still in the room. They were, so she continued. "I'm going to need your help." Chloe listened intently. "The police aren't able to do anything to help me. Nigel would have to kill me or come real close before the authorities would step in." Chloe nodded her understanding. "Now that Nigel knows that I'm pregnant, I don't believe he'll leave me alone." Her eyes became misty. "The only way I can protect myself, these babies, and my family is for me to go away."

"You just lost me." Chloe had a puzzled expression on her face. "What do you mean, *go away*?"

"I need to go somewhere where Nigel can't get to me. I don't feel safe in my house anymore."

Chloe grabbed her and held her close. "I'm so sorry that this is happening. Were you thinking about going out of town to stay with relatives?"

"No." She wiped her wet face with her hands. "I'm seriously thinking about having myself voluntarily committed to a psych ward."

"Forget it." Chloe was adamant. "There's no way I'm going to let you do that. What about your husband? You already know he's not going to go for that. And what about Autumn? Did you think about her? She needs you."

Lyric felt herself becoming more upset. Her heart was racing. "That's all I've thought about. I'm doing this for them. When we were on vacation, I could've sworn I saw Nigel. I don't know if I imagined it or if it were real, but it upset me nonetheless. I thought about what it would do to my family if Nigel killed me."

Chloe halted her hands in the air. "Stop talking like that. He's not going to kill you. You can't think like that."

Lyric tried to reason with her. "I know you don't agree with me on this. I'm sure you think it's extreme; so do I," she admitted. "The truth of the matter is that you've never been raped or stalked." The tears freely flowed. "I was violated in my home. Every day I'm reminded of that. As if that wasn't enough, my attacker stalked me. Whenever I leave the house, I have to look over my shoulder. I've become paranoid. And to make matters worse, I just might be pregnant with babies that don't belong to my husband." She ran her fingers through her hair and tugged.

Chloe tried to console her. "I'm not going to claim to know how you feel, because I don't. I can't even imagine what you must be going through. But what I do know is that you believe in God. Now is the time to hold on to your faith. You're mature enough to know that when things happen in life, most of the time it's not even about you. It's about using your testimony to help somebody else.

"You were raped. God knows that's terrible. But you're still alive. You're still here to be a blessing to other women who have been assaulted."

Lyric blew her nose with the used paper towel on the counter. "I understand that. It's just that I'm in emotional turmoil right now. I'm going through a lot."

"Look." Chloe gave her a warm smile. "The devil is a liar. The enemy has no new tricks, only new faces. You're being attacked because you're a child of God, and you had a breakthrough. As soon as you gained some insight into whom you are and what you want to do with your future, the enemy got angry. He can't stop what God has for you, but he sure can distract you." She held Lyric's face in the palms of her hands. "You should be praising God right now. Laugh at the devil. He's no match for God." She lightly squeezed Lyric's cheeks, trying to get her to crack a smile.

"I know you're right." Lyric sighed. "I was on an emotional high when I found out about the boys. I felt as if a prayer had been answered."

"And then the devil spoke to Nigel and told him to send you this." She held up the feeding set.

Lyric realized that she was still wearing the bracelet and asked Chloe to unclasp it. She placed it back in the box.

Chloe continued. "He wanted to steal your joy. Don't let him," she pleaded.

"I won't." Lyric paused. "Michael told me that he got a gun."

"What?" Her eyes became as wide as two half dollars.

"That's another reason why I wanted to have myself committed. I don't want Michael to do something that could land him in jail."

Chloe sighed. "You need to forget about that whole committing yourself idea," she said seriously. "You're my dearest friend, and we always keep it real, right?"

"Right," Lyric agreed.

"You don't want to do anything that will make you appear unstable. You're a mother; you've got to put your kids first. I don't trust a whole lot of people, and you know that. I've seen how people can use stuff against you when it suits them. Don't give anyone that kind of power over you."

Lyric knew that Chloe had a point. That's why she liked talking to her. She told her what she needed to hear, not necessarily what she wanted to hear. She had not totally abandoned the notion of going away. She simply needed to figure out how to do it without making herself seem like an unfit mother.

make Taylor a millionaire, and we always keep it that right."

"Right," Ilene agreed.

"You don't want to do anything that will make you a quick millionaire, you're a millionaire, you got to put your ass first. And I don't trust a whole lot of people, and you know that. I've seen how people treat each other. I just met you, but it still sums up. And I also know that kind of power over you."

Ilene knew that Chloe had a point. That's why she liked talking to her, she told her what she needed to hear, not necessarily what she wanted to hear. She had not forth with found the solution of each answer. She simply needed to figure out how to do it without making herself seem like an ungrateful.

Nineteen

Michael was still disturbed by his earlier conversation with Lyric. Something needed to be done about Nigel.

"Hey, Mike," Keith said as he entered the break room, interrupting Michael's thoughts. He poured himself a cup of coffee before joining Michael at the table. "I heard through the grapevine that you and the misses are having twin boys." A wide grin spread across his face. "Congrats, man!"

Michael was surprised at how quickly the news had spread. He had only told a few people at work. He had planned to tell Keith anyway, but that was the first chance they'd had to talk.

"Thanks." Michael smiled, remembering that he had something to smile about. He reached into his coat pocket and pulled out a congratulatory cigar that he had purchased from the gift shop and handed it to him.

"You ready for the long nights and poopie diapers?" he teased. "Twelve years is a big gap between kids. You've probably forgotten more than you remember." He shook his head. "Better you than me, partner."

"Don't joke too hard," Michael warned. "You know how women are. I wouldn't be surprised if Chloe started talking about having another baby."

Keith nearly choked on his coffee. "Nah, man. My wife knows the deal. We agreed; one is enough." He took another sip. "So when are we going to get together for a golf game? It's been awhile."

Michael pushed back his chair and stood up. "Let's do that." He paused. "I've been spending more time around the house with Lyric being pregnant and all. But I'll figure something out."

"It's all good, man. I know how it is. Handle your business."

Two hours later, Michael left the hospital and headed home. During the drive, he called Guy and asked him for a favor. He wanted Guy to let him know when Nigel got home. Guy agreed.

When Michael drove up to his estate, he sat in the garage for a couple of minutes. He had to prepare himself for the emotional outburst he was sure to come from Lyric. He needed to be strong for her. He couldn't let her know how upset he really was. He put on his game face and entered his residence.

"Daddy's home," he announced, trying to sound cheerful.

The smell of baked chicken engulfed his nostrils. His stomach growled. He heard Lyric traipse down the stairs. As soon as he saw her face, he could see the worry all over her beautiful countenance. He held her close and assured her that he had her back. He planted soft kisses on top of her head as she melted in his arms.

"I'm glad you're home," she admitted. "Autumn is finishing up her homework. Dinner's ready; I know you're hungry."

He was amazed at how well Lyric seemed to pull herself together for the sake of her family. She was always putting their needs ahead of her own. That's one of the many things he loved and admired about her.

He braced himself. "Okay, let me see the package you received."

Massaging the back of her neck, Lyric said, "They're in the garage. I threw them in the trash."

He furrowed a brow, surprised to hear that. "All right then. Let's eat."

Lyric summoned Autumn to come downstairs for dinner. They each fixed their plates before taking their seats at the table. Michael said grace, and they ate. During dinner, Autumn shared her excitement about the twins. She talked about school and her extracurricular activities.

After dinner, Michael's cell phone vibrated. He checked the caller ID and saw that it was Guy. He answered, and Guy told him that Nigel was at home. That was all he needed to hear. He hung up the phone and went upstairs to retrieve his gun and loaded it. He told Lyric that he had a quick errand to run. While in the garage, he removed the pricey items from the garbage that Lyric had discarded and placed them on the seat of his car. As he backed out of the driveway, he ordered a pizza for pick up.

Twenty minutes later, he picked up his pizza and drove to Nigel's place. It took him an additional twenty minutes to get there. He set the bracelet and the feeding set on top of the cardboard box. He got out of the car and secured the gun in the waistband of his pants. He put on a baseball cap that he kept in his gym bag in the backseat and carried the pizza to the door and rang the bell.

"Who is it?" he heard Nigel ask.

"Pizza delivery."

"I didn't order a pizza," the man yelled. "You've got the wrong house."

Michael rambled off the address and explained that the pizza was already paid for. He said that he couldn't take it back.

After a brief moment of silence, Nigel reluctantly unlocked the door. Michael got into a football-type position and used his shoulder to shove the door open as soon as Nigel cracked it. He dropped the box on the ground and punched Nigel in the face. Nigel stumbled backward. He regained his footing and charged at Michael like a raging bull. The two men tussled and knocked over furniture. When they fell on the floor, Michael landed on top of him. He proceeded to choke Nigel, causing him to go in and out of consciousness. Just when he was about to squeeze the life out of him, a voice told him, "Don't throw your life away for him."

He clenched his jaw and loosened his grasp. He released a barrage of cuss words. Nigel coughed to catch his breath. Michael stood up and pulled out his gun. With the weapon pointed at Nigel, Michael said, "If you ever come near my wife or family again, I will kill you." His tone was serious. There was fire in his eyes. He kicked the pizza box. "And take your gifts, you sick, twisted, son of a—" He lowered his head and walked out, leaving Nigel on the ground struggling to breathe.

"That chump sucker punched me!" Nigel fumed. He stood in the living room and assessed the damage. The coffee table was shattered. Glass was everywhere. He could not believe that he had fallen for the okey doke. That whole pizza delivery was a crock. He had underestimated Mr. Stokes. He wouldn't make that mistake again.

This meant war! Mr. Stokes had started it, but Nigel was determined to finish it.

Nigel had a fleeting thought to call the police. He nixed that idea. The police were not his friends. Even with him being battered, bloodied, and bruised, they'd find a way to blame him for being attacked. Since he had sent Lyric some presents, he knew they'd somehow say he provoked Mr. Stokes.

He bent down and picked up the diamond bracelet that he had especially picked for the love of his life. His heart ached for her. He didn't fault her for her husband's actions. He knew that Mr. Stokes was jealous of him and the relationship he shared with Lyric. Why else would he go into such a jealous rampage? he thought.

Mr. Stokes's antics solidified Nigel's belief that he was indeed the man for Lyric. Her husband was losing his grip on her. That's why he had returned the gifts instead of Lyric returning them. He refused to believe that Lyric willingly gave back his tokens of love. He felt the need to rescue her from her controlling husband.

Surprisingly, the pizza was still in the box, and it felt warm. Not a single slice had touched the floor. Nigel picked up the box and took it into the kitchen. He figured that if Mr. Stokes had wanted to poison him, he wouldn't have gone through the trouble of starting a fight. He removed a couple of slices and nuked them in the microwave. No sense in letting a good pizza go to waste, he reasoned.

Michael's hands were shaking. His knuckles were bruised. He couldn't believe that he had almost killed a man. He stared at his hands. The very hands he had used to save lives had nearly taken a life. The scary part for him was that he was so consumed with rage that every fiber of his being wanted to choke the life out of Nigel. A part of him still wished that he had.

He drove home on auto pilot. His mind kept wandering back to Nigel. He hoped that Nigel wouldn't be stupid enough to retaliate. He thought about ways to ruin his business. Maybe if his business went under, he'd leave town. Then he thought about the twins. There was no way he was ever going to let Nigel come near them.

When he arrived home, he hurried into the house. He caught a glimpse of his reflection in one of the hallway mirrors. His shirt was disheveled and he had a bruise on his cheek. He sighed, hoping that Lyric wouldn't interrogate him to death. As soon as he reached the top of the stairs, Lyric came walking down the hallway.

"I was online getting ideas for the nursery," she said. "I know it's not a big deal to you, but what do you think of a pastel green and yellow colored nursery?"

He turned his back toward her and walked into the bedroom as he spoke. "I'd have to see it." He felt jittery and couldn't get away from her fast enough.

She followed him into the bedroom. "What's going on with you?" she asked. "You're acting strange."

"Nothing," he lied. He walked into the bathroom with Lyric nipping at his heels. He could see her reflection in the mirror.

"I don't believe you. What's up?" She put her hands on her hips, giving him attitude. "Where did you go?"

"Where's Autumn?"

She folded her arms across her chest. "She's in the game room, playing."

He turned to face her, and she gasped. "I got into a little scuffle."

She covered her mouth with her hand. Then she touched the bruise on his face, causing him to flinch. "What have you done?" She sounded afraid.

He closed the bathroom door and locked it. "I'd rather leave you out of it. You worry too much." He took off his shoes.

"You can't leave me out of it," she said sternly. "I'm your wife, Michael. I want to know what's going on."

He swallowed the lump in his throat. He took off his shirt and placed the firearm on the sink counter. The disappointed look in her eyes was more than he could bear. She shook her head as tears escaped from her eyes. The silence was deafening.

He told her where he had gone and what he had done. He assured her that he never fired the weapon. He further explained that when he left, Nigel was alive. She gave him a disapproving look. She didn't say anything. She simply unlocked the door and left him alone.

His heart dropped. He wished that she would've said something. At least he would know what she was thinking and feeling. Her not saying anything was really bad. Was she so disappointed in him that she couldn't think of any words to express her sentiments?

He hurried up and took a shower. He wanted to put the earlier events of the evening behind him. When he got out of the shower, he put on a T-shirt and boxers. He unloaded the gun and locked it back up.

Lyric came into the room carrying a bucket of ice and an ice pack. "I thought you could use these," she said as she handed the items to him.

His heart rejoiced, thankful that she still cared.

Twenty

Lyric was now seven months pregnant and on bed rest. According to her obstetrician, she had an overactive uterus. She had started having contractions, and the doctor admitted her to the hospital to stop the early labor. After being released, she was told to stay in bed. She was grateful that all of her test results had come back normal, and the twins appeared to be healthy. They were progressing normally.

It was July. Lyric hadn't been able to go to Lenox Mall and witness the Fourth of July fireworks like she did every year. Instead, Michael had carried her down the stairs, and she sat on a lawn chair to watch fireworks. Although she didn't like the Atlanta heat, she missed going to Lake Lanier. She especially missed going shopping with Chloe.

Autumn was out of town. She was spending her summer vacation with Erica in Irvine, California. Erica was going to come stay with them after the birth of the twins. Lyric missed her daughter. She looked forward to Autumn's nightly phone calls telling her about all of the fun things she and her grandmother were doing. They had spent a lot of time in Los Angeles. In the time that she had been there, they had gone to Universal Studios, the Kodak Theatre, The Hollywood Museum, Sony Pictures Studio Tour, whale watching, shopping on Rodeo Drive, and of course, the beach.

To help out, Michael hired a housekeeper, Consuela, and a cook, Milton. Lyric felt safer having them in the house.

"Good morning, Mrs. Stokes," Consuela greeted. "How are you feeling?"

"I'm fine; I just wish I could get out of bed." Lyric adjusted her pillow and sat up.

"Milton asked me to bring breakfast up to you." She placed the serving tray on Lyric's lap.

Smiling, Lyric said, "Thank you. I feel like a queen." She inhaled the scrumptious egg white vegetable omelet. "Please tell Milton that I said the food looks and smells delicious."

Consuela nodded her head. "Can I get you anything else?"

"No, I'm good."

She left, and Lyric blessed her food before taking a bite of her wheat toast. She was fam-

ished. She appreciated the thoughtful touches
Milton added to every meal. His presentation
was always impeccable. Her plates looked like
something out of a restaurant. He even took
the time to give her a fresh flower in a tiny glass
vase every morning. That really brightened her
day. With breakfast and lunch, he always gave
her a side of fruit. And he never served her
concentrated juices. Only freshly squeezed or
juiced in the juicer. He had spoiled her. She was
convinced that she didn't want to let him go,
even after the twins were born.

Lyric finished every bite of her breakfast. She
removed the tray from her lap and set it next to
her. Her Bible was resting on the nightstand,
so she picked it up and read a passage from the
book of Psalms. After reading, she closed her
eyes and prayed. When she finished, she slowly
got out of bed and went to the bathroom. Her
bladder seemed to stay full. She then brushed
her teeth and washed her face.

As she waddled back to the bed, her lower
back hurt. She felt as big as a double wide trac-
tor trailer. She had already gained thirty-five
pounds. Her doctor had told her that with twins,
she could easily gain twice that amount. Lyric
didn't want to hear that. No matter how much
Michael complimented her and told her that she

was beautiful, she didn't buy it. She didn't feel the least bit attractive. Hopefully she wouldn't get the mask of pregnancy and wide nose.

Lyric no longer desired to comb her hair or put on make-up. She was in desperate need of a relaxer but couldn't get one. Because of that, her hairstylist would come over once a week to wash and flat iron Lyric's hair. Her hair had grown down to the middle of her back. Lyric wasn't feeling the long hair anymore, so she had her beautician give her a nice shoulder length bob with brown highlights.

She crawled back into bed. Before she pulled up the covers, she noticed that her thighs were no longer tight and toned. They had become loose and flabby looking. She wanted to cry. She wondered whether her body would be able to bounce back. She had been much younger when she had Autumn; her metabolism was faster. Now she was older. She had heard that muscles had memory, and she prayed that was true. To make matters worse, she was retaining water. She could tell by the puffiness around her ankles. Disgusted, she covered up her lower extremities.

Consuela came back into the bedroom to open the blinds and take the tray. "It's a beautiful day outside," she said, letting in the sunlight.

Hearing that didn't make Lyric feel any better. She frowned.

"Sorry." Consuela saw the look on Lyric's face. She removed the tray and placed Lyric's laptop on the bed next to her and booted it up. "Remember to ring the bell if you need anything."

"I will. Thanks."

Consuela left Lyric alone. At the beginning of the summer, Lyric had enrolled in an online program at an accredited school that would allow her to get her wedding consultant certificate. She had originally expected to complete the course in nine months. Since being confined to the bed, she usually devoted the better part of her days completing coursework. At the pace she was going, she'd be done in half the time. That motivated her to do even more. She went to work.

That weekend, Lyric stayed in bed while her beautician came over early to apply her make-up and style her hair. After she left, Lyric slowly got out of bed so that she could put on her clothes. When she finished, Michael carried her downstairs into the great room and sat her in a chair. The pressure between her legs made it difficult to walk. The balloons that Chloe had strategically placed around the room for the baby shower looked cute, she thought.

"Can I get you anything?" Michael asked.

She shook her head. He announced that he was going upstairs to change clothes. She felt a dull ache in her side. She asked the boys to take it easy on her as she rubbed her round belly. She couldn't wait to drop that load.

Just then, Chloe entered carrying a large cake. "Hey, lady." She grinned. She walked over and showed Lyric the sheet cake. It was decorated with blue booties and plastic adorable little brown babies wearing blue diapers. The words "Congratulations, Lyric and Michael" were scribbled on top.

"I like it," Lyric said. "Thanks for throwing me a shower. I was going stir crazy staying in bed all day."

Chloe kissed her on the cheek and took the cake into the kitchen. When she returned, she was nibbling on a cold shrimp. "You should see the spread Milton prepared for the brunch."

Lyric smirked. "You know I can't see it. Just tell me."

Chloe touched her shoulder. "I forgot." She sat down. "Let's see." She rolled her eyes on top of her head. "He has some of everything." She counted on her fingers. "All sorts of pastries, muffins, eggs, waffles, crepes, pancakes, bacon, sausage, home fries, fruit, and mimosas." She licked her lips. "But he's making a special shrimp and grits dish especially for you." She pointed her finger at Lyric for effect.

"So that's why you're smacking on a shrimp."

They both laughed. The doorbell rang, and Chloe answered. The handsome man dressed in a brown shirt and brown shorts handed her a package. As soon as she saw the box in Chloe's hands, her heart pounded. She silently prayed that it was not from Nigel. She hadn't heard anything from him since the day her husband confronted him, and she hoped that wasn't about to change. Chloe beamed as she handed Lyric the parcel.

"It's from Stella." Chloe looked pleased. "I spoke to her recently. She and Brad are living together in New Jersey. It's official; they're getting married!" She sounded excited.

"That's wonderful news," Lyric said sincerely. "I'm happy for her."

"She wanted me to apologize to you for not being able to attend the shower. She sends her love." She waited for a moment. "Don't just look at it; open it," she instructed.

Lyric sucked her teeth and sighed. "You're so impatient," she joked as she ripped open the present. It contained several adorable, coordinated outfits. The ladies "oohed" and "aahed" as they sorted through the clothes. She then tore open the envelope containing a greeting card. Inside of the card was a $500 gift card to Blue Genes. She silently read the card and tucked it back in the envelope, along with the gift card. She set the package to the side. "That was nice of her," Lyric said.

Not long afterward, Michael joined them. Lyric thought he looked darling in his beige linen pant suit. He greeted Chloe with a friendly hug. The three of them chatted briefly about the co-ed shower.

Chloe checked her watch; it read 10:30 A.M. Their conversation was cut short when some of the guests started arriving, including Chloe's husband. Chloe was the perfect hostess. She welcomed the guests and escorted them inside. She took the gifts and placed them in a corner. Everyone hugged, kissed, and congratulated Lyric and Michael. Lyric perked up when she saw Dr. Little and her husband. She hadn't seen her since being put on bed rest.

"You look lovely," Dr. Little said, kissing her on the cheek. "Pregnancy definitely agrees with you."

Lyric thought that with all of the stress she had been under, she was certain she looked five years older. Perhaps having Consuela and Milton around had helped eliminate a lot of her concerns. She was glad to hear that she didn't look as hard as she thought she did. She thanked Dr. Little.

The smell of tasty breakfast foods wafted through the air. Consuela ushered the forty guests into the kitchen so that they could fix their plates. Milton fixed Lyric blackened jumbo pan seared shrimp served over extra creamy cheese grits. He personally served it to her. He always made her feel so special.

As the guests sat down to eat, Consuela handed them glasses of mimosa. She gave Lyric a glass of pineapple juice. The sweet, tangy drink quenched Lyric's thirst. Lyric looked around the room at her distinguished guests. Her friends and associates included doctors, lawyers, executives, a psychoanalyst, and even a judge. She found it funny the way they were practically licking their plates because the food was so good. She had to admit that Milton had done a fantastic job. She didn't feel an ounce of shame when she asked Consuela to bring her seconds.

Everyone had fun eating and getting caught up. Chloe implemented one game, Diaper Olympics, and it was guy friendly. There were two infant-sized dolls that needed pretend diaper changes. She divided the group in half, men versus women, and did a relay race. Each person had to take the baby, rush to the table, pull the diaper off, use a wipe, powder, and then diaper them again. Then they had to take it to the next person in line. The women got a hoot out of watching the men.

When it came time to open the gifts, Lyric and Michael took turns. They received lots of big ticket items, including: twin car seat strollers, a playpen, walkers, bassinettes, and swings. They also racked up on clothes, gift cards, diapers, and wipes. Chloe hooked Lyric up with a designer diaper bag, breast pump, Dr. Brown's bottles, bottle warmer, diaper genie, a wipes warmer, and several outfits.

Three hours had passed, and the party came to a close. Michael and Keith put the presents in the nursery. Michael carried Lyric upstairs and set her in a comfy chair in the babies' room before he and Keith went to play golf. Chloe stayed behind and hung the clothes in the boys' closet. She put the T-shirts and onesies in drawers, and stacked the diapers in the diaper stacker. She placed the wipes, powder, petroleum jelly, and diaper rash ointment on the changing table.

Lyric loved the look and feel of the nursery. The painter had painted the ceiling and walls sky blue with white clouds. The furniture was natural wood. She couldn't wait until the twins occupied the crib. She felt a kick, and she asked Chloe to come over and feel it. Chloe stopped what she was doing and placed her hand on Lyric's over-sized belly. When she felt the movement, both women giggled. Lyric felt a surge of excitement. She fell deeper in love with the twins.

Twenty-one

Sunday rolled around, and Michael felt an overwhelming desire to go to church. He had been praying to God for strength and reading the Bible for instruction. Although he didn't like going to church, his longing to be obedient to what God wanted him to do was greater. He checked the clock and realized that he had enough time to attend the mid-morning worship service. Without disrupting Lyric's sleep, he got dressed and headed out the door.

Once at church, he parked in the crowded lot. As soon as he approached the doors to the building, two greeters spoke to him. He smiled back at them and went inside. He walked down the hall before entering the sanctuary. An usher offered him a seat up front, but he elected for something closer to the back. He didn't want people looking at him. Besides, the video cameras were in front of the church, and he felt that people in the front rows had to put on a show for the television and

Internet audiences. He wasn't in the mood for
that. He just wanted to worship in peace. If he
didn't feel like standing up or waving his hands,
he didn't have to.

He sat down just as one of the associate ministers addressed the congregation. It was time for
opening prayer. Placing his Bible on the vacant
chair next to him, he stood to his feet. He closed
his eyes as the church did a collective prayer.
When the minister finished leading the prayer,
everyone said a collective "Amen" and sat down.

People were still entering and walking around
while the choir sang Fred Hammond's song, "All
Things are Working Together." The music ministered to Michael's spirit. When they finished
their musical selection, it was time for altar call.
In previous times, Michael would've remained in
his seat. This time he felt the urge to lay down his
burdens at the altar. Along with a crowd of other
people, he walked to the front of the church. He
held hands with the people standing on both
sides of him and closed his eyes.

Although a minister led the prayer, Michael
found himself saying a personal prayer silently.
He asked God to forgive him for where he had
fallen short as a husband and father. He then
repented for reacting to Nigel in the flesh. Hanging his head, he invited the Lord into his heart.

He confessed to his Heavenly Father that he couldn't make it without him. He asked the Lord to step in and handle the situation with Nigel. He humbly admitted that there was nothing he could personally do to Nigel that could compare to what God could do.

In the background, Michael heard the minister say, "For the battle is not yours, but God's." He clenched his jaw to stop the tears that threatened to fall if he had opened his eyes. Releasing the woman's hand standing to the right of him, he lightly pressed the corners of his eyes so that no tears would be shed.

Michael realized that he had felt the presence of the Lord, but he wasn't about to cry in public. He had already humbled himself by going to church without Lyric's prompting and praying to God for help. Although he felt vulnerable to the Holy Spirit, he refused to appear weak in front of man.

At the end of the prayer, Michael went back to his seat and enjoyed the services. When the preacher stood behind the podium and said, "Sometimes, if we are to succeed and win victory, the Lord has to be the one to fight the battle," Michael nearly fell out of his seat. The preacher continued.

"This is the way it must be to win the victory over sins." He stepped from behind the podium and picked up his Bible. "Only through what God has done can we win the victory. We cannot redeem ourselves from our sins. We have no price we can offer. That battle must be the Lord's!" The minister set his Bible down and flipped through the pages. He instructed the congregation to turn to 2 Chronicles 20:1-29. He then stated that the title of his sermon was: The Battle is Not Yours, but God's.

Michael laughed to himself. "I get it," he said in a barely audible tone. He felt as if the Lord were speaking directly to him. He vowed to himself, and God, that he was going to cast his cares upon Him.

Twenty-two

The morning of September 4, Lyric woke up to a bed so drenched that she thought that she had wet it in her sleep. She got up and took a shower. To her surprise, water continued to trickle down her leg. Then it dawned on her. Her water had broken. She wasn't due for three more weeks.

Michael had already gone to work, and Autumn was at school. She put on her clothes before yelling for Consuela to come to her aid.

As soon as Consuela entered the room, Lyric said, "I think my water broke."

Consuela panicked. "Oh my God! We need to get you to the hospital."

Trying to remain calm, Lyric said, "I need you to call Michael. Tell him that I'm in labor."

She felt a contraction and panted. It nearly knocked her off her feet. Consuela asked if she was all right. Lyric held up her hand, indicating that she needed a moment. Consuela yelled at the top of her lungs for Milton to come upstairs.

He proceeded in a hurry. When he saw Lyric doing the Lamaze breathing techniques, he immediately took charge.

He looked at Consuela and said, "Call the birthing center. The number and doctor's name are next to the phone. Let them know that we're on our way."

When the pain subsided, Lyric reminded, "Don't forget to call my husband."

Consuela nodded her understanding and got on the phone. Milton grabbed the pre-packed hospital bag and stopwatch from next to the bed and helped Lyric down the stairs. With each step, Lyric felt pressure between her legs. Halfway down the stairs, she had a contraction. She squeezed Milton's hand so tight that his bones cracked. When the pain subsided, Milton asked her how far apart the contractions were. She shrugged her shoulders. He immediately set his watch so that when the next contraction hit, he'd get his answer.

Once Milton had gotten Lyric successfully down the stairs, he grabbed some towels from one of the bathroom closets. He tucked them underneath his arm while ushering Lyric to her car. He placed them on the passenger seat before helping her inside. Just as he was about to toss the bag in the backseat, it fell on the ground. He bent down to pick it up and threw the bag in the car. He then drove Lyric to Rockdale Medical Center in Conyers.

During the drive, Milton clocked Lyric's next contraction as having occurred ten minutes from the previous one. The pain caused a lone tear to roll down her cheek. Milton tried his best to comfort her by telling her that everything would be all right.

Lyric wasn't in the mood to talk. All she could do was moan. She simply stared out the window during the ride, wondering how she could've forgotten how painful childbirth was.

Approximately fifteen minutes later, they arrived safely to their destination. Lyric felt another contraction while they were in the parking lot. She doubled over in pain. She thought she was going to die; it hurt so badly. When it passed, Milton helped her inside.

Once inside, they checked in. One of the staff members escorted Lyric to her room. Milton waited in the hall while they examined Lyric. They determined that she had dilated 4 cm. The nurse came out and told him it was okay for him to go inside. When he entered the room, Lyric had changed into a hospital gown and she was resting in bed. An IV was attached to her hand. He told her that he would sit with her until Mr.

Stokes arrived. Lyric appreciated his kindness, but she couldn't have cared less who was there with her. All she cared about was getting the babies out.

An hour later, Michael showed up. He thanked Milton for staying with Lyric. He hurried over and kissed Lyric on the forehead. She felt like telling him to get away, but she could barely speak. She was so uncomfortable that she didn't want to be touched.

After Milton left, Michael did his best to comfort Lyric. He fed her ice chips and wiped the sweat off her brow. He tried to hold her hand, but she pushed him away. He called Chloe to tell her that Lyric was in labor and to ask her to bring Autumn to the hospital after school. Chloe agreed. He then called his mother. Erica had previously purchased a ticket, and she reminded Michael that she was already scheduled to fly out the following morning. According to Erica, she had a dream that Lyric would go into labor three weeks early. And she was right.

Another contraction hit, and Michael hurried off the phone. Lyric was begging for drugs like an addict. Originally, she had wanted to have a natural birth. That's why she opted for a private room instead of a regular hospital room. Her intent was to relax in the whirlpool. She thought that would ease the contractions. With a twin birth, her doctor didn't recommend it.

To Lyric's dismay, the pain was so intense that she forgot all about her birthing plan. The last thing she wanted to do was sit in a tub. Lyric felt like screaming. In an effort to bear the pain, she gritted her teeth. If she and the contractions were in a fight, she'd be the loser, hands down. Michael spoke to her in a loving and calm manner. He encouraged her to relax and breath.

"How am I supposed to relax, Michael, when I feel like I'm being ripped in two?" she yelled.

He lowered his head and didn't say anything. At one point, the pain was so intense that Lyric asked for a voluntary C-section. The nurse told her she couldn't have a cesarean unless it was an emergency. Unhappy with that response, Lyric begged for an epidural for the umpteenth time. The nurse called the doctor so that she could check Lyric's cervix again before calling the anesthesiologist. The doctor checked, and Lyric was dilated enough to get the epidural. Lyric was thankful to hear that. Not long afterward, the anesthesiologist arrived and administered the drugs. Lyric was so happy to see the anesthesiologist that she thanked him profusely. She smiled for the first time since being admitted. Once the epidural kicked in, Lyric couldn't even feel the contractions.

An hour later, to everyone's surprise, Lyric had dilated to 10 cm. The babies were ready to come. The doctor and nurse turned the bed into a birthing bed complete with stirrups. They gathered at the foot of the bed and instructed Lyric to push. She did as she was told. Each push wore her out. She had forgotten how much work labor really was.

"I can see the baby's head," the doctor said.

Lyric was glad to hear that. She was ready to get them out. Three pushes later, the doctor guided the first baby out. Michael cut the umbilical cord. He counted the fingers and toes and gave a good report to Lyric. He told her that they were halfway there. She felt encouraged, especially after she heard the baby cry.

The doctor told them that the second baby had slipped back into the birth canal. Lyric tried not to panic. She silently said a prayer of protection that she had learned when she used to attend Hillside International Truth Center under the leadership of Dr. Barbara King. In her mind she said, "The light of God surrounds us. The love of God enfolds us. The power of God protects us. And the presence of God watches over us. Wherever we are, God is, and all is well."

The doctor immediately stuck her entire forearm up the birthing canal and guided the baby back. She told Lyric to give a big push like she was having a bowel movement and hold it. She did. The doctor announced that the baby's head was out. She tried to get the baby out, but he was stuck. Lyric could see the distressed looks on everyone's faces, but she refused to panic. She trusted God and silently recited the 23rd Psalm. When she got to the end, the second baby came out.

The doctor reacted with a sense of urgency and cut his umbilical cord instead of letting Michael do it. She handed the baby to the nurse as Michael looked on. When Lyric heard the second baby cry, she silently thanked the Lord.

Michael came over and kissed Lyric on the lips. He told her that she had done a great job. He informed her that the twins had all of their limbs and appeared to be doing fine. They smiled at each other, and he went to see about the boys. Lyric breathed a sigh of relief; she was exhausted. She leaned back on the pillow as the doctor stitched her up and cleaned up the afterbirth.

Lyric glanced over at the nurses cleaning up the babies. They were underneath heat lamps as the nurses wiped them off and washed their hair. They looked like little dolls. She silently thanked God for them.

Later that evening, Chloe arrived at the hospital with Autumn and Heavyn. They entered the room carrying a vase filled with colorful flowers, helium-filled balloons, and stuffed animals. They set the gifts down before going over and hugging and kissing Lyric. They completely ignored Michael, who was sleeping in a chair. They congratulated her and made goo-goo eyes at the babies.

As the twins slept peacefully, Autumn rubbed their backs and touched their tiny hands. She looked at Heavyn and said, "You can tell that Logan is my mother's child. He looks just like her." She pointed and smiled. "He's got my mom's nose."

Heavyn concurred. "I wish they'd open their eyes. I want to pick them up."

"You'll have plenty of time to do that," assured Chloe. She said to Lyric, "We didn't plan to stay long. Just wanted to drop the stuff off to you and let you know that we were thinking about you." She looked at the boys. "They are absolutely adorable."

"Thanks. You girls are so sweet to me."

"The babies are pretty big," Chloe observed.

"Yes, our firstborn, Logan, weighed in at 8 pounds, 3 ounces, and he was twenty-three inches long. Landon weighed 8 pounds even, and he measured at twenty-two inches."

Autumn looked like a proud big sister. "So Logan is the oldest. By how many minutes?"

"Seven." Lyric went on to tell them about the labor and delivery and that she was breastfeeding. She was so tired that she couldn't stifle her yawn.

Chloe stood up and told the girls that it was time to leave because Lyric needed her rest. She told Lyric not to worry about Autumn because she would take care of her. That made Lyric feel good. She knew that Chloe meant what she said. Whenever Autumn was in Chloe's care, Lyric didn't worry. There was one thing she knew for certain, and that was Chloe treated Autumn just like her daughter. She was thankful to have such a loyal friend.

After Nigel realized that Lyric had gone to Rockdale Birthing Center in Conyers, he couldn't stop thinking about her. He called the Center to confirm. The only thing they verified was that she was there. When they patched him through to her room, he hung up. He felt enraged. He should've been there to witness the birth of his child. Did he have a son or a daughter? he wondered. Did the baby look like him or Lyric? Maybe a combination of both. He needed answers.

The results for the newborn screening tests came back normal. Lyric and Michael were glad to hear that. When Michael left to go and get something to eat, the doctor stayed behind to talk to Lyric in private.

"I didn't want to say anything in front of your husband," she admitted. Lyric braced herself. "I know that you were a rape victim, so I want to be as sensitive as I can when I tell you this." She looked Lyric in the eyes. "When the babies were born, they were a little jaundiced. Since your blood type is B negative, we checked both babies. What we found out is that Logan is O positive and Landon is AB negative. We don't understand how that could happen. Because if one of the babies is AB negative, then the father would have to be A type. That wouldn't be possible if the other baby is O positive."

"Okay." Lyric wondered why the doctor would make a big deal out of that. Lots of siblings don't have the same blood types. Lyric sat up in the bed. "So what are you saying?" She sounded serious.

The doctor softened her tone. "Conception can happen when a woman releases multiple eggs during ovulation. If she has more than one sexual partner within the same time period, sperm cells can fertilize two separate eggs," the doctor explained.

Lyric scratched her head. "What?"

"Heteropaternal superfecundation is extremely rare. That's when fraternal twins have different fathers. It can happen if a woman has contact with more than one partner within one menstrual cycle. DNA testing would establish paternity."

Lyric's eyes became misty. She looked over at her babies as they slept peacefully. She looked at all of the flowers and balloons decorating the room and felt overwhelmed. Michael entered the room, smacking on a sandwich. Lyric looked at him and burst into tears. He hurried to her side and tried to console her. When he asked her what was wrong, she blurted out that they needed to get DNA testing.

He stared at the doctor. "What did you say to her?"

The doctor told him the same thing she had said to Lyric. Michael then informed the doctor that unless there was a medical necessity, he didn't want DNA testing for either of the boys. The doctor assured him that they hadn't identified any other health issues with the babies. With that, she apologized and left them alone.

Lyric didn't want to contradict Michael in front of the physician, so she waited until they could talk in private before expressing her true feelings.

"Honey, I love you just for being you." She patted his hand. "These are our babies no matter what." She pressed her lips so tight that they formed a thin line. "Because of that, I want to get the paternity test."

He stood up and turned his back to her.

"Michael, please," she pleaded. "We need to know for us. We should know what we're dealing with." She sighed. "What if Nigel has a hereditary medical condition? If we bury our heads in the sand, it's not going to make it go away. We've got to be proactive instead of reactive." He turned to face her. She could see the sadness in his eyes. "At least if we know the paternity for sure now, it can't come back to haunt us. Not knowing would eat us alive. We'd always wonder."

"You're right," he relented. "But I want the test performed confidentially by an outside lab. I don't want it to be a part of their medical records."

She agreed. He sat next to her and embraced her. She hoped that they'd be able to survive this.

Twenty-three

They were now ready to take the boys home.
They thanked the staff for being so accommodat-
ing and hospitable. Michael loaded up the car
before coming back to get his wife. The nurse
rolled Lyric outside in a wheelchair. Lyric was
surprised to see a brand new Lexus SUV parked
along curbside.

"Surprise," Michael laughed. "Do you like it?"
He helped her into the car and assisted with
buckling the babies in their infant car seats.
"Don't worry; I didn't get rid of your Saab. I
know how much you like having a convertible;
plus it's paid for."

Lyric knew that they needed a bigger vehicle
to accommodate their expanding family, but
she wasn't ready to part with her car. She was so
glad Michael bought an SUV instead of a mini-
van and still kept her ride. "I love it," she said
sincerely. "You thought of everything."

They pulled up to their house and immediately noticed two "Congratulations it's a boy" stork yard signs. When they entered the house, they were greeted by Chloe, Erica, Milton, and Consuela. A large banner read: WELCOME HOME, LOGAN AND LANDON! Lyric grinned when she saw it. Michael placed the car seats on the couch. Milton congratulated the couple and helped Lyric take a seat on the couch. Consuela kissed her on the cheek and excused herself so that she could get back to work.

"Congratulations!" Erica said, giving Michael a hug. She bent down and kissed the babies on their cheeks. "They are so handsome." She read their identification bracelets. "Baby Landon reminds me of his grandfather. And he looks just like Michael did when he was a baby." She pointed at his chin. "He even has Michael's dimpled chin."

When Landon opened his eyes, Chloe threw a receiving blanket over her shoulder and picked him up. She sat on the couch cuddling him. Erica was hovering around. It was obvious that she wanted to hold the baby. Chloe inhaled that fresh baby scent and turned the newborn over to his grandmother.

Milton said to Lyric, "I made you baked chicken breasts, wild rice, and broccoli for lunch. Are you hungry?" He gave her a friendly expression.

"Ah-hem," Erica said, clearing her throat. "She should probably watch the carbs. She's got quite a bit of baby weight to lose."

The room became silent as all eyes were on Erica. No one smiled. Landon closed his eyes and dozed off.

Erica continued. "What? I wasn't being mean. I was just saying."

"Don't start," Michael chastised.

Milton plastered a smile on his face and said, "She looks great. Now if you'd like for me to hold the carbs on your lunch, I'll be happy to do that." He winked at Lyric and went into the kitchen to fix the plates.

Lyric nearly laughed at the tactful way Milton put Erica in her place. Baby Logan awoke, and he whimpered. Chloe took him out of his seat and rocked him for a moment before handing him to his mommy for nursing. After getting his fill and being burped, he dozed off to sleep. Chloe took him out of Lyric's arms and placed him in his bassinet.

A few minutes later, Lyric did the same thing to Landon when he woke up. When she finished, the grownups went into the informal dining area and ate lunch. Chloe initiated the conversation by asking Erica about her temporary move to Atlanta.

"I would do anything for my son," Erica explained. "When he asked me to come here to help with the twins, I was glad to do it. Since I'm retired from nursing, I have the time."

Lyric cut a piece of tender chicken breast and stuffed it in her mouth. Milton had seasoned it just right. "Did you find someone to rent out your house?"

"I sure did," Erica said, stabbing her broccoli with her fork. She looked at Lyric. "Michael told me that you completed your training to become a certified bridal consultant."

"Yes, I did." Lyric was proud of herself for accomplishing her goal. She had worked hard.

Erica finished her vegetables. "I'm glad you're going to work. Personally, I never understood why you stayed at home even after Autumn went to school. A woman is supposed to be her husband's helpmate. Those days of the man taking care of a woman are long gone. A woman should help make the load easier for her husband by contributing. Why stress the man out?"

Lyric didn't know what to say. She felt embarrassed. Not because she had elected to stay at home and raise a family. Rather Erica's mean-spirited comments made her think that perhaps Erica was jealous that Lyric had the option to stay home. Erica tried to make it seem as though

Lyric didn't contribute anything to her marital relationship, but Lyric knew that was a lie.

"Mom," Michael intervened. "No disrespect, but you need to lay off of Lyric. She does plenty around here, and she doesn't need to justify her contributions to anybody. She's my wife, and whatever arrangement we have, that's between us. It's not for anybody to judge." He patted Lyric's hand. "Besides, I like being able to take care of my family."

Erica's face looked as sour as the lemons used to prepare the freshly squeezed lemonade they were drinking. Lyric turned her head and mouthed the words "Thank you" to Michael. They ate the rest of their meal in silence. When they finished eating lunch, Consuela cleared away the dishes. Milton pulled Lyric and Michael to the side while the others made their way to the family room.

"Mr. and Mrs. Stokes," he began.

"Please call me Lyric," she interrupted. "All of my friends do." She gave him a warm smile. She appreciated his professionalism, but she didn't think they needed to be that formal. She had told him previously to call her Lyric, but he never did.

"And you can call me Michael."

"Lyric, Michael," he sounded as if he were trying to get used to saying their names. "I didn't get a chance to mention this on the day that I took Lyric to the hospital." He looked Lyric in the eyes. "But when I dropped your bag on the ground, I saw something blink underneath your car. I waited until I got back to the house to check it out. I'm glad I did." He paused. "It was a tracking device."

Lyric nearly collapsed. Her legs felt like wet noodles. Michael grabbed her and held her up. She pressed her body against the table for support. "Are you serious?"

Michael seemed floored. As if a light bulb went off in his head, he said, "I'm not a gambler, but I'd bet everything I own that Nigel is behind it." He looked at Milton. "What did you do with the device?"

"I didn't move it, because I wanted the two of you to see it."

"You did the right thing," Michael assured him. "We'll get to the bottom of it. Thank you."

Milton left the couple alone while he cleaned up the kitchen. Lyric dreaded the thought of Nigel following her. In her spirit, she knew Michael was right. When had Nigel installed the device? she wondered. How long had he been tracking her whereabouts? She told Michael to get that tracker off her car right away. The whole thing creeped her out.

Twenty-four

Erica got settled in to the in-law suite. When decorating the living quarters, Lyric made sure that it was comfortable, yet nicely decorated. Erica's favorite color was red, so that was the primary hue.

Although Erica treated her daughter-in-law badly, Lyric still wanted her approval. She never understood what she had done to make Erica dislike her so.

Erica watched the twins as Lyric sterilized the baby bottles. When she finished, she sat down in her meditation room and pumped. She was amazed at how much milk she was able to supply. She felt like a cow. She stored the milk in the freezer and checked on the boys. They were resting peacefully, and Erica was reading *Ebony* magazine.

Lyric hated to admit it, but Erica was a god-send. She watched the babies every morning so that Lyric could sleep in. Since Michael worked outside of the home, Lyric was usually the one getting up with the infants in the middle of the night. She had actually learned how to position the twins so that she could feed them at the same time.

She also had a mini-refrigerator and bottle warmers next to her bed. That way Michael could lend a helping hand, if he so chose.

Having Erica around also gave Lyric the time she needed to work on her business plan and get the ball rolling on becoming an entrepreneur. Lyric didn't know what she'd do without her help.

The phone rang, and Lyric answered.

"Baby," Michael greeted. "I forgot to tell you. I'm expecting a plainly wrapped package. When it comes, please put it in the bedroom. It's the testing kit."

Lyric agreed, and they ended the call. She went back to doing more Internet research. Not long afterward, the doorbell rang. She thought it was the delivery guy dropping off the materials for the DNA testing. When she opened the door, her jaw dropped. She could hear her heart thumping loudly against her chest. She wanted to slam the door, but she was too shocked to move.

"Aren't you going to let me in?" the familiar stranger said.

She unlocked the glass door and invited the man she used to call "Daddy" inside. Now he was simply Henry Alexander. He looked the same as she had remembered, except for some creases in his forehead. She hadn't seen the man in twenty years. Not since he drove drunk and killed her mother in a car accident. He spent five years in prison for vehicular homicide. She never wrote him once.

"How did you find me?" she asked.

"Can't you at least show your old man some love?" He reached out to hug her, and her body stiffened. He backed away. "You look so pretty."

She stood there, angry. Tears welled in her eyes. She had pushed him out of her heart. She had no love to show him because she had no love for him. In her mind, he was the man who took her mother away from her. Lyric was only sixteen at the time. She had to live with her maternal grandmother until she went off to college. She never got over that.

While in prison, Henry wrote her regularly. She never opened any of his letters. She stored them in a box and hid them in the back of her closet. She still had the unopened letters.

When he got released, he tried to reach out to her. He had called, but Lyric rejected him. She changed her telephone number. She asked her grandmother and the rest of her family members not to give Henry her address or new number. She had moved on with her life and wanted nothing to do with him. It was too painful for her. That still didn't stop family members from occasionally giving her updates about him, even though she never asked.

"Seriously, what are you doing here?" She closed the door behind him and locked it.

He took off his hat and held it in his hands. "Your husband, Michael, called me."

"He did what?" She sounded surprised. "Why would he do that?"

"Can we sit down and talk?" he said sincerely.

Lyric hesitated for a moment. She wasn't sure if she wanted him to stay. If they sat down, she was concerned that it would prolong his visit. His timing was lousy. The last thing she wanted was to give Erica more reasons to dislike her. Over the years, Michael had simply told his mother that Lyric's mom had died in a car accident. Out of respect for Lyric, he didn't tell her the details about Henry being the one driving the car.

"Why are you being so mysterious?" She walked into the sitting room, and he followed.

"You have a beautiful home."

Lyric thanked him.

He placed his hat on the table and continued. "I know that you never really forgave me for what I did." He shook his head. "I still haven't forgiven myself. It haunts me every day of my life. Lord knows, if I could change it, I would. But I can't."

Lyric felt her bottom lip quiver as her eyes welled with tears. As much as she wanted to hate him, she couldn't. She had asked God to help her forgive him a long time ago. She had to. Holding on to the grief and pain nearly cost Lyric her sanity. She didn't know what she was feeling right now. A part of her wanted to hug her father and tell him that she had forgiven him. Another part of her wanted to slap his face and yell at him for hurting her so deeply.

In a low tone, Lyric said. "What do you want from me?"

"Even though you never wrote me back, I refused to give up on you. You were, and always will be, my little girl."

Hearing those words tugged on Lyric's heartstrings. She couldn't stop the tears from flowing. Henry got out of his seat and held her.

Erica entered the room. "I thought I heard voices in here." She stood there, staring at the two of them. "Are you all right, Lyric? Who's this?"

Lyric parted her lips and let out a breath. "This is my father, Henry Alexander," she introduced, wiping her face. "That's Erica, my mother-in-law."

Henry stood and shook Erica's hand. She eyed him curiously. "Wow, isn't that something. It's only taken what? Fifteen years to meet you."

He didn't say anything.

Lyric said, "We were talking. Would you give us a little while longer, please?"

"Sure." She eyed him up and down. "Nice to meet you," she said before turning on the balls of her feet and leaving them alone.

He cleared his throat. "She's something else."

"Tell me about it," Lyric mumbled.

He sat back down next to her. "Listen, Lyric. I know I wasn't the best father. I had a lot of problems, alcohol being the biggest one. I used to mask my problems instead of facing them." He hung his head and wrung his hands together. "While I was locked up, I had plenty of time to reflect on my life. What I came to realize was that most of my problems stemmed from my childhood." He had a solemn expression. "My mother died when I was ten years old. That left a void in my life, especially since my father didn't show affection." He looked her in the eyes. "I guess you could say I didn't get the nurturing that I needed to be a caring man. As a teenager, I used to smoke weed and get high. I started drinking when I was around seventeen or eighteen years old. I didn't stop until . . ." His eyes became wet, and he hid his face in his hands. "Lyric, as God is my witness, I've been sober for the last twenty years."

She removed his hands from his face. She was shocked to see him crying. Come to think of it, she couldn't remember ever seeing a man cry like that before. She thought back to her childhood, and she couldn't think of a time when she had seen Henry cry.

As much as she tried to detach herself from him, she couldn't. She felt his pain, and she felt sorry for him. She put her arm around his shoulders and said, "I forgive you, Daddy."

The fact that she called him "Daddy" made him cry even harder. Seeing him crying like that made her cry too.

"I've waited so long to hear you say that," he sobbed. He wiped his runny nose with the back of his hand.

Lyric got up and grabbed a box of tissue from out of the bathroom. She handed it to him.

He blew his nose. "Your husband really loves you."

Wiping her face, she said, "What do you mean?"

He stood up and paced the floor. "Right before your wedding, he found me." Lyric was speechless. "We had a nice long talk. I told him about your childhood and how I had failed you. I told him that he'd better not hurt you, and he promised he wouldn't. We actually kept in touch. We'd talk on the phone, or he'd send me pictures." He stopped pacing. "Autumn is a beautiful young lady. I have so many pictures of her." He smiled. "I even have copies of her report cards. She's very smart." He walked over to Lyric and sat beside her. Holding her hand he said, "You're a good mother. I'm so proud of you."

Lyric felt herself getting all choked up. She couldn't understand why, but Henry's validation actually meant something to her.

"Congratulations on the twins, Logan and Landon. Michael is so proud of them." He cleared his throat. "That's why I'm here." He squeezed her hand. "Michael thought you were at a place in your life spiritually where you'd be more willing to let me in."

Lyric thought for a moment as a lone tear ran down her cheek. "Are you ready to meet your grandsons?"

Lyric could not believe that Henry was at her house. She felt as if she were dreaming. She went into her bedroom to gather her thoughts. She knelt down on the side of her bed and prayed for wisdom, knowledge, and strength.

When she returned downstairs, she saw an incredible sight. Henry was holding Landon. He was grinning and talking to the baby, calling him little man. Erica sat next to him, feeding Logan a bottle. For Lyric, that moment was priceless. She joined them.

"Henry, uh, Dad," she corrected, "do you want to stay for dinner?"

"I would like that very much," he eagerly accepted.

"Where are you staying?" Erica asked.

He told her that he had checked into The Four Seasons Hotel in Buckhead.

"That's nonsense," Erica said. "You're Lyric's father; you should be staying here."

Lyric blinked quickly. She could not believe Erica's nerve. How was she going to invite someone to stay at someone else's house? It's not even like she knew Henry. He was a virtual stranger to her. Since she had put Lyric in a precarious predicament, Lyric felt that it would've been rude of her not to extend an invitation for him to stay in one of the guest bedrooms. It's not like they didn't have the space to accommodate him.

"Erica's right. You should stay here," Lyric said.

She saw Henry's face light up. "Thanks, but you don't have to. I don't want you to feel obligated to let me stay here."

Lyric felt like saying, "Okay," but she knew that wasn't right. Instead, she said sincerely, "No, I insist. It'll give you the opportunity to spend time with your grandkids. Besides, it'll give us a chance to get caught up." She couldn't believe those words had come out of her mouth with such ease. The Holy Spirit was really ministering to her. She checked her watch and realized that she needed to pick up Autumn from cheerleading practice. "I have to pick up Autumn," she announced. "You two will be all right staying here together. Won't you?"

Erica told her to go on. They'd be just fine. Lyric grabbed her keys and purse. She kissed the babies on top of their heads, not without noticing how comfortable Erica seemed around Henry. She admonished the thought and walked out the door.

When Autumn got in the car, she leaned over and kissed her mother on the cheek. Lyric drove them to Dairy Queen. Autumn ordered a banana split, and Lyric got a strawberry sundae. They ate inside of the establishment.

"So what's up, Mom?" Autumn asked. "You never eat ice cream unless it's something serious. Did something happen?"

Lyric bit her lower lip. "You know me so well." She exhaled. "Where do I begin?"

"Try the beginning," she said, her words dripping with sarcasm.

Lyric dipped her spoon in the cold treat and placed a scoop in her mouth. She enjoyed the sweet taste as it melted in her mouth. She wondered how she should break the news to Autumn. "My dad's at the house," she decided to just come right out and say. In this instance, the take-it-like-cough medicine approach worked better for Lyric.

Autumn chewed a piece of banana. "For real? When did he get in?" She didn't seem surprised.

"Okay, that's not the response I expected," Lyric admitted. "You don't seem the least bit surprised. What's up with that?"

Setting down her spoon, Autumn said, "Daddy lets me speak to Grandpa at least once a month. I've been talking to him since I was old enough to speak."

Lyric tilted her head to the side. "Why didn't you tell me?" She was upset that Autumn had been keeping that from her.

"Calm down. Daddy told me that I shouldn't keep secrets from you. He said that this was different. When it came to Grandpa, you didn't want to have a relationship with him. But he explained that just because you weren't talking to him, didn't mean that we shouldn't. He told me that he had been praying that one day you and your dad would reconcile. In the meantime, he thought it would be best if we didn't tell you about Grandpa until you were ready."

Lyric calmed down a bit. She understood Michael's reasoning, but she didn't like it. Not one time had Michael slipped up about being in contact with Henry. She prayed that her husband hadn't been keeping anything else from her. She realized that a certain amount of secrecy or privacy was good for a relationship. It was her hope that Michael had been forthright about the other things in their relationship.

"One more thing," Autumn said, licking her spoon. "Grandpa attended Grandpa Logan's funeral. I'm surprised you didn't see him."

Lyric lost her appetite. She had to get out of there. "Let's go," she said as she grabbed her purse. Michael had some serious explaining to do.

When Lyric and Autumn returned home, Erica and Henry were laughing like two old friends. They were sitting in the same spot as when Lyric had left. Only this time they were sipping coffee, and Landon and Logan were sleeping.

"Come over here and give your grandpa a hug," Henry said as soon as he saw Autumn. He sat his coffee cup on the table.

Autumn put down her book bag and embraced him. "It's nice to see you."

He broke away from her and said, "You look like a model with your pretty self." He then kissed her on the cheek.

Autumn blushed. She went over and hugged Erica too. Logan opened his eyes. Just as Autumn was about to pick him up out of his bassinet.

"Go wash up. Then you can play with the baby," Lyric said.

Autumn did as she was told. Lyric excused herself to go wash her hands as well. Then she returned and draped a receiving blanket over her shoulder and picked up Logan.

She looked into his doe eyes and her heart melted. She kissed his cheek and inhaled his powdery scent. She could tell that he was ready to eat by the way he kept turning his face into her chest, so she used the blanket to cover herself and nursed him.

Autumn noticed her mom feeding the baby and quietly took a seat on the couch next to her. When the baby finished suckling, Lyric burped him and changed his diaper. She lightly rubbed his belly after laying him on his back to sleep.

Then Landon awoke, and she repeated the process.

Erica and Henry were having a private conversation. Lyric looked up whenever Erica squealed with delight or Henry chuckled.

"You didn't tell me that you had such a charming father," Erica said, squeezing Henry's thigh.

Lyric wanted to throw up. She hoped with everything in her that Erica wasn't flirting with Henry. By the sultry look in Erica's eyes, she was doing just that. Just then, the doorbell rang. Lyric remembered about the package and insisted she'd get the door. She adjusted her bra and handed the partially sleeping baby to Autumn.

After signing for the delivery, Lyric hid the DNA testing kit in her bedroom behind a pillow on her bed. She didn't want anyone to accidentally stumble upon it.

She had mixed emotions about the testing. A part of her felt sad. The reality that Nigel could very well be the biological father of one of her twins made her sick to her stomach. She stood in the middle of her bedroom a moment longer to compose herself. She didn't want to be around her children while she was in such a foul mood.

To get herself out of her funk, she thought about the good things in her life, like her family.

Now that her dad was back, she was being given another opportunity to have a relationship with him. She made up in her mind that no matter what the test results proved, Landon and Logan were her babies. That's all that mattered. She loved them.

A few minutes later, Lyric felt comfortable enough to join her family. Before she even entered the room, she heard Henry telling a story about her.

"She was such a stubborn baby," he said. "She wanted what she wanted when she wanted it."

Everyone laughed as Lyric rounded the corner. Henry continued to share more stories about her childhood. She felt a tightening in her chest. She didn't like Henry talking about the past. It put her on the defensive. His recollection of her childhood was much different than hers.

While Henry sat there telling funny stories, Lyric tried to conceal her discontent. The phone rang. It was a welcomed distraction. Lyric answered on the second ring. As soon as she heard Chloe's voice on the other end, she went into another room to talk in private.

"You're never going to believe the type of day I've had," Lyric said, exhaling. She went on to explain the unexpected visit from her dad and Michael's hand in it.

Chloe sounded surprised. "Wow! I don't know what to say." Lyric admitted that she, too, had been at a loss for words when she found out. "Keith is home now." Lyric heard Chloe and Keith exchange pleasantries and a kiss. Chloe apologized for the interruption and offered to come over.

"No, you stay with your husband. We'll hook up later." Lyric discontinued the call.

The smell of lasagna caught her attention. She had been so distracted that she hadn't paid any attention to Milton slaving away in the kitchen. She clutched the phone in her hand as she followed the scent.

Milton finished tossing the salad and placed a few slices of buttered bread on a tray. "Dinner smells delicious," she said. He smiled at her. "My dad is here, so we're going to need an extra setting at the table." He nodded his head in agreement.

Fifteen minutes later, Michael came walking through the door carrying a bouquet of rainbow colored roses. He handed the blooms to Lyric. She smirked at him, trying to hold on to her negative feelings. When he leaned over and kissed her on the cheek, the warmth of his soft lips softened her resolve. No matter how hard she tried, she couldn't stay angry with him. She replaced her smirk with a genuine smile and thanked him.

Michael greeted Autumn and Erica and raised a brow when he saw Henry. "How's it going?" he asked, looking Henry in the eyes.

"All is well, son." Henry stood and gave his son-in-law a manly hug.

Erica chimed in. "Henry's going to be staying with us for a little while."

Michael stepped back. "Is that right?" He couldn't hide his enthusiasm.

"Yes." Henry beamed. He looked at Lyric; she was taking a whiff of her flowers. "Your wife was kind enough to invite me to stay."

Lyric felt every eyeball in the room on her. She didn't say anything. She simply retrieved a Waterford crystal vase from the German Shrunk and went into the kitchen to fill it with filtered water.

While in the cookery, Milton said, "Those are some beautiful flowers."

"Michael got them for me," she said proudly. She separated the assemblage with her fingers. "We're ready to eat."

"Not a problem."

They ate dinner in the dining room. When they finished, Henry left to go check out of his hotel room. Michael showered, and Lyric and Erica washed up the babies and put on their sleepers. They fed them, and the twins fell asleep. Autumn chatted on the phone with Heavyn.

Lyric joined Michael in their bedroom and closed the door. Michael seemed tense.

"You want me to give you a massage?" Lyric offered.

He climbed on top of the bed and lay on his stomach. "That would be nice."

Lyric grabbed a bottle of massage oil from the night-stand and mounted her frame on top of his. She poured the oil in the palm of her hands and rubbed her hands together. "The kit came," she said as she massaged his back. He grunted. "Are you ready to tell me why you've been keeping in touch with my father for all these years?" Kneading his shoulders like dough, she waited for his response.

He blew air between his lips. "I know you think your father is a monster; he's not. When you told me about him and what he did, I became curious. I had to see for myself. I needed to know if he was really that bad."

She stopped massaging him. "You didn't believe me?"

He carefully turned his body over so that he could look at her. "Of course I believed you. He was somebody that hurt you. As your man, I needed to know what I was dealing with. I had a bunch of questions. After all, I was marrying a woman with unresolved Daddy issues." She got off of him and folded her arms across her chest. He sat up. "Listen to me," he reached out and touched her. "I didn't contact your father to hurt you. I did it because I love you."

She squinted her eyes. "Then why didn't you tell me?"

"Because you weren't ready," he said seriously. Her eyes became wet, and he hugged her. "Baby, your father is a good man." Lyric's body tensed. "He's made a lot of mistakes, and he's paid for them. He doesn't drink anymore. He even has a relationship with the Lord."

"Really?" She buried her head deeper in his chest.

"Yes. You should be proud of him. I've never seen anybody work to change as hard as he has." He stroked her arm. "He's a different person. You should give him a chance." She sniffed. "I don't know if Henry told you, but he's a successful boat trader. He lives in Hilton Head, South Carolina."

"Is he married? Does he have any other children?" She bit her lower lip.

He kissed the top of her head. "No, baby. He chose not to remarry or have other kids because he didn't feel he was worthy of love after what he had done. He told me that he didn't want to risk messing up somebody else's life like he did with you and your mother."

Tears streamed down Lyric's cheeks. "And what about Autumn? Why did you involve her in your deception?"

"Deception?" he repeated, raising his voice. "That would imply that I intentionally set out to do you wrong. You need to understand something. Henry has, and always will be, a part of you. I wanted Autumn to know her grandfather."

"Did you tell her what he did?" she asked.

"No," he admitted. "I didn't have to. Henry asked me if he could tell her, and I agreed."

Lyric lightly pushed him. "You did that without consulting me first? How could you? I should've been there."

He squeezed the bridge of his nose and closed his eyes. "I didn't have a problem with it. I thought she should know where she came from and why you had such a problem with her grandfather. That way she could make her own judgments about him."

"I didn't think I did, but I love him."

"I know you do."

Nigel couldn't believe that there were two birth announcement signs in Lyric's front yard. Two babies?

Boys? He always thought that he was more potent than the average man. Now he had proof. He stuck his chest out proudly.

He also wondered about the older man he saw coming out of Lyric's house. The guy was extremely tall. He could've easily been six feet eleven. He looked like a giant and was built like a linebacker. He decided not to waste any more time thinking about the old guy. He needed to figure out a way to see his sons.

He fixed himself a turkey sandwich with potato chips. He ate in the living room. The television was on, but he wasn't paying attention. It was simply background noise. He wondered whether he should take Lyric to court and sue for custody. He scratched the side of his head.

"That's not a good idea," he said to no one in particular. "If I do that, she'll accuse me of rape again."

He bit and chewed his sandwich. Then he thought about taking Lyric and the boys away. Perhaps he could talk to her and give her the opportunity to run away with him on her own. He'd only force her to go if she didn't willingly cooperate. He was certain that once she got to know him better, she'd grow to love him. She had to; they were meant to be.

He finished off his sandwich and washed it down with a soda. He thought about Lyric's

husband and daughter. Knowing Lyric the way
he did, he figured she'd feel guilty leaving her
marriage and daughter. He expected her to be
sad for a while, but she'd have to get over that.
Lots of people leave their old families behind
when they find new love. Besides, it wasn't like
Mr. Stokes couldn't take care of his child.

A fleeting thought crossed Nigel's mind. What
if the babies weren't his? He quickly dismissed
the notion. He and Lyric were meant to be; it was
kismet, he reasoned. The babies had to be his.
Nigel was convinced that it was in the best interest of those babies to be raised by their mother
and real father. He wasn't about to move out of
the way so that Mr. Stokes could play Daddy to
his seeds. Wasn't going to happen.

As for baby girl, he wasn't completely heart-
less. He didn't have any problem letting Lyric
maintain a relationship with her daughter.
Provided it didn't cause any strife between him
and Lyric. If baby girl had any delusions about
her parents getting back together, then she was
in for a rude awakening.

He crunched on some salty chips before
checking the status of the tracker on Lyric's car.
He found it strange that her car hadn't moved
since she'd been home from the hospital. He
wondered what was up.

Twenty-five

Two weeks had passed since the birth of the twins. Lyric and Michael decided to wait a couple of weeks before taking the DNA tests. They wanted to bond with the babies first. Michael seemed nervous as he used the buccal swabs to collect sample cheek cells for Logan and Landon. He rubbed the inside of their cheeks. Taking the samples was painless and not traumatic to either of the babies. Still, it was obvious that Michael didn't really want to do it.

Lyric refused to collect her own sample for fear of botching something up. She insisted that Michael do it. He then gathered samples from his wife and himself.

"I'll send these to the lab today," he told his wife.

She kissed him on the lips and assured him everything would be okay. "Did you want to go with us to their doctor's appointment?"

He shook his head. "My mom's going with you. You'll be fine." He kissed the boys on their chubby cheeks and got ready for work.

Two hours later, Lyric and Erica arrived at the pediatrician's office with babies in tow. The doctor took their weight, height, and head circumference. Both boys had grown. They repeated the newborn screening tests. The doctor told Lyric and Erica that the boys were healthy and progressing normally. That made Lyric feel good.

After the doctor left the room, a nurse entered to give Logan and Landon their first Hepatitis B vaccination. Both boys screamed at the top of their lungs after being poked with the needles. Lyric was so thankful that she had given her babies Tylenol before their immunizations to help prevent fever and reduce pain. They immediately fell asleep.

During the ride home, Erica broached the subject of Henry. "Why is your relationship with your father so strained?"

Lyric parted her lips. She knew that Erica would eventually ask; she just wasn't prepared to answer. "It's complicated. I really don't feel like discussing it."

Erica looked out of the passenger window for a moment. Then she glared at Lyric. "I know you think I don't like you." Without missing a beat, she continued. "The truth is, for the longest time I wasn't crazy about you. Not because you did anything to me. The fact that my son loved you so much made me feel insecure." She played with her hands. "Michael is my only son; we've always been close. I wasn't prepared for him to go off to college and fall in love so quickly. You were the first serious girlfriend he ever had. And for him to marry you," she shook her head, "that threw me for a loop."

"We were in love," Lyric explained.

"I see that . . . now." She sighed. "I realize that Michael is devoted to you. Over the years, his commitment has only gotten stronger. I can tell by the way he looks at you." She leaned her head against the headrest. "He told me that you are the love of his life." She pressed her lips together. "And I believe him."

"Why are you telling me this now?" Lyric sounded serious.

Erica held her head down. "After I saw you with your father, I realized that you had a lot of hurt and pain going on. I felt bad about the way I've treated you." She touched the top of Lyric's hand. "I'd like for us to start over."

Lyric swallowed the lump in her throat. She was taken aback. "I don't know what to say."

"We're family. I was wrong to be so hard on you. I'm a Christian woman, but I haven't treated you with the love you deserve."

Lyric kept her eyes on the road. She didn't want to look at Erica. She wondered whether God was testing her. First her father. Now this. Dare she even ask, what's next? She felt as if the world were going crazy. Erica had to be one of the most difficult people she knew, and here she was apologizing. She didn't want to seem skeptical; however, she was certainly going to proceed with caution when it came to Erica. Perhaps if she didn't have any expectations regarding their relationship, then she couldn't be disappointed, she figured.

Gripping the steering wheel, Lyric said, "That sounds all fine, well, and good, Erica. Please forgive me for being a bit leery."

"Sweetheart, I don't blame you."

Sweetheart? Erica had never referred to Lyric in such an endearing way. Lyric almost choked on her own spit.

Erica continued. "I don't expect our relationship to mend overnight. We've got years of damage to work through. I just hope you'll give me a chance to make things right between us."

Lyric drove into her subdivision. All sorts of thoughts went through her mind. She found herself asking the trendy question, what would Jesus do? Although it sounded cliché, she decided to take the high road anyway. Life was too short, and tomorrow may not come.

She thought about the scripture Matthew 5:44. It states, *But I say unto you, Love your enemies, bless them that curse you, do good to them that hate you, and pray for them which despitefully use you, and persecute you;*

Lyric sighed and said, "I'm willing to try."

A wide smile spread across Erica's face. "That's all I ask."

Lyric drove slowly down her street. As she neared her house, she spotted her neighbor, Vendela Johnson, standing outside. She was happy to see that Vendela was back from her month-long trip in Paris, France. She usually traveled overseas three or four times a year. No matter where she went, she brought back souvenirs for Lyric and Autumn. She shared exciting stories and took great pictures. Lyric couldn't wait to hear about her latest holiday. They waved at each other, and Lyric pulled into the driveway.

As the garage door ascended, Vendela came over. Lyric rolled down her window and greeted her neighbor.

"I heard you dropped the load," Vendela said, laughing.

Lyric stuck her head out the window. "Yes, I did. They're in the backseat."

Vendela came closer and caught a glimpse of the sleeping babies. "They're gorgeous!" she squealed.

"Thank you," Lyric said. "You remember my mother-inlaw, Erica."

She waved and said, "Hey, Mama Stokes."

Erica acknowledged her.

"How was your European vacation?" Lyric asked.

"Incredible!" Vendela said. "I got back last night. I brought you and Autumn souvenirs. I'll bring them over later. If Carlton would let me, I'd move us to Europe." Her husband, Carlton, was a senior partner at a major law firm.

"You know there's no way he's going to move and leave his practice."

"A girl can dream, can't she?" Vendela half joked. "I'll let you go and get those babies inside. Take it easy."

As Vendela walked away, Lyric pulled the car into the garage. She and Erica unloaded the vehicle and carried the babies inside. The twins were still sleeping, so they carefully placed them in their bassinettes. They sat in the great room and resumed their conversation.

Since Erica seemed to be in such a good mood, Lyric decided to ask her some questions. "Why did you have a problem with me not working outside of the household?"

Laughing a nervous laugh, Erica said, "I was jealous."

Lyric did a double take. She didn't know what she had expected Erica to say, but not that. She looked with astonishment at her mother-in-law. She raised a brow. Unable to conceal her amazement, she said, "You were jealous of me?"

Erica wrung her hands together. "I'm not proud of it. And if you tell anybody I said it, I'll deny it," she joked. She stopped smiling and said in a serious tone, "Getting old isn't easy." She had a faraway look in her eyes. Lyric pretended to clear her throat. "When I was young, I used to walk into a room and heads would turn. Being around you reminded me that I was no longer the youngest or the prettiest woman in the room. Here you were this pretty young thing who had my son's nose wide open. The mere fact that my son was willing to give you everything he had didn't sit well with me. He was so in love with you that he wanted to take care of you. I was threatened by you." She shifted in her seat and faced Lyric. "Although my husband was everything I ever wanted in a man, I still had to work. That's why I was so jealous of you."

Lyric was speechless. She appreciated Erica's transparency. Seeing Erica in such a vulnerable state made her respect her. She reached out and hugged her. For the first time ever, Erica said to Lyric, "I love you."

Twenty-six

Lyric felt numb as Michael held the DNA test results in his hand. It was official. Logan was not Michael's biological child, 100% exclusion. As for Landon, there was a 99.99% inclusion. Michael was Landon's father for sure.

She could hear her heart beating loudly in her ears. She felt like curling up in the fetal position and dying. No matter how much she had tried to prepare herself for the possibility of such devastating news, nothing could've prepared her for the feelings of overwhelming anger and disappointment that she felt. She tried not to cry, but she could not stop herself.

In an effort to console Lyric, Michael held his wife close as she sobbed uncontrollably. While she was crying, she felt something wet drip on her bare shoulder. She looked up, and Michael quickly wiped his wet eyes.

Seeing Michael so distraught shattered Lyric's heart like broken glass. In spite of her relationship with the Lord, she couldn't help but wonder why life had thrown her such a curve ball. For a brief moment, she felt sorry for herself and her husband.

When her grandmother raised her, she had been strict. She taught Lyric how to be a refined young lady and encouraged her to abstain from sex until marriage. The temptation to give in to her flesh had been overwhelming. Meeting Michael had been a prayer answered. That was one of the reasons why she got married so young and after a short courtship. She knew right away that Michael was the one. She was thankful that she had saved herself for her husband. That made their connection even stronger. She had given him the most precious part of her.

Lyric felt like screaming at the top of her lungs, "Why, God, why?" She tried to live right, she reasoned. She had never been promiscuous. She hadn't cheated on her husband. So why was she in a position to need a paternity test? Even worse, she felt, was that she was married and her children had different fathers. That's not what she wanted.

Just as she was sinking deeper into her pity-party, the Holy Spirit ministered to her.

"For my thoughts are not your thoughts," the voice said, quoting Isaiah 55:8-9, *"neither are*

your ways my ways. For as the heavens are higher than the earth, so are my ways higher than your ways, and my thoughts than your thoughts."

She felt convicted. She chastised herself for feeling betrayed by God. As good as God had been to her, she realized that she had no right to challenge Him. Ephesians 2:8-9 came to mind. *"For by grace are ye saved through faith; and that not of yourselves: it is the gift of God: Not of works, lest any man should boast."*

Lyric reminded herself that everything happens for a reason. More than ever, she needed to hold on to her faith.

"We'll get through this," Michael said, interrupting her thoughts. "Lots of people come into the world under less than desirable circumstances. That doesn't make their lives any less valuable." He squeezed the bridge of his nose. "Logan's my son, and I love him no matter what. He's innocent in all of this. He shouldn't be punished for the sins of his father." He held her hand and looked her in the eye. "This," he held up the piece of paper in his left hand, "doesn't change anything for me. I'm just as committed to you and devoted to our family as I ever have been." He bent over and kissed her glossy lips. Folding the document in half, Michael said, "I'm going to put this in the safe." He removed the portrait from the wall covering the safe and keyed in the pin number. He placed the document inside.

"Do you think we should take my dad out to dinner or have Milton prepare a special feast for his last night in town?" Lyric asked, trying to change the subject.

Michael locked the safe and re-hung the painting. "We might as well eat here so that the whole family can attend."

Nodding her head in agreement, Lyric said, "Believe it or not, I'm going to miss him."

She ran her finger along the edge of her dresser. She had finally gotten used to the idea of having her father around. No matter how many questions Lyric had about the past, Henry was willing to answer. She appreciated his candor, as well as his patience.

And she couldn't deny that he was great with her children. Autumn obviously adored him. She enjoyed being her grandfather's little girl, and he spoiled her to no end. He had taken her out to eat, to the movies, and shopping. The sound of his deep, yet soothing voice calmed crying babies.

Michael smiled knowingly at Lyric before announcing that he was headed to work. He hugged her again. "Are you going to be all right?"

"Of course," she assured him. "Go to work. Just make sure you're back in time for dinner."

He winked at her and left. Alone in her bedroom, Lyric picked up her Bible. She read a few chapters from the book of Psalms. When she finished, she got down on her knees and prayed.

Later that evening, the family gathered around the dinner table. Milton had prepared Cornish game hens, yellow rice, buttery spinach, and rolls. Henry talked about his boating business and how much he would love to have the family come visit him. He wanted to take everyone on a boat ride. He owned a yacht that he named Leading Lady Lyric. When Lyric heard the name of his boat, her eyes became misty. She got up from her seat and hugged her father's neck.

Everyone told Henry how much they were going to miss him. They finished their meal, and Milton served coffee. That's when Henry excused himself from the table. A few minutes later, Henry returned with gifts. He handed small boxes to Lyric, Autumn, and Erica. The women were delighted. They could hardly contain their enthusiasm as they unwrapped and opened the presents.

"Daddy, this is gorgeous," Lyric said of the heart-shaped diamond encrusted pendant dangling from a platinum necklace. She stood up and kissed him on the cheek. Henry smiled proudly as he clasped the chain around Lyric's neck. She touched the jewelry as it rested against her chest.

When Autumn opened her gift, she marveled at the round ruby basket weave heart locket set in white gold. She thanked her grandfather.

Erica's jaw dropped when she saw the pear-shaped diamond stud earrings that Henry had gotten for her. "This is exquisite, Henry. You shouldn't have."

Henry smiled. "Just a token of my affection. I'm glad you all like your gifts." He turned to face Autumn. Looking her in the eyes, he said, "I'll bet you're wondering why I got you rubies instead of diamonds." Autumn crinkled her brow and nodded her head. "The Bible poses the question, *Who can find a virtuous woman? for her price is far above rubies*. I got you rubies to remind you that you're virtuous. Diamonds may cost more, but rubies are rare."

Autumn couldn't help but smile. She hugged Henry and asked him to help her put on her necklace. She promised to never take it off.

Although Michael had told Lyric that Henry was saved, Lyric was nonetheless surprised that he was familiar with the scripture Proverbs 31:10. Watching the interaction between Autumn and

Henry solidified Henry's place in Lyric's heart.
She genuinely loved him.

The following morning, Michael and Henry
had a private exchange. Lyric couldn't hear what
they were saying. Judging by the looks on their
faces, she knew it was serious. She wanted to
interrupt and find out what was going on. Out of
respect and consideration for her husband, she
decided against it. She figured that if Michael
wanted her to know, he'd tell her.

Not long afterward, the family ate breakfast
together and bid Henry a tearful farewell. Henry
vowed to keep in touch and not stay away too
long. As soon as Henry pulled out of the driveway, Lyric missed him.

Michael pulled Lyric to the side and told her
that he had confided in Henry about the situation with Nigel. Lyric was shocked, yet relieved.
At least now she was privy to their conversation.
She trusted Michael. If Michael trusted Henry
that much, then she believed in her spirit that
she could trust Henry too. Michael further
explained that he had given Henry the tracking
device to take back to Hilton Head with him.
They decided not to give it to the police because
they didn't think the police would do anything
about it. Therefore, Henry agreed to discard it.
They hoped it was enough to throw Nigel off.

Nigel checked the tracking system and was shocked to discover that Lyric was in Hilton Head, South Carolina. What was she doing there? he wondered. Were the twins with her? Had she finally wised up and left her husband? Was she coming back? He had more questions than answers. He needed to get to the bottom of this. It didn't make sense to him that she would travel so soon after giving birth. He was wound up, so he decided to take an impromptu trip to Hilton Head to see for himself.

Less than four hours later, Nigel arrived in Hilton Head. According to the tracker, Lyric was in an empty parking lot. He looked around and didn't see her car anywhere. None of it made sense. Then it dawned on him. Somebody must've discovered the tracker. The thought of someone trying to outsmart him infuriated him.

He thought about some of the people who associated with Lyric and would know her whereabouts. Dr. Little was at the top of his list. He quickly dismissed that notion because Lyric hadn't gone to see her in quite some time. Whatever she had been dealing with must've been resolved or more manageable, he reasoned.

He then thought about her best friend. Maybe if he followed her, he'd get some insight into what was going on with Lyric. He nixed that idea. He didn't have time to waste. He turned his car around and headed back to Georgia.

Suddenly it occurred to him. At some point Lyric would want to have a baby dedication for the boys at her church. Those things were usually scheduled in advance. He could pretend that he was a relative and call up to the church and find out if and when the Stokeses' baby dedication ceremony was scheduled.

He checked his watch. The time read 5:00 P.M. It was still business hours. He dialed information and got the telephone number to the church. He placed the call. When the church secretary answered, Nigel went on his fishing expedition.

"Hello, ma'am." Nigel sounded so polite. "My brother and his wife recently had twins and they mentioned getting the babies dedicated. They gave me the information, but I misplaced it." He chuckled. "Since I'm traveling from out of town, I want to make sure I have the right date and time. I'm too embarrassed to call my brother back and ask him again. Don't want him to think I'm irresponsible. Can you help me?"

"Sure," the lady said. "What's the family's name?"

Nigel breathed a sigh of relief. "The last name is Stokes."

There was a brief pause while the secretary checked the books. When she came back on the line, she informed Nigel that the dedication was in five weeks. As she rattled off the date and time, Nigel scribbled down the details on a piece of crumpled up paper from his console. At the end of the exchange, the secretary congratulated him, and he thanked her. Nigel got off the phone feeling smug. One point for him.

Twenty-seven

Lyric woke up feeling happy and excited. She snuggled up next to Michael who was lightly snoring. The twins were sleeping peacefully in their bassinets next to her bed. She could not believe that the boys were already two months old. Time had flown by. She had been exercising five days a week for the past five weeks. The baby weight was coming off slowly but surely. She still wore a girdle, but her stomach was noticeably smaller. She was glad that she and Michael had resumed having marital relations after getting the green light from her gynecologist at her six weeks checkup. She had missed the closeness that she felt whenever she and Michael had intimate encounters. Lyric felt a sense of normalcy. Her life was finally coming back together.

It was Sunday morning, and the boys were having their baby dedication ceremonies at church. She had their white smocked christening shortalls laid out with unisex christening booties. Since Lyric's favorite color was red, she insisted that family and friends all wear red to the ceremony.

Henry came back specifically for the occasion. He had arrived on Friday. Other family members who came from out-of-town included Lyric's eighty-year-old maternal grandmother, Mema, her mom's sister, Tiffany, Michael's two younger sisters, Mahogany and Malika, along with their husbands and five children between them.

Lyric's eight-bedroom house was filled to capacity. Having converted one of the rooms to an office, they were one bedroom short. Somehow they made it work. Mema and Aunty Tiffany shared a room. Mahogany and Malika shared rooms with their husbands. The girls all slept in Autumn's room. The two boys slept on the sofa bed in the nursery. One thing Lyric really liked was that her nieces and nephews were well-behaved. Erica allowed Henry to stay in the spare bedroom in the in-law suite.

Ordinarily, Lyric didn't like having a house full of people. She preferred not having to entertain guests all the time. It seemed like whenever people stayed over, Lyric went out of her way to make sure they were comfortable. She felt as if she were running a bed and breakfast. She had to cook, clean, and be hospitable. Having

Consuela and Milton's help made tending to the guests a lot easier. She really appreciated them, especially now.

The intercom next to her bed buzzed. She pressed the button and Milton announced that breakfast was ready. She nudged Michael, and he grunted. She shook him and told him that it was time to eat. They both got out of bed and went into the bathroom to splash water on their faces and brush their teeth.

Before leaving their bedroom, Michael slipped on a pair of lounge pants and a T-shirt. He picked up the baby monitor so that he could carry it downstairs. He wanted to be able to hear if the babies woke up while they were eating. Lyric wrapped her frame in a long, satin bathrobe. She checked on Landon and Logan. They were fine. Since she had fed them not that long ago, she figured they wouldn't wake up again until after she had eaten.

As soon as they opened the door, scrumptious smells engulfed their nostrils. Michael went downstairs. Lyric walked down the hall and knocked once on the closed bedroom doors, announcing that it was breakfast time. Her grandmother and aunt were already awake and fully dressed. She greeted them with hugs. They followed her downstairs.

Milton had really outdone himself, Lyric thought. He had a lavish spread fit for a queen. The menu was similar to the one at Lyric's baby shower. Additionally, there was miniature quiche, smoked salmon, hickory smoked country ham, bagels, and French toast.

When Milton saw her, they exchanged pleasantries. He acknowledged each guest as well. He informed them that the formal dining room had been set up for the adults. The casual dining area was for the children.

It didn't take long before everyone trickled into the eating areas, including Erica and Henry. Michael blessed the food, and everyone fended for themselves. Over breakfast, there was small talk about the christening and the importance of family.

Mema looked across the table at Lyric and said, "Suga, it does my heart good to see you and your daddy together. It dang near killed me to see you holding onto grudges for so long." She cleared her throat. "Lawd knows if I can forgive him for what he done, you sho' can. I prayed to the Lawd above that I'd live long enough to see the two of you come together. Ain't God good?" She said that more like a statement than a question.

The room had an uncomfortable silence. Everyone stuffed their mouths so that no one had to speak. Henry stared at his half-full plate. Finally, Tiffany said, "Momma, no one wants to hear about family drama. We're here for a special occasion. Let's focus on the positive." She shifted in her seat. "Lyric, I'm so proud of you. I know my sister would be proud of you too. It amazes me how much you're like your mother. Your mannerisms, and even your smile, are just like hers."

Henry glimpsed at Lyric from the corner of his eyes. She glanced back at him. With a warm smile, she said, "I'm my mother's child."

She didn't say that to hurt Henry. She was simply acknowledging the similarities. She realized that although she spent the bulk of her life trying to be different than her mother, she was a lot like her. Now that she had accepted that fact, it was easier for her to cherish her mother's memories.

For so long, Lyric blamed her mother for staying in an emotionally abusive relationship with an alcoholic. Because of that, she didn't respect her. When her mother died, Lyric was angry at her and partly blamed her. Lyric believed that if her mother had been strong enough to leave Henry, she'd still be alive. Therapy and prayer helped her overcome those feelings of resentment.

After breakfast, everyone got ready for the ceremony. Landon and Logan woke up, so Lyric breastfed them. When she finished, she and Erica washed up the babies and put on their clothes. Then Lyric got dressed.

When it was time to go, everyone got into their vehicles and formed a caravan. Michael drove the lead car. Everyone followed him to the church.

Once at the place of worship, Lyric and Michael met with the pastor briefly to discuss where they should stand during the ceremony. Afterward, they sat with the rest of their family and friends near the front in reserved seating. Lyric spotted Chloe and Keith, and waved at them.

When it came time to do the dedication services, the minister stood front and center in the sanctuary. Michael stood immediately to the pastor's right with Lyric standing next to her husband, and Autumn standing next to her. Lyric and Autumn each held a baby in their arms. The godparents, Chloe and Keith, along with Mema, Erica, and Henry, stood to the minister's left. The rest of the family members came forward. The minister acknowledged all of them.

The minister said, "Children are a gift from God. Psalm 127:3 proclaims that: *Sons are a heritage from the Lord, children are a reward from Him.* As believers we are called to recognize that children belong first and foremost to God. God in His goodness gives children as gifts to parents. They not only have the awesome responsibility of caring for this gift, but also the wonderful privilege of enjoying the gift. Because children belong to God and are given by grace as gifts to parents, it is only proper and appropriate that children be dedicated back to God.

"We are told in 1 Samuel 1 that Hannah presented her son, Samuel, to the Lord. In Luke 2:22 we read that Mary and Joseph brought their baby, Jesus, to the temple in Jerusalem in order to present Him before the Lord. In the same way, Lyric and Michael Stokes today bring their sons, Landon and Logan, presenting first themselves, and then their sons before the Lord our God.

"Accompanying them in making this commitment are Landon and Logan's godparents, Chloe and Keith Washington. And witnessing this as well is Autumn Stokes.

"Mr. and Mrs. Stokes, I call your attention to the commands of God recorded in Holy Scripture. Deuteronomy 6:4-7 tells us: *Hear O Israel: The Lord our God is one. Love the Lord your*

God with all your heart, and with all your soul, and with all your strength. These commandments that I give you today are to be upon your hearts. Impress them on their children. Talk about them when you sit at home and when you walk along the road, when you lie down and when you get up.

"Ephesians 6:4 says: . . . *fathers, do not provoke your children to wrath; instead, bring them up in the training and instruction of the Lord.* God's instructions are plain.

"Mr. and Mrs. Stokes, love God with every ounce and fiber of your energy and teach Landon and Logan to do the same. As you love God, one another, and Autumn, you will model before Landon and Logan a wonderful love for God that they will want for themselves.

"Mr. and Mrs. Stokes, by coming forward before God and His people, do you hereby declare your desire to dedicate yourselves and your sons, Landon and Logan, to the Lord? If so, please respond by saying 'we do.' "

In unison, Lyric and Michael said, "We do."

The preacher continued. "Having come freely, I ask now that you enter into the following commitment in the presence of God and His people." Lyric handed Landon to Michael as a sign of his spiritual headship in the family. "So that Landon

and Logan may walk in the abundant life that
Christ offers, do you, Mr. and Mrs. Stokes, vow
by God's help and in partnership with the church,
to provide Landon and Logan a Christian home
of love and peace, to raise them in the truth of
our Lord's instruction and discipline, and to
encourage them to one day trust Jesus Christ as
their Savior and Lord?"

"We do," Lyric and Michael said.

"Modeling this kind of love cannot be done
alone. It requires the help of others. For this
reason, Mr. and Mrs. Stokes call upon the help
of Chloe and Keith Washington. I now direct
my questions to you. By coming forward before
God and His people, do you hereby declare your
desire to help Lyric and Michael Stokes fulfill the
vow they have just made by becoming Landon
and Logan's godparents? If so, please respond by
saying 'we do.' "

Chloe and Keith replied, "We do."

"Having come freely, I ask now that you enter
into the following commitment: So that Landon
and Logan may walk in the abundant life that
Christ offers, do you vow by God's help, to encourage, through praise and correction, Mr. and
Mrs. Stokes in their effort to raise Landon and
Logan in the fear of the Lord, to uphold them in
prayer, and if anything should happen to Lyric

and Michael, to assume responsibility in helping Landon and Logan receive our Lord's guidance and instruction?"

In a serious tone, Chloe and Keith said, "We do."

"Finally, I ask that the church make a vow as well. There's an old proverb that says 'it takes a village to raise a child.' Parents have first responsibility. But parents need the help and support of the community. So I direct my questions now to the church. By being present in God's house today, do you hereby declare yourselves to be the children of God because you trust in Jesus Christ alone for the forgiveness of sins and the gift of eternal life? If this is true, please respond by saying 'we do.'"

The church collectively said, "We do."

"Would you please stand?" The pastor instructed the congregation, and they stood. "Having come freely, I ask now that you make the following commitment to those who stand before you: So that Landon and Logan may walk in the abundant life that Christ offers, do you vow by God's help, to be faithful in your calling as members of the body of Christ, to help Lyric and Michael Stokes be faithful to God, and to help teach and train Landon and Logan in the ways of the Lord so that they might one day trust Him as Savior and Lord? If you accept this responsibility, please respond by saying 'we do.'"

The congregation said, "We do."

At the end of the liturgy, Lyric silently thanked God for her precious gifts, Logan and Landon. As she and her family exited the sanctuary, her eyes locked with Nigel's. He was coming out of the restroom. Lyric yelped, almost dropping Logan. He stood there, staring at her with a scowl on his face. Lyric handed the baby to Chloe and asked her to take the family outside.

When the coast was clear, Lyric hurried over to Nigel with Michael nipping at her heels. He tried to grab her arm, but she jerked away from him. Standing inches away from Nigel's face, she yelled, "How dare you harass me in a place of worship." Then she spit in his face.

He wiped the saliva away with the sleeve of his shirt. She inched away from Nigel, never taking her eyes off of him. Michael stepped between them in an intimidating stance. He didn't speak. Instead, he balled his fists, clenched his jaw, and stared into Nigel's eyes.

A crowd gathered and one of the associate ministers broke through to find out what was going on. Nigel cut his eyes at the minister.

Without missing a beat, Lyric said, "This guy is a stalker and he has an active restraining order against him."

Nigel raised a brow. He seemed surprised and disappointed by Lyric's outburst. Without saying a word, he left abruptly.

Lyric felt her insides quiver as Michael grabbed her hand and escorted her out of the church. "You should've waited for me before going up to him," he said.

"I'm sorry," she said sincerely. "I just got caught up in the heat of the moment." She squeezed his hand. "When I saw him, I lost it."

Chloe walked up to them. "Are you all right?"

Lyric hugged her friend. "I'll be fine." She sighed. "I'm not going to let him ruin my mood or this day. I refuse to give that nutcase any power over me."

They started walking in the direction of their cars. "What was he doing here?" Chloe asked.

"He didn't say. He just stood there looking stupid," Lyric explained.

Chloe shook her head. "No one in your family suspected anything. I told them that you and Michael wanted to talk to the pastor alone. They didn't question it."

They both thanked Chloe for her tact. Lyric appreciated Chloe's thoughtfulness. Thinking quickly on her feet was one of Chloe's strengths, and Lyric liked that about her.

When they made it to their cars, Lyric spotted Nigel's work van as it came around the corner. Goosebumps popped up on her arms. Her fine hairs stood at attention. She wished she had a brick; she would've thrown it at him.

Twenty-eight

Lyric, Chloe, Vendela, and Skyler spent their Saturday morning at the country club. Skyler had recently joined the club. She immediately notified Lyric. When Lyric found out, she invited Skyler to hang out with her and her friends. That was Skyler's first outing with the other ladies. They paired up and played a game of doubles tennis. Lyric and Chloe won two out of three sets.

After running around the court and breaking a sweat, the ladies went into the locker room and showered. They then went into the dining room for breakfast.

Vendela sipped her cranberry juice. "I think it's great that Lyric and Chloe have gone into business together."

"I couldn't agree more," Skyler said, buttering a piece of wheat toast. "So tell us more about this venture."

Lyric and Chloe exchanged glances. Lyric said, "After I got my six-week check-up, we got our business license. I turned my basement into an office. We have everything." She sounded excited. "Business line, fax line, computer, color laser printer, copier, business cards, stationery, and lots of wedding books." She chuckled. "Now all we need are clients."

Chloe sliced a piece of her strawberry crepe with her fork and took a bite. "We're going to place ads in Atlanta-based bridal magazines. We're also planning to participate in bridal shows." She dangled her fork in the air. "We're currently in the process of establishing relationships with event rental companies, banquet halls, caterers, florists, photographers, and videographers. That way we can utilize them, and they can refer people to us."

"Good for you," Vendela said. "Word-of-mouth can be the best advertising. And it's free." They laughed. She reached inside her purse and pulled out a small notepad and ink pen. "My sister, Kayla, recently got engaged. Here's her phone number." She jotted down the information. "Be sure to let her know that I referred you." She handed the paper to Lyric.

Accepting the note, Lyric said, "Girl, thank you." She folded the sheet and tucked it in her purse.

"Hasn't she been living with the same guy for the past four years?" Chloe asked.

Vendela stuffed her mouth with mixed fruit. "Yes. According to my sister, they wanted to wait until she graduated from law school before tying the knot. I guess that gave him enough time to get whatever was in his system out. He's finally ready to commit. Or at least he says he is." She rolled her eyes. "You know how those NBA players can be."

"She's marrying a baller?" Skyler asked, wiping the corners of her mouth.

"He plays for the Atlanta Hawks." She eyed Lyric. "So you know that'll be good for business. High-profile clientele always adds a certain level of prestige to any organization." She smacked her lips. "Just think about the referrals you'll get. And the media coverage." Lyric nodded her head, imagining the possibilities. "Like I always say, it's not what you know, but who you know." She turned and faced Skyler. This was her second time meeting her. The first time they met was at Lyric's baby shower. "So, Skyler, how did you become a psychoanalyst?"

Skyler placed her fork on her plate and gave a broad smile. "My dad had, and still has, a great influence on me. He has a PhD and was a rocket scientist."

"A rocket scientist?" Vendela sounded intrigued.

"Yes," Skyler said. "I realized at an early age that I liked smart men and that I wanted to be smart. My dad and I would read the newspaper together and discuss current events. He would tell me that there was nothing more attractive than a beautiful woman with brains." She sipped her coffee. "That stuck with me. I studied hard and graduated from high school when I was fourteen years old. I went straight to college at my mom's alma mater, New York University. After graduating, I attended NYU School of Medicine. Then I enrolled in the NYU Psychoanalytic Institute." She rested her hands on the table. "I decided to become a psychoanalyst because the human mind fascinated me. I liked thinking outside of the box and helping people. It gave me a sense of accomplishment. I felt as if my life had purpose, meaning."

"And tell them how you met your hot, sexy, fine husband, Donovan," Lyric said, propping her elbows on the table and holding her face in her hands. Chloe threw her cloth napkin at her, playfully reprimanding her for her comment. "What?" Lyric feigned innocence. They all laughed.

Skyler assured her that she had taken no offense to Lyric's remark. She admitted that she totally agreed with Lyric's assessment of her husband. She then explained how they met. Taking another sip of coffee, Skyler said, "Donovan and I met six years ago while we were both living in New York. I was twenty-eight, and he was thirty. I was working as an assistant clinical professor at NYU. We were at a Jewish deli located on Second Avenue in the East Village. While we were waiting for our lunch orders, we struck up casual conversation and ended up sitting together." She had a pleasant look on her face as she appeared to remember fondly. "Donovan told me that his family had migrated from Jamaica to New York during the Jamaican slave trade. He had a PhD and worked as a product development chemist."

"Fine and smart," Chloe teased.

Laughing, Skyler said, "I was immediately attracted to him because—it's true—women are attracted to men who remind them of their fathers."

"That's sweet," Vendela interjected.

Skyler looked at Vendela and Chloe. "I already know how Lyric and Michael met. Please tell me how the two of you met your husbands."

Vendela parted her lips and exhaled. "Well, my story was no fairytale." She shook her head. "When Carlton and I met, he was already married and had two kids." She halted her hand. "No, we didn't have an affair. I worked as a paralegal at his law firm. He was fifteen years older than me. I wasn't immediately attracted to him. Not because he wasn't attractive." She leaned back in her cushiony seat. "My mother raised me to believe that messing with another woman's man was a no-no. As long as he was married, there was no chance he was going to get with me." She tossed her shoulder-length hair over her shoulder. "So we became platonic friends." She took a sip of ice water and moved a piece of ice around in her mouth until it melted.

"About six months later, he told me that he was filing for divorce." She chuckled. "I actually tried to talk him out of it." With a faraway look in her eyes, Vendela continued. "My parents got divorced when I was young, and I know firsthand how much the kids suffer. I encouraged him to try and work it out. He promised that he would. At least he did until he found out his wife was having an affair with a friend of his." She looked at the ladies. "After that, all bets were off. We started seeing each other and got married a year later."

"Wow," was all Skyler could say. "Did his children accept you?"

"Eventually," Vendela admitted. "The typical stepparent stuff." She shrugged.

"Do you have any children of your own?" Skyler asked.

Vendela shook her head. "Carlton didn't want anymore." She sighed. "That's fine with me, though. He has a ten-year-old daughter and eight-year-old son. I love those children very much. When I get the occasional feelings of nurturing, I take it out on them," she said sincerely.

"Don't break out the violins," Lyric joked, looking at Vendela. "You're only twenty-nine years old, and you have more money than you could ever spend. On top of that, your husband adores you. Kids or no kids, you're the baddest chick. And you've got the flattest abs to prove it."

They erupted with laughter. When the laughing died down, everyone looked at Chloe, waiting for her to share her relationship story.

"I guess I'm next," Chloe said. "Keith and I met at a night club." She laughed. "That was before either of us was saved," she clarified. "We dated on and off for two years before deciding to get married. Neither of us had ever been married before, and we didn't have any kids. We went down to the courthouse and did it. No frills, no thrills, no bells and whistles. As a matter-of-fact, we were so casual with the whole thing that I wore a pink jogging suit, and he wore jeans."

"You're kidding," Vendela said.

"Nope. We were young and in love." With a starry look in her eyes, she said, "We were foolish enough to think that was enough." She raised a brow. "Since we both only worked part-time, we had to move in with his momma. It didn't take long before we realized that love wasn't enough. We were broke all the time. We literally had to go around the house scraping coins together just to have enough money to go to the movies. We got tired of that mess. So we both went back to school. At the time I had an associate's degree. Keith had finished three years of college. I majored in nursing so that I could land a good paying job while Keith was in med school. That's my story."

Vendela flexed her wrist and checked her watch. "As much as I love kickin' it with you ladies, I must leave you now." She stood up. "I have an appointment for a facial." Blowing kisses at them, she said, "Kiss, kiss," and left.

"I should probably get going too," Chloe announced, scooting back her chair. She stood and hugged both ladies before leaving.

"You're not in a hurry, are you?" Skyler asked Lyric.

"Not really. Michael told me to enjoy myself and not worry about the twins. He's helping his mom, and Autumn is helping him."

"Good. That gives us a chance to talk." She leaned in closer and said, "So what's been going on?"

Lyric looked around to make sure no one was eavesdropping on their conversation. When she felt comfortable that no one else was listening, she lowered her voice and said, "Is this on the clock or off the clock?"

"Just two friends talking," Skyler assured her.

Lyric went on to tell her about Nigel placing a tracking device on her car, the paternity issues with her sons, Nigel showing up at the babies' dedication ceremony, and her reconciliation with Henry.

Skyler was floored. "I don't even know where to begin." Lyric could tell her mental wheels were rolling. "So what happened to the tracker?"

"Michael admitted to me that he had given the tracker to my dad for him to take back to South Carolina with him. He wanted to throw Nigel off my scent."

Staring Lyric intently in the eyes, Skyler said, "Now that Nigel has seen the babies, he's going to up the ante, raise the stakes. He's going to do whatever it takes to be with you." She bit the corner of her lip. "I wouldn't put anything past him now. He's desperate. Nigel thrives on control. Right now he realizes that he's not in control." She reached out and grabbed Lyric's hand. "You need to be extra careful. Don't go anywhere alone. Not even to run simple errands."

Lyric tilted her head to the side. "I'm tired of this," she admitted.

"I know." Skyler sighed. "I shudder to think what he had in store for me the day he attacked me at my birthday party. It still gives me chills." She gave a faint smile. "I'm praying for you." She squeezed her hand and continued. "You know that if you need me, I'm here for you."

Lyric extended her arms and hugged her. "I know." She couldn't help but wonder when the nightmare would finally be over.

Twenty-nine

Lyric and Chloe were excited about their meeting with Kayla. It was the week of Thanksgiving. Erica had taken the two-and-a-half-month-old twins for a stroll at the park. Autumn was at school. Michael was at work. Milton prepared finger sandwiches and punch to be served upon Kayla's arrival.

Prior to the scheduled in-person meeting, Lyric had faxed Kayla a pre-wedding planning questionnaire for her to complete and fax back. Based on Kayla's answers, Lyric was able to put together ideas for possible locations, a theme, and color scheme. She had stacks of bridal books on-hand.

Lyric and Chloe waited in the sitting room. They chatted briefly about their ideas for Kayla's wedding. The doorbell rang, interrupting their conversation. Lyric answered. She was surprised to see Vendela standing next to Kayla. Vendela's five feet seven frame appeared to be much taller than usual standing next to Kayla, who looked every bit of five feet three with heels on. Although short in stature, Kayla had a larger than life persona. She was a walking billboard for the latest fashion designers. Everything from her large sunglasses to oversized handbag was name brand. And she wore an expensive looking, 100% human hair weave that stopped at her waist.

Extending her hand, Lyric said, "It's nice to meet you, Kayla." They shook hands. "Come on in." As both women entered the house, Lyric said to Vendela, "I wasn't expecting to see you today."

Doing her best Jimmy Walker impression from the seventies sitcom, *Good Times,* Vendela said, "Well, you know, what can I say. I had to support my little sister. I couldn't leave her hanging."

Kayla giggled and playfully tapped her sister on the arm. "Can't take you anywhere."

The scent of Kayla's sweet-smelling perfume lingered in the air. Lyric showed them to the sitting room, and Chloe greeted them. The sisters sat next to each other on the couch. Milton entered, carrying refreshments. As Milton exited the room, Vendela checked him out. Her eyes seemed fixated on his broad shoulders and muscular arms. She twisted her mouth. "Nice, very nice." She was obviously admiring Milton's good looks.

"Don't make me call Carlton," Lyric teased. "Now let's get down to business." She retrieved some papers from a manila folder. Looking over the paperwork, she said to Kayla, "You've given me some general information about your wedding day, let's get some specifics." She picked up her favorite Montblanc writing instrument. "Tell me your vision for your wedding day."

Kayla seemed reflective for a moment. "Ever since I was a little girl, I dreamed of my wedding day. My dress has got to make me look like a princess. I want romance and elegance. I plan to have a large bridal party with at least 250 guests." She paused for a moment. "Remember the wedding scene in Tyler Perry's movie, *Madea's Family Reunion?*" They all nodded. "Something like that would be perfect for me. That had to be one of the most beautiful and luxurious weddings I think I've ever seen."

The other ladies agreed. Lyric took notes. Vendela munched on a sandwich.

"That helps," Lyric said, sipping on some rainbow sherbert and ginger ale punch. "When we spoke, you said that you didn't have a firm date yet. Has that changed?"

She grabbed a sandwich. "Yes. We want to get married on New Year's Day."

"Not *this* New Year's," Lyric and Vendela said in unison.

"Of course not," Kayla laughed. "We have over a year to plan."

Lyric breathed a sigh of relief. They went on to discuss the wedding budget, food, liquor, and music. They looked through a slew of pictures to get a feel for the right gown, headpiece, bridesmaid dresses, and flowers. Kayla joked that she wasn't trying to break any records for having the longest train. Especially since none of the record holders stayed married. The ladies got a kick out of that. They completely agreed with her decision. They went on to pick out a color scheme and theme. As for the location, Kayla wanted a church wedding. She was receptive to the idea of having the reception at a banquet hall.

Lyric was happy with the progress they had made. She felt confident that she and Chloe would be able to pull off the event. Two hours later, Kayla signed a contract, hiring Lyric and Chloe as her official wedding planners. Additionally, she wrote a sizeable check to get the ladies started.

As soon as Kayla and Vendela walked out the door, Lyric and Chloe jumped up and down, screaming. They could no longer contain their excitement. Milton rushed into the foyer and

asked if they were all right. Lyric assured him
that they were fine. She shared with him the
good news. He congratulated them. Lyric then
asked him to fill two champagne glasses with
sparkling apple cider so that they could toast to
their success. He did as he was told.

Lyric and Chloe stood in the kitchen and
clanked their glasses together. "To the beginning
of great things," Lyric said. Chloe concurred, and
they sipped their drinks. They were so elated that
they were tempted not to cash their first business
check. After second thought, they cancelled that
notion. Instead, they went into the office and
made a copy of the bank draft and framed it.

Thirty

It was Thanksgiving Day. Henry had arrived that morning, and he and Lyric were sitting in the media room talking. Nearly three weeks had passed since they had seen each other. He expressed his concerns to her.

"La La," he said.

That was the nickname he created for her when she was little. He used to call her that and she loved it. Hearing him say it again made her feel as if their relationship had progressed to the next level. No one else called her that. It had been so long since she'd heard it; she almost forgot he even referred to her that way. She felt comfortable with him. The more time she spent with him, the more convinced she became that he was a changed man. She had developed genuine feelings for her father. She loved him. And she trusted him. In her heart, she knew he had her best interest, as well as that of her family's.

Henry continued. "I've been worried about you."

"Why?" She eyed him incredulously.

He held both of her hands. "Michael told me about Nigel when I first came to visit." She sat quietly and listened. "I know what he did to you, and I know about the twins." He squeezed her hands. "Keeping that secret was eating Michael alive. He needed someone to talk to; someone that would keep his confidence. I'm the only person he told." He put his arm around her. "And I'll take it to my grave." He kissed the top of her head. "He also gave me the tracking device so that I could get rid of it. He wanted to go to the police, but I convinced him not to. Without proof, that was just one more thing to get frustrated about." He rubbed his hand along her arm. "I'm here for you, La La. Whatever you need, just tell me. Daddy's here."

His words warmed her heart. She felt as safe and protected in his embrace as she did in Michael's. She was convinced that he truly loved her the way a father should love his daughter . . . that agape kind of love. She believed wholeheartedly that Henry would do anything, or sacrifice everything, for her.

Lyric made the rounds of calling family members and friends to wish them a happy Thanksgiving. Since Malika and Mahogany had flown down from Las Vegas, Nevada, and San

Fernando Valley, California, respectively, just weeks earlier for the baby dedications, they both decided to skip Thanksgiving and come back for Christmas. They were a close-knit family. Their mother expected them to spend at least one of the major holidays with her every year. They happily obliged.

For the past two years, Mema hadn't been as mobile as she used to be. She had knee and hip replacement surgeries. Lyric knew that she wouldn't be back for Thanksgiving. She hadn't expected her to travel again so soon after visiting just weeks prior. She was thankful that she had been able to attend the ceremony.

Lyric had wanted to have Mema move in with her and her family so that she could recuperate after the first surgery, but Aunt Tiffany stepped up to the plate. She rented out her condo in Buckhead and moved into her mother's house in Columbia, South Carolina. Whenever Lyric was going to visit Mema or Mema was coming to visit her, Lyric eagerly anticipated spending time with her. Being around Mema made Lyric feel like a kid again. Besides that, she made the best sweet potato pies they had ever eaten. No one else's pies even compared.

When Lyric finished making her phone calls, she went into the nursery. She asked Autumn to

help her with the babies. Lyric sat in the rocking
chair and sang lullabies as she nursed Logan.
Sitting in a comfy chair, Autumn fed Landon
with a bottle. His tiny hand gripped her finger.

Once the babies had their fill, Lyric and Autumn washed them up and put on their clothes.
When they finished, they kissed them on their
chubby cheeks and lay the boys in their bassinettes.

Lyric looked at the clock on the nursery wall.
It read eleven o'clock. Chloe and her clan were
supposed to come over at one. Besides Keith
and Heavyn, Chloe was bringing her mother,
Mrs. Lovejoy. Lyric figured that she had enough
time to get a workout in, so she changed into a
sports bra and spandex pants. She went into her
home gym and got on the elliptical trainer for
thirty minutes. She did some weight lifting and
abdominal exercises. Afterward, she showered
and changed into a white and blue knee length
dress with a thick belt to give the illusion of a
smaller waistline. Her hair was still pretty long,
so she brushed it and wore it straight down. She
walked around the house in a pair of fuzzy pink
house-slippers. She didn't like to put on shoes
until she absolutely had to. Oftentimes that
meant five minutes before guests were expected
to arrive.

She went downstairs. Consuela had the house sparkling from top to bottom. Michael and Henry were in the library discussing the Greek Classics. She made her way into the kitchen. Her mouth watered at the mere aroma of the Cajun turkey. Milton and Erica were putting the finishing touches on the meal. Clearly Milton didn't need Erica's help, but she insisted. She wanted to feel as though she had contributed to the festivities, so she made a broccoli casserole.

"The food looks and smells good," Lyric said. "The guests will be here shortly." She poured herself a cup of eggnog and took a sip. "Mmmm. This is some of the best nog I've ever tasted." She licked her lips.

Milton smiled proudly. "Family recipe."

Erica chimed in. "Milton and I have been getting acquainted." She patted him on the back. "I thought I was a good cook." She laughed. "Milton has taught me a thing or two. He really knows his way around the kitchen."

"That's why we hired him," Lyric said playfully, draining her cup. The milky drink tasted so good she felt like licking the remnants from the porcelain. "Erica, you make a mean casserole, but I'm surprised Milton let you anywhere near the kitchen. He prefers to do it all, alone."

Erica boasted. "I can be quite persuasive when I want to be."

Not long afterward, Chloe arrived with her crew. Keith joined Henry and Michael in the library. It was a warm seventy degrees outside, so Autumn and Heavyn sat around the outdoor swimming pool, dipping their feet in the water. The ladies went into the family room and chatted. It was Erica's first time meeting Chloe's mom, Juanita. Lyric had met her lots of times. Whenever she was in Florida, she tried to stop by and visit Juanita. It didn't matter whether Chloe was with her or not. She also saw Juanita during Juanita's Atlanta stops.

"So, Juanita, did you drive or fly from Florida?" Erica asked.

In a breathy tone, Juanita said, "I flew. I can't stand that long drive." She massaged her knee. "Being cramped up that long is bad for my knees."

"I understand," Erica said.

Lyric could tell that Erica was trying to get a feel for Juanita. Juanita looked like the definition of fun. She had big, curly hair, a face full of make-up, and colorful clothes. One could tell just by looking at her that she was a real beauty in her day. There was nothing understated about her. She didn't look tacky. In fact, she looked vibrant and full of personality. Her style worked for her.

Juanita clapped her hands. "Put on some music. This is supposed to be a family gathering. Let's get this party started." She stood up and pretended to dance by herself. "Liven it up."

Lyric and Chloe laughed. They were used to her antics. They knew that she didn't mean any harm. Erica had a look of sheer horror on her face. Lyric wanted to tell Erica to chill and not judge Juanita.

Several years ago, Juanita had a brain aneurysm. By the grace of God, she survived. The doctors told her that she should've been dead. After completing physical therapy and speech therapy, Juanita's life changed. She promised to live each day to the fullest. She told Chloe and Lyric that she was going to take advantage of the second chance at life God had given her. They saw an immediate change in her. She became more outgoing. If she felt like doing something, she did it. If she felt like going out, she went. She seemed to enjoy her life.

Lyric picked up the remote and turned on the TV. She selected the music channel, R&B and Soul. As the melodic tunes played in the background, the men entered the room.

"What's all the ruckus about?" Michael asked.

Just as Lyric was about to speak, Juanita froze in her tracks. Juanita covered her open mouth with her hands. Staring at Henry, she finally said, "Henry Alexander! What in the world are you doing here?" She let out a loud squeal before leaping into his arms. She wrapped her slender arms around his neck and planted a wet kiss on his cheek.

Lyric and Chloe exchanged perplexed expressions. Chloe shrugged her shoulders and mouthed the word, "What?"

Henry placed his hands around Juanita's waist and gently pushed her off him. "Juanita?"

"In the flesh." She did a model turn. "What's it been? Ten years?"

Henry scratched his head. "At least."

Lyric couldn't take it any longer. "How do the two of you know each other?" she demanded.

Henry and Juanita looked devilishly at one another. "Ahem." Henry pretended to clear his throat. He looked at his daughter who was staring at him, waiting for an answer. "We're old friends."

Juanita playfully punched him on the arm. "Who are you calling old?"

"Definitely not you, babe." He winked at her.

"Dad," Lyric said, inserting her arm through his, ushering him into the other room, "come with me." They entered the sitting room, and Lyric interrogated him. "What's up with you and Chloe's mom?"

"Chloe's mom?" He plopped down in a chair. Lyric kneeled down beside him. "Look, La La, I'm not going to lie to you. Juanita and I met while I was in Saint Petersburg visiting a friend of mine. He owned a yacht and threw a party. Juanita was one of the guests. There was chemistry between us. We ended up spending my remaining days in Florida together. Nothing ever came of it because of the distance."

"So," she said carefully, "were you and Juanita intimate friends?"

"That's not your business," he said seriously. "I never claimed to be a saint." He patted her on top of her head and stood up. "I had no way of knowing she was your friend's mom. Let's get back in there." He reached out his hand; she accepted. They walked back into the family room together.

Autumn and Heavyn came in; they wanted to know when dinner was going to be served. Lyric was still in shock. The thought of her father messing around with Chloe's mom made her stomach churn. She realized that Henry probably hadn't been living like a monk for all these years, but Juanita? Of all the people on the planet, why did he have to make the beast with two backs with her best friend's mom? That was so nasty, she thought. Every time she looked at the two of them, she imagined them in compromising positions. She couldn't help but wonder what attracted the two. Was it purely physical? she wondered. Admittedly, Juanita was attractive. But her personality was a direct contrast to Lyric's mom. Maybe it was their past addictions that bonded them. She pondered the thought. She turned her attention toward Autumn.

"I'll let Milton know that we're ready to eat," Lyric said.

Everyone congregated into the dining room. Michael blessed the food. Over dinner, Michael and Keith shared their latest surgery successes. Henry talked about boats. Although Lyric couldn't keep her mind off Henry and Juanita, she noticed that Erica wasn't saying much. She seemed deep in thought. Her eyes occasionally darted back and forth between the unlikely pair. There was a certain sadness in her eyes that led Lyric to believe that her feelings were hurt. Or was that disappointment? Lyric couldn't help but wonder whether there was something going on between Henry and Erica.

Thirty-one

After the Thanksgiving Day drama, Lyric and Chloe had a heart-to-heart talk about their parents' rendezvous. They both agreed that whatever happened between their parents was in the past and none of their business. They had a good laugh about it.

For weeks following, Lyric and Chloe worked tirelessly on Kayla's wedding plans. They were trying to accomplish as much as they could before businesses closed for the Christmas holiday. While meeting with vendors, they were given referrals, resulting in two more clients. They were elated. In honor of their achievements, they went to lunch at Chloe's favorite restaurant, City Grill in downtown Atlanta. Chloe ordered Grouper, and Lyric chose grilled tenderloin wedge. When they finished their meal, they walked out to the street. A guy dressed in a holey, perspiration stained, long john shirt with baggy jeans and a twisted belt approached them.

They immediately clutched their purses. The guy looked like a crack-head. Lyric positioned her keys between her index and middle fingers. She was prepared to use them as a makeshift weapon.

"Hey," the dirty looking man with a scruffy beard said; his breath assaulted her nostrils. The smell of week old garbage, two-day old cabbage, and an old batch of collard greens came to Lyric's mind as her eyes watered. The foul stench of his breath was competing with all of them. "This is for you." He held an envelope in his hand. He smiled, revealing yellow teeth; one of his front teeth had a gold trim. Lyric found it hard to believe that he had ever sat in a dentist's chair, especially since his teeth looked like they hadn't been brushed in at least six months.

Holding her breath and taking a step backward, Lyric halted her hand and shook her head. She was indicating no to more than just the envelope. She was wondering how someone's breath could smell so awful. She felt like saying, "Stop talking and get your stink breath out of my face." Instead, Chloe spoke for both of them. "No, thanks," she said. They tried to walk away.

"A guy gave me twenty-dollars to give this to you," he insisted, shoving the envelope at her.

Refusing to accept it, the parcel fell on the ground. Lyric looked at the guy as if he were on crack. She wasn't about to pick it up. For all she knew, it could've been laced with a bomb or anthrax. "I don't want it," Lyric said sternly. She ushered Chloe by the arm and they hurried away.

Both ladies looked over their shoulders, making sure the guy hadn't followed them. He didn't. They made it to their car and locked the doors behind them.

"What was that about?" Lyric said. Her hand trembled as she placed the key in the ignition.

"I don't know, but that guy scared the daylights out of me. I couldn't tell if he wanted to rob us or ask us for some money." She looked around, making sure the guy was nowhere in sight. He wasn't.

Lyric backed out of the parking lot and headed to I-75 going south. She then got on I-20 east. She drove to her house. She and Chloe still had more work to do.

Once at home, Lyric noticed an unfamiliar car parked in front of her house. "Erica must have company," Lyric said, pulling into her driveway.

As soon as the ladies entered the house, they were shocked and appalled by what they saw.

Erica smiled and said, "Nigel stopped by to drop off some Christmas gifts for the twins. He told me that—"

Cutting Erica off before she could finish her statement, Lyric said, "I don't care what he told you. Get that mad man out of my house."

Erica's eyes widened to the size of half-dollars. She began to stutter. Nigel picked up his jacket. "I didn't mean to upset you. I'll leave."

Chloe pulled out her cell phone and snapped a picture of him. "Want me to call the police?" she asked Lyric.

"Yes." She never took her eyes off Nigel. "He's violating his restraining order."

Chloe dialed 9-1-1.

"There's no need for things to get ugly." He raised his hands in surrender. "I just came over to see my kids and drop off some presents."

"*Your* kids?" Lyric and Erica said in unison, emphasizing the word your.

"Obviously you didn't read the note I sent, telling you that I'd be here when you got home." He looked at Erica. "You didn't know? I'm the father of those babies."

Erica grabbed her chest as if she were having heart palpitations. Lyric felt as if she were having an out of body experience. She picked up a lamp and tossed it at Nigel's head. He moved out of the way, causing the lamp to hit the fireplace and shatter. She ran over to him and started clawing at his face and eyes.

"Hurry up and get here!" Chloe yelled after giving the authorities her information. She hung up and joined Lyric in her attack on Nigel. Erica picked up the babies and moved them out of the way.

"I'll kill you for spreading such lies," Lyric screamed.

"What's all the commotion?" Milton asked as he entered the room. When he saw Lyric and Chloe punching and kicking Nigel, he stepped in. He tried to pull the women off of Nigel.

"Don't grab us!" Chloe said. "Grab him. He's the perverted stalker."

"Say what?" Milton snatched Nigel up by his collar. "Did he hurt you, Mrs. Stokes?" he said, staring boldly into Nigel's dark eyes. He seemed to be saying, "Give me a reason to punch his lights out."

"He did," Lyric admitted. Her throat was scratchy, and she sounded hoarse. "We've already called the cops." She repeated that Nigel was in violation of his restraining order. She adjusted her disheveled clothing.

Nigel kneed Milton in the groin. Milton doubled over in pain. "Get your hands off me," Nigel fumed. He gave a sadistic smile. Lyric thought he was going to try and kill her. She prayed that he didn't have a gun. "Lyric, I've done nothing but love your crazy self." He pointed a finger at her. "I'm telling you now. You're pushing me to the limit. You're trying my patience." The whites of Nigel's eyes were red. Milton stood up and punched Nigel in the gut and in his right eye. Nigel fell flat on his back. As soon as he hit the ground, he made a moaning sound, and his body jerked several times. Then he passed out.

Erica placed the babies back in their bassinettes. When Lyric heard the police sirens in the background, she couldn't open the door fast enough to let them in. The police entered and Nigel was still knocked out. One of the officers immediately called the paramedics, and the other handcuffed Nigel.

The officers then took statements from all of the conscious people in the room.

Lyric went first. "I have no idea what Nigel was doing here. All I know is that when my friend Chloe and I came home, Nigel was waiting. My mother-in-law had let him in." She pressed her lips together. "He violated the restraining order that I have against him."

Erica chimed in. "The only reason I let him in was because he told me that he was a friend of my son and daughter-in-law. He had an armful of gifts for the twins and seemed pleasant enough, so I believed him. He wasn't even here for thirty minutes before Lyric came back." Her eyes became misty. "Lord knows I never would've let him in here had I known the truth." She hung her head. "I'm so sorry."

Lyric patted her hand and assured her that it wasn't her fault. Nigel moaned again. He seemed to be waking up. The paramedics arrived and examined him. While the paramedics tended to Nigel, Chloe and Milton gave their statements. Chloe echoed everything Lyric had said. The only thing she added was that she was the person who called the police.

Milton backed up Erica's recollection of events. He explained that he was in the kitchen and heard the exchange between Erica and Nigel at the door. He further explained that he did not realize there was a problem until he heard raised voices coming from the family room.

The police didn't even bother to ask how the fight started. The fact that Nigel had violated a restraining order and was on the property illegally was enough for them to haul him in. Besides the bruises, the paramedics didn't find anything seriously wrong with Nigel. Especially after he tried to break free. The police took him into custody and off the premises.

***

Erica and Chloe decided to stay with Lyric a while longer. Once Milton was convinced that Lyric was all right, he went back to preparing dinner. Lyric excused herself so that she could call Michael at work. He was with a patient, so she hung up without leaving a message. Although she was highly upset, she figured it was probably best to tell Michael what happened face-to-face. When she re-entered the room with Erica and Chloe, she told them that Michael had been unavailable and that she'd talk to him when he got home.

"After that episode, I almost feel like taking a drink," Erica said half-jokingly.

"You don't drink," Lyric admonished.

"I know. That should tell you how bad it was."

Chloe chimed in. "I second that."

Lyric was relieved that Erica hadn't pried and asked her why she had a restraining order against Nigel. She wasn't ready to disclose that bit of information to her just yet.

Consuela had gone grocery shopping and to pick up the dry cleaning during the entire Nigel saga. When she got back, they helped her clean up the mess. She didn't ask any questions.

No longer in the mood to concentrate on work, Lyric suggested the three of them watch a movie in the twelve-seat home theatre. They watched the dramatic comedy, *The Women*.

After watching the film, Chloe realized that it was close to time for Heavyn to come home from school, so she left. When Autumn got home, she greeted her mother and grandmother with hugs. She checked on her adorable baby brothers and kissed them. They were asleep. Autumn grabbed a snack from the fridge and went to her room to complete her homework. As soon as Michael walked through the door, Erica said her goodbyes and went to her quarters.

Without giving Michael a chance to relax and unwind, Lyric said, "You will never believe the kind of day I had." She sighed.

He had a concerned look on his face. "What's wrong?"

"Well, it started out as a good day." She plopped on the couch. "Chloe and I went out to lunch to celebrate getting some new clients. As soon as we left the restaurant, some guy looking like a crack addict stepped to us, trying to shove an envelope in my face."

Michael loosened his tie. Sitting next to Lyric on the couch, he said, "Are you serious?"

She nodded her head. "We hurried up and got away from him. But wait," she held up a finger, "it gets worse."

He squeezed the bridge of his nose. "I'm almost scared to hear it."

"When we got to the house, you'll never guess who was here with your mother and the boys."

Exhaling, Michael said, "Who?"

Lyric grabbed his hands and looked him in the eye. She went on to tell him all about Nigel showing up at the house with gifts, how he paid the guy to deliver the envelope to her, the brawl, including Nigel getting knocked out by Milton, and the police taking Nigel away.

"Now that's some mess," Michael said, shaking his head. "Why didn't you call me?"

"I did, but you were with a patient. I didn't leave a message."

He sighed. "I'll have to thank Milton for stepping in and being a man. Is everybody all right?"

"For the most part," she admitted. "We were pretty shaken up." She paused for a moment. "What are we going to tell your mother? I'm sure she has a lot of questions."

He smoothed his goatee. "We almost *have* to tell her now." He pressed his back against the cushioned surface.

"You were the victim of a crime. What happened to you wasn't your fault. It's not like you had an affair and brought a baby home. We don't have anything to be ashamed about. Neither one of us did anything wrong." He touched the side of Lyric's face. "Every family has secrets. I'm telling you now; Logan is not going to be our dirty little secret." His tone sounded serious. "I love Logan just as much as I do Autumn and Landon, maybe even more."

Lyric tilted her head. She had a look of surprise on her face. "What do you mean, 'maybe even more'?"

He pressed his palms together. He looked as if he were about to pray. "Autumn and Landon will always know their place in the family." He gestured toward her. "You're their mother." With four fingers pointing at himself, he said, "And I'm their father. No one can deny that or dispute it. When it comes to Logan, we have to treat him better and love him more. If we don't, he could one day feel as though we didn't love him the same or as much as his brother and sister because he was different. I, for one, don't want that to happen. I never want him to question his place in this family or in my heart."

"Honey, I understand what you're saying." She moistened her lips. "I agree with a lot of what you said." She rested her hand on her chest. "It's just that I don't want us to make the mistake of being too lax with Logan out of guilt. We shouldn't feel obligated to shower Logan with extra attention or love simply because of the circumstances surrounding his conception. If anything, we should treat him the same way we treat his siblings. That way, Autumn and Landon won't resent him and think he's our favorite child. I want our children to be close. As long as we treat all of them fairly and love them equally, I think they'll be fine."

He nodded his understanding. He kissed his wife on the forehead. "I'm about to take a shower before dinner."

"Want to relax in the Jacuzzi after the kids go to bed?" She gave a wicked grin.

"Sounds like a plan." He went upstairs.

Lyric saw some movement coming from one of the bassinettes. She picked up Landon and cradled him in her arms. She figured that he was probably hungry, so she immediately nursed him. She didn't want to give him a chance to cry and wake up his brother. When she finished feeding him, he was still awake and in a playful mood. She spread out an activity mat on the floor and placed him on his back. He had fun hitting and grabbing at the dangling blocks and links. He especially got a kick out of seeing his reflection in the baby mirror.

While Landon enjoyed his playtime, Logan awoke. Lyric fed him too. When he finished nursing, Lyric kissed his belly. He laughed. She loved hearing her babies laugh, coo, and babble.

She placed him on the floor with his brother. They immediately held hands. Lyric admired their closeness.

A few minutes later, the babies started getting fussy. She picked them up, and they stopped. Autumn entered the room and snatched Logan up, freeing him from Lyric's embrace. Holding him close to her chest, she took him upstairs. Not long afterward, she returned with a miniature book. She sat on the couch next to her mother and read a story to the twins. Autumn's love for her baby brothers was evident. Seeing Autumn with her brothers solidified Lyric's own yearning for a brother or sister. She knew it was too late for that, but it didn't stop her from wanting it just the same. Thank goodness she had Chloe, Mahogany, and Malika to fill that void.

Later that evening, Michael and Lyric relaxed in the hot Jacuzzi with the jet bubbles in full blast. Michael lightly massaged Lyric's shoulders.

"This feels so good," Lyric said, closing her eyes.

"The Jacuzzi or the massage?"

"Both." He kneaded her shoulders a while longer, easing the tension from the nape of her neck. He slid his palms over her soft skin and kissed her on the collar. She turned around to face him and rested her arms around his shoulders. "I love you." She planted a wet kiss on his lips."

"Love you too." They splashed water at each other and laughed. They sat and watched their legs float in the water. "After the New Year, I want us to reduce Consuela and Milton to part-time. Between you and my mother, we no longer need the full-time help. It's not like you're still on bed rest."

Lyric pretended to pout. "If we must, then we must. Just know that I'm doing it under protest." She thought about how much she was going to miss Milton's delicious cooking every day.

"I've been thinking about this for the past few weeks," Michael said. Lyric looked at the side of his face. "We should call a family meeting. Christmas is a few days away. We should tell my mom the truth about the twins." He sat silently, waiting for her response.

Lyric swallowed the lump forming in her throat. "Did you pray about this?"

He smiled at her. "Actually, I did. This wasn't an easy decision for me. In the midst of reading the Word and praying to God for answers, that revelation came to me. More specifically, I was told that this situation is bigger than us. The twins didn't come to us as a source of pain. They came to us to strengthen our relationship with God."

Lyric didn't realize that she was crying until Michael used his thumb to wipe away her tears. She leaned in and kissed him. "I trust you."

Thirty-two

The day after Christmas, Lyric and Michael called a family meeting. Malika, Mahogany, and their families had flown back home. Lyric and Michael had spent time in prayer asking God to give them the right words to say to Erica. They also prayed that the Lord would soften their hearts. They gathered in the family room. Lyric led the meeting.

"You're probably wondering why we called this meeting," Lyric said. Michael sat next to her, holding her hand. Without waiting for a response, she continued. "There's no easy way to say this, so I'm just going to say it." She told Erica about Nigel attacking her and stalking her. She was in tears as she told the story. Erica cried too. She got up and hugged Lyric afterward.

"I hope he pays for what he did to you," Erica said, patting Lyric on the back. Wiping away her tears, Erica continued. "That's a horrible thing for you to have to go through. There are no words to express how much I loathe that man. Do you know if he's still in jail for violating the restraining order?" She had a look of disapproval on her face.

"No," Lyric said. "My attorney showed up at Nigel's bail hearing and told me that his bail was set at $5,000. Nigel paid ten percent and was released."

Erica shook her head. Michael told Erica that there was more to the story. Since Lyric was so visibly distraught, he explained the paternity of the twins.

"Sweet, Jesus!" Erica said. "It doesn't seem fair that such a precious child had to come from such a beast." She blew her nose in a tissue. She had a solemn expression. "It doesn't matter to me. Logan is still my grandson. It's not his fault." Lyric couldn't help but smile. Erica said seriously, "You weren't planning on telling Autumn any of this, were you?"

Lyric shook her head.

"Good," Erica said. "We don't want to mess up her head with grown people's problems. Let her stay a kid for as long as she can. There are some things you shouldn't discuss with children. This is one of them." Erica hugged Michael and Lyric. "I'm proud of both of you for the way you're holding your family together."

With all of the outpouring of support she received from Erica, Lyric was relieved that she no longer had to shoulder that burden. Trying to keep that secret was eating away at her. Although logically she knew that she had done nothing wrong, there was a part of her that felt ashamed and guilty. It reminded her of a story that her mom told her a long time ago.

Aunt Tiffany had caught Lyric's mom kissing a boy at school. Aunt Tiffany held that over her head for weeks. She would make her do chores and whatever else she asked of her just so that she wouldn't tell their mother. One day, Lyric's mom had enough. She was tired of being blackmailed, so she told on herself. After she confessed, she didn't get in nearly as much trouble as she had imagined she would. In fact, Mema had been quite understanding.

From that, Lyric learned that most of the things she feared weren't justified. And if they were justified, they weren't usually as bad as she thought.

After the family meeting concluded, Lyric and Michael met with Consuela and Milton to tell them that they would be switching to part-time at the beginning of the New Year. Consuela and Milton seemed disappointed until Michael handed them their year-end bonuses. They perked up after that.

Later that evening, Erica came back to the main house. She seemed distraught. She told Lyric and Michael that she needed to fly back home to tend to her house. Apparently, the tenant died suddenly. They told her that they understood. Lyric didn't know what she was going to do without Erica. It was like having a full-time nanny. With Milton and Consuela on a part-time basis, she was about to discover what it really felt like to be a working mother. The thought made her shudder. The realization intimidated her. Could she handle it?

Thirty-three

Erica was back in Cali, and Lyric enrolled the boys in daycare for four hours a day. It was a difficult decision for her to make, especially since the babies were only five months old. But it was necessary. Otherwise, she wouldn't be able to go on appointments or get any work done.

In an attempt to maintain order and balance in her life, Lyric went back to creating daily schedules and adhering to them. She posted a calendar on the side of the refrigerator to remind her of any and all appointments. She also carried a day planner.

On the days that Milton wasn't working, Lyric even found time to prepare dinner. As for keeping the house clean, she elicited Autumn's help. Together they straightened up on the weekends. That kept things in order until Consuela arrived and did the deep cleaning. Admittedly, Lyric was proud of herself for managing her household so effectively.

Lyric was in a good mood. It was Valentine's Day, and Michael had roses delivered to the house. She stopped working early and went to pick the boys up from daycare. When she got back home, she checked the mail. After putting the boys in their playpen with a few toys, she shuffled through the letters and found an official-looking document. She quickly opened it and skimmed the contents. The letter was regarding a court date for Nigel. Although the court appearance was a few weeks away, she made a mental note of the date. As far as she was concerned, nothing would keep her away. Even if he weren't being charged for her rape, she'd settle for the violation of the restraining order. She welcomed any disruption to his life.

Later that evening, Michael had planned a romantic time for his wife. Lyric was elated. Consuela offered to babysit. She wasn't married and wasn't in a serious relationship, so she didn't mind. Lyric and Michael gladly accepted. Heavyn even came over to hang out with Autumn, freeing her parents up to have a romantic excursion as well.

That night, Michael took Lyric to her favorite restaurant, Bone's. Lyric feasted on crispy Halibut with oyster mushroom and lemon butter sauce. Michael delighted his taste buds with lemon chicken with capers and mushrooms.

A couple of hours later, they went home. Autumn and Heavyn were watching movies in Autumn's bedroom. They were ready for bed. According to Consuela, the twins had not long ago dozed off. They thanked her and paid her before she left.

Alone in their bedroom, the couple was feeling amorous. Michael inserted a Luther Vandross CD in the CD player. Lyric couldn't help but laugh as Michael tried to woo her with his sweet talk and smooth moves. Swaying their bodies to the rhythm of the music, Michael held his wife close to him. They kissed passionately before revving themselves up for a night of passion.

Thirty-four

Nigel couldn't stop wondering how things had gone so terribly wrong between him and Lyric. He loved that woman, yet he had to spend time in jail, pay fines, and still had a pending court date behind some nonsense. All because he wanted to give his children their Christmas presents. What was so wrong with that? he wondered.

Nigel picked up Lyric's picture off his night-stand and glared at it. For the past several weeks, he had been even more careful when he watched Lyric and the boys from a distance. He even went as far as renting cars on a couple of occasions. He didn't want to risk someone spotting his car and calling the cops. A week ago he purchased a cheap car from one of those "Buy-Here, Pay-Here" places so that he wouldn't bring attention to himself when he watched Lyric. Following her around wasn't nearly as easy without the tracker on her car, especially now that she had meetings. Because of that, he no longer knew her comings and goings.

He puckered his lips and kissed Lyric's image. "One more chance. That's what I'm going to give you," he said.

He tossed the picture on his unmade bed. He went in the bathroom and shaved. Then he splashed on some smell good. Checking himself out in the mirror, he thought he looked handsome. He knew that Mr. Stokes was out of town because he had seen him loading up the car in the middle of the night. To confirm it, he followed Mr. Stokes to the airport. Nigel was prepared to take full advantage of the opportunity. He was going to get through to Lyric one way or another.

Chloe was in the middle of preparing spaghetti and meatballs for dinner when her cell phone rang. She started not to answer, because everyone close to her knew not to call her during mealtime. Whatever it was had better be an emergency. She felt around in her purse, which was perched on a barstool, and retrieved her phone.

"Hello," she said with attitude.

"Is this Chloe Washington?"

"It is. Who's this?"

She placed a lid on the pan containing the meatballs and sauce. The smell of ground chuck, tomatoes, garlic, and herbs engulfed her nostrils.

"This is Ms. Emerson at Ever Lovin' Daycare. You're listed as an emergency contact for Logan and Landon Stokes."

Chloe felt a tightening in her chest. She wondered why the daycare would be calling her instead of Lyric. Trying to remain calm, she stopped stirring the pot of boiling noodles.

"Are the twins all right?" she whispered into the receiver, because she did not want Heavyn or Autumn to overhear her conversation.

"The boys are fine. It's just that it's after closing time and no one has come to pick them up. We tried to reach Mr. and Mrs. Stokes, but were unsuccessful."

"Oh." She felt thankful that the twins were all right. Chloe wiped her hands on a dishrag and licked the spaghetti sauce off her lips. "I'll be right there."

She hung up her phone and tossed it back in the bag. Heavyn was upstairs with Autumn. They were doing homework together, and Autumn had planned to stay for dinner.

She yelled up the stairs. "Girls, I have to make a quick run. The meatballs and sauce are ready. I just need you to turn off the pasta in five minutes and drain them in the colander. Got it?" She waited for a response.

With a concerned look on her oval-shaped face, thirteenyear-old Heavyn came halfway down the stairs and asked, "Is everything all right?"

Autumn stood barefoot behind Heavyn. Chloe removed the scrunchy from her hair, freed her ponytail, and shook her head.

"I'm not sure yet," Chloe replied.

"Want us to wait for you to get back before we eat?" Heavyn gave a half-smile.

"No, help yourselves." Chloe turned on the balls of her feet, picked up her purse, and left. She was so distracted that she barely heard the girls say "goodbye" to her. She sensed in her spirit that something was wrong. Never had Lyric been late picking the twins up from daycare. Never.

While in the garage, Chloe hurriedly placed two car seats in the back of her black Lincoln Navigator. She thought it was a good idea to have her own set after the twins were born. Besides, she took her role as their godmother seriously.

Chloe climbed inside of the SUV and called Lyric's house phone. No answer. She dialed her cell. Nothing. As a last ditch effort, she tried Michael's phone, even though she knew he was in Dallas, Texas, at a medical convention. Again, nothing, zilch, nada. Her mind was on overload as she drove the ten miles to the twins' school.

When she arrived, there were only two cars in the parking lot, a used Toyota Camry, and a Honda Civic. Chloe felt panicked as she hopped out of her truck and sprinted into the building. She was slightly winded when she entered.

"Thanks for coming, Mrs. Washington," the center director said from behind a desk.

Before Chloe could respond, the daycare worker came up to her with a baby on each hip. They looked so cute dressed in matching tees and jeans, she thought. She felt like crying as she rubbed their backs.

"Thanks for staying with them," Chloe said, looking at the brown skinned lady with jet black shoulder length hair. "I'm sorry about this. I don't know what's going on."

The director offered a wan smile as Chloe picked up the diaper bag and adjusted the strap over her left shoulder. Then she took Logan out of the worker's arms. The daycare worker, carrying Landon, trailed Chloe to the car, and they strapped the boys in.

She decided to ride by Lyric's house to make sure everything was okay. Although the boys only lived five miles away, Chloe drove the speed limit and with extreme caution. She didn't want to risk getting into an accident, and in her current mental state, she just might have one.

This was not like Lyric. No way would she not pick up the kids. Something was terribly wrong, and it terrified her to think of what.

As soon as Chloe pulled up in front of the house, she spotted police cars and an ambulance parked in the driveway. The two-story tudor that was normally inviting had an ominous feeling tonight. Chloe's heart began to race, and even in the cool of the vehicle, beads of sweat formed on her forehead. She wrung her hands together and looked into the backseat at her round-faced, dimple cheeked godsons. The twins were drooling and babbling. None of their gibberish registered with Chloe. Somehow she hoped that looking at them would give her the strength she needed to get out of the car. Then she did what came natural for her to do when faced with a crisis; she prayed.

In a low voice, Chloe said, "Lord, make me strong enough to handle whatever is going on in this home. If something has happened to Lyric, please let her be all right. Her children need her, and so do I. In Jesus' name, I pray. Amen."

She thought that leaving the boys in the car was the right thing to do, just in case. Just in case of what, she wasn't sure. She rolled down the driver's side window and removed the key from the ignition.

Looking at the boys, she said, "I'm going to see what's going on, but I'll be right back to get you. Don't mess with anything and stay in your seats. Okay?"

Chloe knew they didn't understand, but she was trying to make sense out of a senseless situation. Trying to put on a brave front for the boys, Chloe forced a smile.

Chloe was not convinced that she would be emotionally strong enough to handle the shock if something bad had happened to Lyric. She swallowed the lump of fear that had pushed its way up from the pit of her stomach to her chest and now her throat and exited the car.

Thirty-five

Lyric awoke. She was in pain. She looked around the unfamiliar surroundings and panicked.

"You're awake," Michael said. He jumped up from his chair. The dark circles under his eyes made him look five years older. He kissed her on the forehead. "Thank God! I'll get your doctor."

"No," Chloe said. "You stay with her. I'll get the doctor." She gave a faint smile.

Michael stroked her hair. His eyes became misty and her lower lip quivered. He balled his fist and dabbed his eyes before any tears escaped.

The attending physician entered. "You gave us quite a scare. You've been in a coma for the past five days."

A coma? Lyric thought. Hearing that sent a frightening chill up her spine. She wondered how her children were doing. Who was taking care of her babies?

The doctor continued. He asked her a series of questions, including her name and the day of the week. Lyric answered most of them correctly. He then asked her, "What was your last memory from the accident?" She had a faraway look in her eye. She didn't answer. "That's okay," the doctor said. "She's in post traumatic amnesia. As she emerges from PTA, the answers will become more accurate to her."

"I want to go home," Lyric said.

The doctor smiled. "Let us run a few more tests. Depending on the results, we'll discuss your possible release." The doctor told her that he was going to order an MRI and EEG, then he left.

Chloe walked over to Lyric and pressed her head against her bosom. Tears flowed freely down her face. "I love you so much. You're my best friend. If I had lost you, I don't know what I would've done. I prayed for you every single day. The fact that you woke up is a miracle." She held her a moment longer before letting her go.

"Where are my kids?" Lyric asked. Her throat was drier than the Sahara Desert.

As if he had read her thoughts, Michael poured her a glass of water and handed it to her. "When I told my mom what happened, she hopped on the next plane. She and your father are with the children," Michael explained.

Michael and Chloe never left Lyric's side. They waited while the medical staff poked, prodded, and ran tests. That night, Chloe went home and Michael slept in a chair.

The following morning, the police waited outside Lyric's hospital room while the doctor reviewed the MRI and EEG results with Lyric and Michael. He announced that Lyric did not have any brain swelling, and her brain activity was normal. She still had two broken ribs and a fractured nose that would cause her great discomfort. He emphasized that she would be in pain. However, he would be able to prescribe some pain medication. He advised her that her multiple bruises would heal. The doctor announced that she was strong enough to talk to the police as long as she didn't feel too pressured or overwhelmed to remember. He then informed her that he would prepare to release her later that day.

When the police officers entered the room, Lyric felt her body stiffen. Michael squeezed her hand and assured her it was all right.

"Mrs. Stokes," the officer said as he walked closer to Lyric. His partner stood next to the door. "We're sorry about what happened to you. We're glad you're alive, though. Do you remember what happened on the day you were attacked?"

Lyric tried to remember but couldn't. Breathing heavily, she finally said, "No, I don't remember."

"Apparently, Mrs. Stokes, Nigel Fredericks broke into your house and attacked you."

Lyric gasped. She swallowed air while forcing back the tears.

"You don't have to worry about Nigel anymore. He's dead."

A lone tear escaped from Lyric's bruised eye and Michael swiped it with his thumb.

"You're lucky, Mrs. Stokes." Lyric had a solemn expression on her face. "Your father told us that when he arrived at your house, Nigel was about to rape you. He stopped that from happening. The two men fought, and Nigel ended up falling over the balcony and onto one of the ropes on your painting. It hung him."

"What's going to happen to my dad," Lyric said faintly, lightly strumming her numb jaw.

"We investigated the incident, and the evidence supports your father's story. Therefore, no charges will be filed against him."

Michael cleared his throat. "Thanks for stopping by, officers. I need to help my wife get ready so that she can get out of here. You understand." He nodded his head.

"Of course." The officer handed Michael a business card. "Thanks for your time." He said to Lyric, "Get well soon."

When Lyric got home, she was so happy to see her children, Henry, and Erica. The twins were asleep in their portable crib. Henry explained that since Lyric probably wouldn't be able to walk up the stairs right away, he decided to assemble the portable bed for the boys so that they could be near their mother. Consuela and Milton were there, but Lyric didn't remember them. She could tell that they were disappointed, but judging by the sincere looks on their faces, she knew they cared about her. They both welcomed her back before leaving her alone with her family.

"Mommy, I'm so glad to see you. I missed you like crazy," Autumn said. She attempted to hug her mom, but Lyric winced in pain.

"Your mom's sore right now," Michael explained, giving Lyric a pain pill and bottled water. He helped her to the couch.

Lyric took a seat and washed down the medicine. She noticed that Henry was sitting next to Erica with his arm around her.

"Something you two want to tell me?" asked Lyric.

"Oh." Henry removed his arm from Erica's shoulder and held her hand. A smile creased his face. "We're seeing each other now."

Lyric gave a warm smile. "Good for you. You both deserve to be happy."

Michael said to Autumn, "Need you to go up to your room for a little while. Grown people need to talk."

"Do I have to?" She had a pleading look on her face. "I really missed Mom."

"I know you did. You can come back when we're finished," Michael explained.

Autumn kissed Lyric on the cheek and left the room. Michael waited a few seconds to make sure Autumn was out of earshot. He then retrieved an envelope from his jacket and removed the document inside. "It's the DNA results. I've been wanting to do this ever since Nigel died." He handed the paper to Lyric. "You want to do the honors."

Grabbing the paper, Lyric stared at it for a moment. She then ripped it into shreds. Michael gathered the pieces and threw them into the fireplace where he set it ablaze.

"No one ever has to know," Erica said.

About ten days later, Lyric started to recover. She slowly got her memory back. She could remember certain things, but not everything. She was having a difficult time recalling names of her friends. That was frustrating for her, but she knew it was only temporary. She didn't have amnesia. She still couldn't recall the accident, though.

Late one night, Lyric had a terrible nightmare. She awoke in a cold sweat, screaming.

"What's wrong?" Michael asked.

Tears mixed with perspiration covered her face. Her nightgown clung to her body like a wet T-shirt. "I remember." She couldn't stop crying.

Michael held her in his arms. "Tell me what happened."

She pulled away from him. She had a faraway look in her eyes. "I had gone through the garage to cut some fresh flowers from the garden. I forgot to close the garage door. For some reason, I didn't feel afraid that day. It was as if I were tired of living in fear." She searched his face for understanding. "While I was working in my office, I didn't even turn on the alarm. I knew that you were out of town at a convention, but I felt comfortable. You had told Milton and Consuela to come over and check on me. They did. That particular day, when I heard someone enter the house, I thought it was Milton or Consuela, so I came upstairs from the basement. It wasn't until I heard Nigel's voice that I knew I was in trouble." She closed her eyes tightly. Biting her lower lip, she said, "The moment I saw him, I knew he was going to try and kill me." She cried some more.

"He told me that if I wasn't going to raise the twins with him, then I wasn't going to raise them with anybody." She licked her dry lips. "I fought him with everything in me. I picked up whatever I could get my hands on and threw it at him. He chased me around the house, and we battled. He punched me so many times in my face that I went in and out of consciousness." She squeezed his hands. "He ripped off my dress and got on top of me. He was going to rape me again. He was tugging on my panties when help arrived." She paused. "At first I didn't know who the guy was that hit Nigel over the head and pushed him off of me because my eyes were nearly swollen shut. It was hard for me to see. I could hear the person repeatedly striking Nigel with an object. I figured it was a gun."

"It was," Michael added. "I had left it with your dad just in case something jumped off."

Lyric bit her lower lip. "I wondered if the person was going to shoot Nigel, because Nigel wasn't going down easily. He kept fighting. Finally, I heard a man scream." Lyric covered her face with her hands. "That's when my dad spoke to me. My dad said, 'La La, I couldn't protect you before. I'll never make that mistake again. Nigel won't be able to hurt you or your family ever again. He's dead. Daddy took care of it.' " Lyric uncovered her face. "He told me that he loved me. He called 9-1-1 before picking me up and carrying me downstairs so that the paramedics could find me faster." She sighed. "While I was lying on the floor, he went upstairs to put away the gun. That's when I lost consciousness again."

"That must've been when Consuela and Vendela found you."

Michael held his wife as she sobbed uncontrollably. In their minds, Henry was a hero. He had saved Lyric's life. They would always be grateful to him.

~ A time to kill, and a time to heal; a time to break down, and a time to build up; Ecclesiastes 3:3

Reading Group
Discussion Questions

1. Do you think it's possible for women who didn't grow up together to be as good friends as Lyric and Chloe? Explain.

2. Were you surprised by Michael's reaction after Lyric told him about what happened to her?

3. Do you feel Michael handled the situation appropriately? If so, why? If not, why not?

4. Under the circumstances, did you feel Lyric made the right decision regarding her unexpected condition?

5. Did you think Lyric should've trusted Erica enough to tell her the truth about her family?

6. What did you think of Henry?

7. Do you believe that the sins of the mother or father can be passed along to the children? Why or why not?

8. How did you feel about Nigel's outcome?

9. Were you surprised by any part of the story? If so, what and why?

Author's Bio

Dwan Abrams is a full-time novelist, freelance editor, publisher, and speaker. She's the best-selling author of inspirational novels, *Married Strangers, Divorcing the Devil,* and *Only True Love Waits*. She's the founder, publisher, and editorial director of Nevaeh Publishing, a small press independent publishing house. She currently resides in a suburb of Atlanta with her husband and daughter.

She loves hearing from her readers via email at:
dwanabrams1@ aol.com.

Visit her on the Web at:
www.dwanabrams.com.

UC His Glory Book Club!

www.uchisglorybookclub.net

UC His Glory Book Club is the spirit-inspired brainchild of Joylynn Jossel, Author and Acquisitions Editor of Urban Christian, and Kendra Norman-Bellamy, Author for Urban Christian. This is an online book club that hosts authors of Urban Christian. We welcome as members all men and women who have a passion for reading Christian-based fiction.

UC His Glory Book Club pledges our commitment to provide support, positive feedback, encouragement, and a forum whereby members can openly discuss and review the literary works of Urban Christian authors.

There is no membership fee associated with UC His Glory Book Club; however, we do ask that you support the authors through purchasing, encouraging, providing book reviews, and of course, your prayers. We also ask that you respect our beliefs and follow the guidelines of the book club. We hope to receive your valuable input, opinions, and reviews that build up, rather than tear down our authors.

What We Believe:

—We believe that Jesus is the Christ, Son of the Living God.

—We believe the Bible is the true, living Word of God.

—We believe all Urban Christian authors should use their God-given writing abilities to honor God and share the message of the written word God has given to each of them uniquely.

—We believe in supporting Urban Christian authors in their literary endeavors by reading, purchasing and sharing their titles with our on-line community.

—We believe that in everything we do in our literary arena should be done in a manner that will lead to God being glorified and honored.

We look forward to the online fellowship with you.

Please visit us often at:
www.uchisglorybookclub.net.

Many Blessing to You!

Shelia E. Lipsey,
President, UC His Glory Book Club

ORDER FORM
URBAN BOOKS, LLC
78 E. Industry Ct
Deer Park, NY 11729

Name: (please print):_____

Address:_____

City/State:_____

Zip:_____

QTY	TITLES	PRICE
	3:57 A.M Timing Is Everything	$14.95
	A Man's Worth	$14.95
	A Woman's Worth	$14.95
	Abundant Rain	$14.95
	After The Feeling	$14.95
	Amaryllis	$14.95
	An Inconvenient Friend	$14.95

Shipping and handling-add $3.50 for 1st book, then $1.75 for each additional book.

Please send a check payable to:

Urban Books, LLC

Please allow 4-6 weeks for delivery

ORDER FORM
URBAN BOOKS, LLC
78 E. Industry Ct
Deer Park, NY 11729

Name: (please print):_____

Address:_____

City/State:_____

Zip:_____

QTY	TITLES	PRICE
	Battle of Jericho	$14.95
	Be Careful What You Pray For	$14.95
	Beautiful Ugly	$14.95
	Been There Prayed That:	$14.95
	Before Redemp-tion	$14.95
	By the Grace of God	$14.95

Shipping and handling-add $3.50 for 1st book, then $1.75 for each additional book.
Please send a check payable to:
   Urban Books, LLC
Please allow 4-6 weeks for delivery

ORDER FORM
URBAN BOOKS, LLC
78 E. Industry Ct
Deer Park, NY 11729

Name: (please print):_____

Address:_____

City/State:_____

Zip:_____

QTY	TITLES	PRICE
	Confessions Of A preachers Wife	$14.95
	Dance Into Destiny	$14.95
	Deliver Me From My Enemies	$14.95
	Desperate Decisions	$14.95
	Divorcing the Devil	$14.95

Shipping and handling-add $3.50 for 1st book, then $1.75 for each additional book.

Please send a check payable to:

Urban Books, LLC

Please allow 4-6 weeks for delivery

ORDER FORM
URBAN BOOKS, LLC
78 E. Industry Ct
Deer Park, NY 11729

Name: (please print):_____

Address:_____

City/State:_____

Zip:_____

QTY	TITLES	PRICE
	Faith	$14.95
	First Comes Love	$14.95
	Flaws and All	$14.95
	Forgiven	$14.95
	Former Rain	$14.95
	Forsaken	$14.95
	From Sinner To Saint	$14.95

Shipping and handling-add $3.50 for 1st book, then $1.75 for each additional book.

Please send a check payable to:

Urban Books, LLC

Please allow 4-6 weeks for delivery